The Second Edition

DARK MATTER TRANSIT

3.

The Terrabot Wars

By

VERNON J. YARKER

For Rosalind

Acknowledgements

FOR THEIR ENCOURAGEMENT TO WRITE

THIS BOOK

TO

Stephanie Adam.

Marieke Verschuuren.

Table of Contents

Chapter 1

ABDUCTION

Vivienne was seated, applying her makeup, when her mobile telephone shrilled loudly on her dressing table. That's early, she thought as she put down her lipstick and reached for the gold telephone to reset it to the speaker mode.

"Am I speaking with the Ambong Representative to the planet Earth?" The caller had used a common Earth slang expression for the Federation of Ambrocognia Mundi Colligation (AMC) and the Ongle System of Planets, the man sounded harried and breathless.

"Yes, I am Vivienne Holder, the AmOn Representative," she replied cautiously, fearing that it may be a nuisance call. "Can I help you?"

"Sorry this is early," her caller left no gap "I am Mark Gelder, Mark for short, Chief of the Global Police Force and I have some very important news to tell you and to ask you if the AmOn authorities can help." He paused.

"Well, I will certainly see what we can do once I know the problem." Vivienne had adopted her professional tone. "Yes, I remember you now," she said. "You spoke at the recent World Congress on the subject of criminal mind; it was an interesting speech which you had researched well."

"We aim to please," he laughed but stifled it for the business in hand and continued. "At 07.05 hours Greenwich Meantime, earlier today, the president of the United World Government was abducted from outside his hotel in London by persons unknown."

"Whew!" Vivienne was plainly shocked. "How and why; was anybody else taken too?"

"No, just the President," Mark affirmed. "Apparently, he was due to return to Bermuda today for tomorrow's reopening, after the summer recess, of Parliament of the United World Government. He had just come out of the hotel and was waiting for his car to draw up when there was a blinding flash of light and a small space craft emerged, probably from the dark matter. The craft was emitting intense waves of blue light which mentally disorientated the witnesses to the extent that they, and the body guard, were unable to render assistance properly. A hatch was thrown open in the side of the spacecraft and a dense stream of a smoke issued from it, presumably to hide the aliens, but it did not deploy properly so it was seen that two helmeted, space suited creatures had jumped out, then bundled the President into the craft which immediately disappeared back into dark matter. The only form of resistance taken was by one of the Presidential guards who managed to loose off a pistol shot at the craft at the point where it disappeared."

"Naturally we will help in any way that we can," Vivienne replied "but is there anything specific that you would like AmOn to do?"

"Ahem," Mark cleared his throat, "as you know the Earth has no DMT abilities yet and we will not be introduced to the technology until the Earth is firmly under one form of government. Currently we are getting there but there are some reluctant countries and of course the religions which each claim to be the true and only religion recognised by God. The consequence of that is that all of the major religions on Earth are scrambling for their religion to be adopted as the official religion of the United World Governent.

"Yes, of course," Vivienne agreed, "although we have the saying in AmOn that there are many religions but only one God."

Mark chuckled. "You try to tell that to some of Earth's religious leaders. Their answer invariably is that they have the necessary proofs and scriptures, with heavenly promises that prove beyond doubt that their's is the only religion to which God listens. Only he will deliver them from Armageddon. It is this bickering, along with dyed in the wool racism and nationalism, that is really hold ng us back from being able to unite the world and being able to fulfil our commitment to AmOn to realise a one Nation' one Government and one Earth to join you in the firmament."

Vivienne sat back in her chair thoughtfully before replying. "I can't really see what the motive could be," she responded. "Ransom seems to be the obvious candidate and, in that case, given the vastness of space and the fact that the pepetrators are using dark matter transit, they could be anywhere in a limitless universe. Offhand there is not much that I can do here. I will have to consult AmOn and I will get back to you afterwards."

"Thanks for that," Mark was relieved. "Meantime the abduction is not being released to the press and only to a select few in the government. It will be explained that it was a security exercise."

Vivienne had been especially selected for the assignment to be AmOn's Representative to the planet

Earth because she had studied politics at university. Since then, she had acquitted herself well in junior ministerial posts in their government. It was a no brainer, too, in-that she was the daughter of Geoffrey Holder who had met and married Imogen after he was involuntarily transported from Earth to the Ongle ship, the QvO. The fact that her father was an Earth man gave her a foot in both camps, as it were, and she would be likely viewed favourably by both cultures.

The distance between AmOn and Earth was nearly half a billion light years, give or take a week, was the usual light hearted quip when distance in space was discussed. Vivienne, however, was able to overcome the communications lag by the use of DMT messenger darts. This type of dart hovered in near space to receive her long distant messages and immediately transferred them to AmOn. When they arrived in orbit there, her messages would be downloaded to the appropriate addressee who replied by the same method. There would be a short delay because of the physical process of downloading and uploading the message but the response in time to a simple question and a reply to it could be achieved within the hour.

Vivienne exercised her right to address her message, reporting the event on Earth directly to the Chairman of the AmOn government; and unusually for an official document it would be in her own handwriting because she personally knew Chairman Wei and his delightful wife Xiu very well; and she had dined with them at their home several times in the past. Both were terribly excited that Vivienne was going to be the AmOn Representative on Earth and they begged her to visit Nanjusi and Taishi in China, to where they had traced their respective ancestors before their capture and enslavement by the Rap empire. They wanted her, mostly, to acquire local works of art with which to adorn the walls of their private quarters in the Chairman's Palace.

The response was fast for official deliberations and it arrived thirty minutes later and was both formal and informal in its choice of language, beginning 'Dear Vivienne', and was signed on behalf of Wei; but in between it tersely said that a DMT vehicle was arriving at Bermuda L.F. Wade international airport and she was to return to the planet Qee in the Ongle system immediately." Huh," Vivienne laughed. "I hope I have time to dress first." She hurried to complete her morning ritual and then she threw a few, must have with me, items into an attache case, followed by a random selection of dresses, underwear plus shoes from her wardrobes. She piled all these into a suitcase and pressed the lid down with her knees until she was able to snap the fasteners with a double click.

Because the technology on Earth was not as highly developed as it was on AmOn, Vivienne was not permitted the many gadgets and devices that would be available in her homeland. In return for future access to these advanced technologies, the people of Earth had been set the task of planetary unification under one Parliament, to have but one Army and to place all of its weaponry under the control of this new Government, and only then could they apply and be accepted as a democratic member of the AmOn Federation. Thereafter, there would be less likelihood that Earth people would employ imparted technical knowhow to wage war on each other. Having met the required integration of all races and governance, the Earth people would be considered mature enough to be given advanced technology and to join AmOn in space. The fear of organised theft, however, had led to the decision that AmOn visitors to Earth were to utilise the facilities of the planet as were available. It is for this reason that Vivienne now stood outside the door to her villa, awaiting a taxi to arrive.

As the taxi approached L.F. Wade airport, Vivienne could see a large grey dome some distance beyond the terminal and she knew that this was the force field to protect DMT craft when they arrived. AmOn had taken no chances and a small detachment of their soldiers were confined within the dome and they had been given the instruction that in case of interference to press the homing buttons of any craft contained within the force field. Once done, the spacecraft contained within the dome would in stantly and automatically return to AmOn. One entered the dome through an ordinary lookalike doorway in the force field and there was a small waiting room where one of the soldiers checked Vivienne's papers. A cough caused her to turn round to see Mark Gelder sitting in one of the arm chairs, he rose to meet her to shake her hand and, as only a woman can, she scanned him fleetingly from head to toe, deciding that she liked him even before they shook hands; then she noticed that he had two suitcases by his feet. He was also much taller than her, he had blue eyes, he was smartly dressed in police uniform and his smile was generous as he took her hand firmly to formally greet her.

"Good morning, Mister Gelder," as she returned the hand shake, "I didn't know that you would be here!"

"Me neither," he laughed. "I had twenty minutes warning in a telephone call from the Vice President. Then I was given ten minutes to pack, then a ride here in a police car, accompanied by flashing blue lights and outriders." They were interrupted by an AmOn soldier who approached them to proffer a hucom to Mark with the advice that, when worn, it would enable him to converse with the people that he was about to meet when he arrived at AmOn. Mark already knew about a hucom's technical ability to translate and convey thoughts direct to the brain of the person one was engaging with. He knew, too, that the device could interact with computers in much the same way. He glanced at it and saw that it was a little thicker than a headband and there were no switches apparent on its surface.

"You had better put it on now," Vivienne smiled. "It's fairly easy to use once you get the hang of it but it takes a long time to become an expert with one. You will make many mistakes. The best way to avoid them is to pair it only with the hucom of the person that you are speaking to; in that way any unexpected results are only shared with one other person. I will show you how to operate it once we get aboard the DMT." Vivienne pointed her hand to indicate the white transit vessel waiting for them to board it.

"Watch," she advised, as she put a hucom on her own head. "I am going to transmit an authorisation code to command it to open its passenger doorway, she pointed to the ship as the gull winged passenger doorway lifted upwards to permit their entrance and a short flight of steps slid down. Two soldiers picked up their cases, easily hefting them into the cabin after them. "The controls are preset," they told them. "All you have to do is close the door and it will transit automatically."

"Wow!" Mark voiced his surprised-on entry. "I had half imagined batteries of dials and computer screens but all we have is a computer screen on the coffee table, also there are arm chairs where I had expected rows of passenger seats orderly lined up; and there are no safety straps. Do we just sit down?"

"You may sit down if you wish," Vivienne laughed, "but we are all ready here."

"Incredible," Mark mock-wiped his brow, "and not even a sensation of movement at all yet we are already half way across the known universe. How is it done?"

"It would take a scientific mind to explain it fully," Vivienne replied. "In essence, we did not move at all in our universe, we submerged into dark matter and re-emerged where we wished to be. In the days of old that did not always happen and storms in dark matter could easily throw a vessel a billion light years off course. Nowadays, a newer embedded navigation system is in place which uses dark matter (DMRD) ripple detectors; the journey is as easy as catching a bus on planet Earth."

"Of course, I have read a lot about DM," Mark replied, "but it was often dry and scientific; unless one knew the terminology, it could be sleep inducing. Is there a simple explanation from the people who use it day by day?" Vivienne thought for a moment and Mark was fascinated by the way she moved her eyes as if scanning a document as she gathered her facts together.

"Best sit down for a moment then; we have not been allocated a landing spot yet, but when they do it is to be on the planet Qeem" she said. But Mark was still in a state of wonder and said, "I really cannot believe that in the past few moments I have travelled across two galaxies."

"Yes, you certainly did," laughed Vivienne as they took opposite arm chairs, then she commenced to explain. "As you already know, dark matter is everywhere in the universe, in everything, through everything and between everything. The scientists in AmOn call it the basic universe; and dark matter is the only constant in the universe. It has no shared physical properties relevant to our universe. I know you know this but I am just confirming, as it is, and to check that we are both on the same page! Dark matter has no length, no depth, nor height nor weight. It is immeasurable by our own physics. You cannot travel through it as if in a propelled voyage of going from A to B."

She glanced at Mark to see if he was following.

"Yes, carry on," he assured her, and she resumed "Because it has no physical properties, anything in it is, in a way, next door or even jumbled together some say. Once you have set your exit bias and press 'commit' it is instantaneous; you are here one moment and there the next. The trick, of course, to not set the biases so that your ship materialises in the midst of a blazing sun or a solid object, but our navigation beacons enable us to avoid that."

"It is certainly a difficult concept to get one's head around." Mark summed up. "All is one and one is all."

"The difficulty is our misunderstanding of physics and the physics of our universe, with an absolute refusal to even contemplate that we do not know it all" Vivienne replied. "To us, anything physical, or the space between, has to be measurable in one way or other. Even we cannot fully explain dark matter but we have learned to use it to get around," Vivienne nodded.

"Does radio communication work within dark matter itself?' Mark was interested but Vivienne shook her head to stop him.

"We can communicate within dark matter, we have to, to be able to challenge our embedded navigational beacons for read-outs so that we can set our biases but that, I am afraid, is embargoed information to which Earth will be given the knowhow when the time comes."

"Oh, sorry," he was red faced, "it was only personal interest not espionage," he grinned, "but I take your point."

"Yes, it is all a bit odd, isn't it," Vivienne said, "but you will get used to it." She tapped the hucom that she was wearing and he re alised that all that time he had been wearing his own hucom so she must have moved her lips silently through their last conversation as a form of training and he had not realised that the words he had thought he had heard through his ears were really heard directly within his brain; at the same time he was broadcasting his own thoughts to her. He reddened. "You did well in that exercise," she said, "and thank you for your complimentary thoughts." Her laughter was crystal clear.

"You could read all my thoughts?" Mark sounded anguished. "Indeed," she said

"All of them?" He flummoxed.

"Don't worry, all women receive those kinds of thoughts," she giggled prettily. "Now think personal relationships and then think 'relationships-block-personal- thoughts. Say it to yourself, not forgetting the hyphens. The hucom will repeat it back to you and you must confirm it. It will thereafter filter your personal thoughts about females from being broadcast to all and sundry."

"I'm sorry," he stuttered.

"Don't be" she replied, "it is quite normal and healthy. The adjustment that you have now made will save you any embarrassment in the future."

Mark had previously seen many news clippings originating in AmOn so he was not surprised to see, through the now open hatchway, that there were robots designed for every physical or clerical purpose attending their craft, some sedate and others scurrying to complete their tasks. "They look to me as if they are an independent society entombed in another society," he observed.

"That just about sums them up," Vivienne nodded. "In general, robots look after themselves and recharge their batteries, as required. They are even repaired by other robots if something goes wrong. It may surprise you to know that many of them have their own virtual clubs and indulge in computer games and competitive sports such as tennis. Humans cannot normally interact in their games because the robot mind is superior to ours when it comes to mathematics and assessing patterns of play. But they never do anything without calculating the most probable result. That, of course, can lead to constant stalemate, in chess for example." She smiled.

"So their chess is somewhat more complex than ours and is played with one-hundred pieces to a side. As I understand it, they get round the stalemate problem by using what they term 'game referees,' which is a bit of a contradiction in terms. If the game will obviously end in stalemate, and most would, then the referee can randomly reposition or remove up to two chess pieces from the board in play. The problem is that they may not be identical pieces. It results in the players having to try to guess how they can cover for that eventuality, for example, if they were to loose a strategic piece. So the conundrum for them is to try to forsee the effect of 'random intervention' and factor it in to their game ; for them, that is the game."

"Sounds very complex to me," Mark said vaguely, "I think that I will need to learn a lot about robots in a short time."

After their craft had settled on the ground the door of the shuttle slid open to reveal steps going down to a hardstanding; two waiting robots ignored the steps and bounded from ground level straight in through the cabin door to ask them what was to be unloaded and Vivienne allowed Mark to evesdrop on her hucom conversation with the robots

"Now you have the gist of what to do, let's put it into practice when we embark on the flatbed passenger transport outside. Please direct it to the Department for Earth Studies; it is known as 'the DES' by one and all. The best way when you are learning to use a hucom is to mentally read it as if reading rom a book. It is a much slower method but it helps to avoid mistakes to begin with."

The porter robots had already loaded the suitcases on and had departed before Vivienne and Mark arrived at the flat bed, of which the load platform was quite close to the ground with two throne like passenger seats mounted on it. "Does one have to wave to the people we pass?" Mark quipped and Vivienne laughed.

"Oh, by the way people call me either Vee or Fifi, once they know me. I think that we may be working together for a few days, at least, so the use of our shortened names may be less time consuming."

"Some people on Earth call their dogs Fifi," Mark explained. "So we had better not call you that!"

"Pity," Vivienne pouted, "I rather like Fifi. It sounds more friendly." She put her hand forward to shake hands and said "Hello, Mark. Welcome to this world,"

"Pleased to meet you, Vee." he shook her hand playfully vigourousy, "But I have no idea what my mission is here. I have been told nothing except that the Vice President of the United World Government told me to be here and to be prepared to stay for up to a week."

"To tell the truth, I do not know much more than you do, but AmOn pay my salary so when they call me back to headquarters, I comply without question; but I suspect that it has something to do with the abduction of your President earlier today. Oh, that leads me to think that we will have to find a wristwatch for you; the days are longer on Qee and, of course, time varies from planet to planet in the system. Mark glanced at the watch he was wearing. "Yes, I wouldn't have thought of that. I am used to days, hours and minutes being the same wherever I am. Will they take Earth dollars here?"

"I doubt it," Vee opined, "but the concept of dividing the day up into very small segments on Earth and wearing it strapped to the wrist predates the concept of it having been thought of here in AmOn. As a result, there is a good trade, from Ongle to the rest of the Federation, for Earth- like time pieces. As you are aware the ancestors of the Ongle people were enslaved abductees from planet Earth and, to some, that gives a wristwatch made on Ongle a pedigree stretching back to Earth. The embargo on exporting advanced technology to Earth generally prevents Earth's trade with AmOn, but should Earth be finally accepted and invited to join with AmOn, so too will they be able to trade with us. Quite frankly you will be able to exchange your 'Made on Earth' wristwatch at any jewellers if you wish but I expect that AmOn will give you an expense account while you are here anyway," she advised him.

"Hitherto, I had regarded it as just a watch but now it has just suddenly become a part of the history of time. I think I will take up your suggestion; at least I will have given something back, if only small," he confided.

"I think they will appreciate that and whoever buys it would probably own the only one with a traceable personal history in the whole of AmOn. Do let me come with you when you pass it on."

"Agreed." Mark gave her a playful salute.

Chapter 2

THE DEPARTMENT OF EARTH STUDIES (DES)

The Department of Earth studies, was a large building, Mark observed, they approached it, and Vee interpreted his look.

"As you will see inside, it doesn't warrant thousands of employees at the moment. They are expecting to expand their numbers as the Earth project grows in importance; eventually it will become the hub between AmOn and Earth on all matters including trade," she said as they alighted from the flat bed. "Leave the cases, they will take them to wherever we end up." She spread her arms and shrugged to indicate anywhere. "Gosh," she added when she looked around, "I wonder what all these military people are doing here, this must be larger than I thought." The fact became increasingly evident when they entered the building where they were scanned by a robot and their identities were checked carefully by a marine seated at a console in the foyer. Satisfied, the marine called a house robot to usher them to a nearby office door where it left them to go inside to announce their arrival to the office occupant; he then returned to invite them to enter.

"There has got to be something very big going on," Vee confided. "The DES is a backwater and you would normally enter and leave it without question. I expect that we are soon to know."

Vee led the way through the door and gave a gasp when she saw the seated occupant who arose as they entered the room in where an attractive lady with an inviting smile came around the desk to meet them and she addressed them by their Christian names. "Good morning, Vivienne and Mark," she said. "My name is Anita and I am so pleased to meet you and welcome you." Vivienne had no problems in recognising Anita and took her hand and shook it, saying. "It it is indeed an honour to meet with the Vice Chief Minister of the Ongle System Of Planets, I had no idea that we were to meet you here on Qee."

"Ah! All will be revealed in a moment," Anita smiled as she released Vivienne's hand and she turned to shake hands with Mark. "It is a pleasure to meet you, Mr Gelder," she said warmly, as he took her hand in his own, noting to himself that it seemed delicate and trusting. Observing inwardly, too, that despite her high office over the nine inhabited planets of the Ongle System Of Planets, she displayed, by demeanour, none of the trappings of power. She was rather pretty, he decided, not with an hour glass figure but with a radiating personality and charm. Everything was right about her, the woman that every man would wish to be married to, he decided, as she returned to the chair behind the carved wood desk in the centre of the room and motioned to them to take the two seats placed before it.

"Funny," Mark mused inwardly. "I am on another planet in another galaxy, yet my Earthly training into decoding involuntary mannerisms still holds good on the planet Qee." This was because he had noted that when Anita sat down to face them she had hooked her thumbs underneath the lip of her desk top, splaying her fingers above the lip. It was a sure sign, he knew, that a person doing this was seeking support and security but may not be aware that they were doing so. "Well,"Anita commenced, "it is time to tell you why we have asked you here."

Vivienne and Mark had already correctly assumed that there must be extreme importance in what was about to be divulged to them and they had both leaned instinctively and attentively forward in their seats.

"Let me see," she fumbled with some papers on her desk as she composed herself. "I have to tell you both that the planet Earth is not alone in this. Yesterday the First minister of the Ongle System of Planets was also abducted from his garden where he was attending to his rose bushes, the only witness to the event being his wife who was sitting in their conservatory. She has told us that there were intense blue flashing lights in the garden and when she looked there was a small space craft on their lawn. It was about six metres long. She saw her husband standing, looking at the craft which had issued a dense blanket of steam or smoke. As she watched, the craft disappeared along with her husband. Naturally she thought it was something to do with an emergency somewhere in the Ongle System but when she asked around nobody knew anything about the event. The President has not been seen since nor has there been any communication from him. This effectively puts me in charge until he can be found."

She had stopped to take a sip of water, then she smiled, shrugged and looked somewhat apprehensively at them. "That was yesterday morning, Ongle time," she said. "Since then we have received a report from the AMC of a similar attempt to try to kidnap The Julate of AMC. By happenstance, the Julate had removed his hucom and was searching in his pockets for a key. To assist him, one of his personal bodyguards stepped forward and held the Julate's hucom. In much the same way, as has happened on Earth, a black craft, of similar size used to snatch the Earth's President and the President of Ongle, landed nearby and issued clouds of steam; and before the party had caught their breath, the craft plus the personal bodyguard had disappeared. So it would appear that whoever these people are, they are using the personal hucoms worn by their targets to identify them. There is a sad twist to this story though. The body of the guard was found in orbit around AMC this morning. They had pinpointed him by broadcasting the hucom's secret transponder code which enabled it to send out a homing signal for them to zero into it, in space. Even more sadly, the body of the guard, when it was recovered, exhibited evidence of having being tortured." Anita stopped and looked at them trying to read their facial expressions.

The meeting had now lapsed into an awkward silence and Mark exchanged glances with Vivienne and she nodded at him and tilted her eyes towards Anita as an indication to him to ask the first question, and he cleared his throat. "Ahem, both shocking and mind blowing I would describe it and not a lot to go on, but my policeman training gives me helpful ideas and that is how most investigations begin. There are just a few clues from which we can build a speculative dossier; and little by little the dossier is expanded as new ideas or facts become available and finally we are at least able to make a fairly informed supposition. I take it there was no ransom note or demand made connected with the abduction?"

"No," Anita nodded her head. "Absolutely nothing at all!"

"Fine," Mark was getting into his tried and tested formula when dealing with a criminal case back on Earth. "Do you know how or where the secret codes for the hucoms of VIPs are kept and if they are kept only as a hard copy or also on computers?"

"Indeed," Anita sounded brighter, "they are kept in the registry of the Military Police back in Ongle and at a similar establishment in AMC; by law they cannot be kept on computers nor can they be downloaded to robots. Each code is single use and all are changed completely every six months, used or not. Mark looked thoughtful when he then asked.

"Are there any dissident or dissatisfied politically motivated groups in AmOn that may have the know how to carry out an operation of this complexity?"

Anita was amused, she had not really expected Mark to adopt his investigative mode so quickly, albeit she could appreciate there were good reasons for him to get everything down in a logical format. She was scheduled to meet with the Ongle police later on but she knew she could now tell them the matter was being dealt with elsewhere "Nothing comes to mind," she advised him, "but, of course, all political persuasions have their opponents; it is par for the course. But the two systems of AMC and Ongle comprise twenty-one inhabited planets, plus Marina and a myriad of lesser satellites and lesser asteroids that are partially occupied, from time to time , so it would be difficult to say really."

Mark smiled. "Well we have the beginnings of a useful report," he advised her. "The most promising aspects are that the villains had not briefed themselves extensively enough before the operation or they would not have relied entirely upon the premise that the person that they wished to grab was not wearing their hucom, so that doesn't indicate a formal training. The second point which interests me is their use of smoke or steam. Was it to conceal themselves or just intended to disorientate the bodyguards or perhaps to deny them a clear shot. If it was both there is an indication that if they were seen they could have been easily recognised. So the culprits are local or perhaps distinctively different in appearance. The most important part, what I would call 'real evidence,' is their use of a, thought to be, protected hucom password to locate their victims. There is always the possibility, of course, that they discovered the password by sheer chance, but to repeat that again for another hoist and another password stretches credibility a bit too far! That is very important seen against the information that you have given to me. Effectively, it means you may only have to scrutinise and assess the loyalty of personnel who have had access to the Registry since that particular password was last changed. which will narrow the field somewhat." Mark drew his hands apart and moved them slightly up and down as if he was weighing up the balance.

"Thank you for that," Anita smiled widely. "We had reached some of your conclusions already. We had already concluded that the smoke or vapour cloud was to conceal their activity; but, as you say, there may also be another reason, we had overlooked that it may have been to conceal their identities. Oh sorry, I forgot, you may wonder why you have been brought here to Qee when the seat of government is over on the planet Ongle. I can tell you that it is a security precaution and my office has been relocated here along with a very heavy military presence. My office here is above ground, but my residence is underground in an area which has connecting service tunnels which have been technically designed to include bends, twists and dog legs to obviate a direct attack by a craft employing DMT. To attempt it would be to risk finding themselves wholly or partially embedded in solid rock. Above ground, Space Fleet will take care of unidentified craft approaching Qee. "Anyway," she looked towards Vivienne and addressed her. "What are your thoughts on this conundrum?" Vivienne, who had been listening intently, gave a start when she realised that she had been given the floor and said:

"I was thinking, if the kidnappers, or whatever their motive, used DMT for their under taking, then our immersed detection devices in the DM would have a transit record of their journey from where to there?"

"Indeed," Anita assured her. "Apparently AMC sent no less than a dozen cruisers to the craft's recorded jump off and return spot but they arrived to find millions of kilometres of empty space, but there was a signature of a poenillium drive which they followed until it reached a large star. The alien ship's engine signature was traceable to the outskirts of the star's corona and then it disappeard.

We have assumed they may have deliberately moved close to the star to obtain a sling shot effect from its gravity. They will have switched off their engines, so there was no residual ion trace. At an appropriate time they would have re-engaged their engines and disguised themselves by joining the normal trade routes. That is the best we have so far,"she smiled. "Now, for the reasons we have asked you to come here" Anita resumed. "Vivienne, we would like you to go back to Earth then make an urgent appointment with the Deputy President who will probably have been sworn in as the President by now, and appraise him under strict 'need to know' parameters of the conversation that has taken place here today. It is very urgent, so a shuttle craft awaits you in front of the building." She stood up and warmly shook Vivienne's hand and wished her a safe journey; and with smiles and waves, as she turned to go, Anita thrust on her a transcript of their recent meeting, for the President of Earth's United World Government, which Vivienne waved in the air as she departed.

"Wonderful girl that one," Anita said as she watched her depart. "You can always trust what you ask her to do will be carried out to the letter."

Anita returned to her chair and Mark sat down in the chair that he had previously used, facing her. Honesty, he thought, was an aurora that seemed to surround her, and her ready smile literally melted the heart; she was well chosen for the job. He smiled back. "That leaves just us two," she stated the obvious. "I must tell you that your own Vice President of Earth's government has given the authority for you to come here and work with us. What has happened since the abductions is that the AmOn government has decided to set up a joint task force to investigate and pursue the perpetrators of these crimes. It is to be centred right here on Qee and specifically in the underground area of the Department of Earth Studies (DES). I am to take it under my wing but I need somebody to manage it and report to me from time to time on the progress that has been made. The balance of feeling between AMC and Ongle is fine provided that they are both treated equally but cries of nepotism are soon heard if the allocation of ministries, or power, appear to favour one star system or the other. Quite frankly nobody else came to mind anyway. We were aware that you have a very illustrious track record on Earth and we want to put you in overall charge of our operation 'Clench.' The choice of that word is because it suggests a powerful grip. Interestingly, too, it means much the same and is pronounced much the same in AMC and in Ongle. Of course, we cannot order you to take up the post so we have brought you here to see if you will take it on. Earth's government has assured us that your job will remain open for you in your absence."

Mark had speculated that there would be a job for him to do after his arrival on Qee and he had surmised that it would be something to do with liaison between the police forces of AmOn and those on Earth, but to be told that he was to be the director of the whole operation caused him to double blink in surprise but, other than that, his experience in dealing with the uneepected kicked in, although he gave no outward sign of his inward astonishment.

"It is quite a responsibility, but thank you for asking me and I accept," he said without hesitation, "but while I suspect that a police investigation under the jurisdiction of AmOn will not be that different from an investigation on Earth, I do have some reservations because there would be dissimilar aspects, too, which give me some concern. Technologically, Earth is still relatively in the Stone Age compared to AmOn. Just the office equipment you use is way advanced of my understanding. I am wondering how I would cope with that. Of course, as time goes by, I would come to grips with it but to maintain discipline and respect among the work force the director of an enterprise must have a good overall knowledge. I could not be seen to be asking too many basic questions about the machines they employ. I am also uncertain about protocols. It is easy to make a sincerely meant but unintentionally rude or disrespectful observation across cultures. How could I avoid these things?"

"That has all been envisaged," she responded and he loved her smile as she said it. "You will be allocated two work related robots. One will be clerical and the other technical; in shop floor terms a cheribot plus a gekobot. Their working names are Mavis for the clerical robot and Earnest for the gekobot. They will assist you and train you on the job. They are humanoid in appearance. You may think it is sexist that Mavis resembles a woman and Earnest a man. This is because of our historical human ingrained perceptions of roles. In reality, though, there are no gender-based occupations these days but the role of women and men in the organic society remains much about the same as it is on Earth; quite frankly we prefer it that way. On the domestic front we have allocated a very experienced house keeper robot who will cook for you and attend to all house hold matters according to your requirements. You will hardly have to lift a finger in that respect," she laughed.

Chapter 3

TAKING COMMAND

Her hand felt delicate, small and perfectly formed in his, as Anita bade him goodbye and called a house robot to guide him to his new quarters in the executive accommodation. "I am just further along the tunnel in apartment number One. Do not hesitate to give me a call if there are problems that cannot be solved without somebody with a little more experience in domestic matters on the planet Qee," she giggled. Then when the house robot arrived she gave it her instructions, telling Mark that the same robot would call upon him to show him the way to his offices. "I will call you soon to see you into your office accommodation. I can tell you now, however, that we have selected ten senior police Officers across the breadth of AmOn to support you. They will each have an open office and support cheribots to assist them. They will report directly to you and nobody else. I have, also, to tell you that our lifts are not conventional, they hardly could be for a descent of five kilometres. In effect they are box-like DMT vessels, programmed to transport passengers to hollowed out rock cocoons below. When your lift reaches a cocoon, a door will open which leads directly into a corridor and from there you may find your way by walking or by hailing a flat top. The house robot will help you."

"That is the first time that I have heard of DMT lifts," Mark grinned.

"I had better brief you more fully," Anita added. "You will appreciate that the cocoons and corridors and open spaces are our Achilles heel, so a word of warning, if we are attacked then all open spaces are covered by automatic poenillium fire. Should that happen, please keep your head down or lose it. In time, our storm troopers will follow on with a mopping up operation to subdue any remnants of the attack."

"How far down, is down?" Mark questioned light heartedly, but Anita took it as a serious question.

"They fire no lower than forty centimetres above floor level. They do this because if they hit the floor there might be ricochets and poenillium splash, maybe even gouge up or penetrate the floor to endanger people in the offices and spaces below. So I would suggest as close as you can get." She stamped her food illustratively on the floor, and her laugh had something of the tinkle of a crystal wind charm to it as she did so and he laughed with her. Mark watched her solemnly as she walked away. She was small and somehow vulnerable looking, yet she carried the weight of being the elected leader of all of the peoples inhabiting the nine inhabited planets of the Ongle System, plus the uninhabited planet Marina. In her own right she was the Commander of armed forces numbering, according to what Vivienne had told him, twenty-million souls with a like number in reserve. She could muster five hundred thousand fighting space ships and another mothballed fleet of a similar size. Those numbers would be jointly doubled if AMC joined the fray. Does it worry her at all, he wondered. He decided that it did. She was still human, he thought, and he felt that he had seen an underlying sensitivity that was concealed by her face of office. She was infinitely more approachable than some of the bull-headed politicians he had met in his professional life.

Mark found that his quarters were only a few steps from the DM lift and the house robot accompanied him to the door of his apartment, briefing him that the entrance code to open the door was XOP51 which he had to punch into the keyboard beside the door. "We do not permit the use of hucoms to activate doors, safes or other password defended access points," the house robot told him suavely, "the point being that there is always a time when one is distracted and when one can forget othey are wearing a hucom which is switched on, with the obvious result!"

"I imagine those are tried and tested reasons and yes, I can see there would be times perhaps when in a hurry that one could easily forget a switched on hucom. "Thanks for your advice;" Mark added. For it was at this point that the house robot bade him a restful night, saying that he would be back to escort him to the suite of offices allocated to the Commander of Operation Clench the next morning.

The accommodation, when Mark saw it, was certainly spacious and tasteful but it rather conveyed an unlivedin atmosphere with no frills or knick-knacks, even the carpets and furniture were coloured neutrally light grey and fawn which came off well but devoid of character. As Mark moved from room to room he was pleasantly surprised to see there was one featureless wall in each of them. In actuality, he was to learn that whole wall was really a screen. When activated it showed a regular rural scene that could be changed through one's hucom with the added ability to zoom in on selected parts of the screen, rather like viewing it through binoculars. At the moment, though, he was being shown a lifelike country scene realistically depicted in 3D. When he later learned to use the zoom effect he could follow the path of a colourful bird or perhaps a robocoter crossing the sky or exotic flower beds with flowers larger than he had ever seen on Earth. It gave a great feeling of relief to not feel so depressively shut away in the bowels of Qee now that he could remain in touch with the day light and nature's whims and temperament ias it happened, minute by minute.

The apartment took some time to explore and he felt gratitude towards Anita because in truth the planet Earth was centuries behind in technology, yet he was being made to feel equal and an asset of value to AmOn. A moment of surprise followed when he heard a sound as he approached the kitchen and he trod warily towards its source. When he was in a position to see right into it he tittered when he saw a humanoid robot dressed in a suit and tie and wearing a pinafore over the suit; and it was wiping down the kitchen surfaces.

"Hello," Mark ventured "I am the new temporary resident in this suite. May I ask who you might be?"

"Hello to you, too," the robot replied affably and it dropped the house cloth it had been holding and turned to face Mark. "I am your domestic robot. I can do anything in the household, cook, clean, launder, make beds, even clean shoes and do the ironing. I have recently unpacked your luggage and it is all stowed in the master bedroom."

"Phew!" Mark blew out his breath, "all that so soon?"

"Yes, all that, I never tire," the robot assured him.

"Well, that's the interview over then," Mark smiled, "I have to tell you that you are hired and you can start right away." He never questioned himself that he was speaking socially to a computer because the robot seemed so lifelike even with an expressive face that creased and wrinkled in sympathy with his mood and what he was saying.

"Thank you, master," the robot gave a mock bow in Mark's direction and he laughed a guttural laugh. "My name is John."

"A robot with a sense of humour, John?"

"Indeed so; we domestic robots are skilled in all household duties including dealing with medical emergencies. We are also programmed to be a social companion to the resident we serve."

"Things are getting better and better by the minute. Perhaps you will train me in the use of the household gadgets we have here?" Mark enquired.

"Yes, I can do that," John replied, "but there is really no need, I can take care of everything."

That night Mark turned in to sleep in a very large bed and for the sheer joy of experimentation he decided to keep his 'all-wall' screen on with the sound switched low and selected something that he could never have done in real life which was to sleep in the open on the edge of a jungle. The camera was preset and didn't zoom or sweep which if anything added to the realism of the backdrop. It was densely dark in places while in other more open areas the moon light from two moons penetrated to the jungle floor. Here and there fireflies flickered their prescense according to whim and now and again luminescent eyes glowed briefly as they were caught by rays of moonlight, then disappeared; but had the creatures gone or were they still there watching him from the darkness. A shiver traced downwards along his spine, leaving his skin cold and sensitive. Occasionally, although electronically muted, but with still quite loud voices, male predatory animals vocalised their claim to dominance, territory and their undisputed choice of females, their claim loudly disputed by other males of their species. Later, the crash of falling trees and glimpses of thrashing tails in the undergrowth with added roars of defiance, signified that the males that had answered the challenge were meeting to fight it out. The security of being in bed and just a bystander was soporific and soon induced Mark to fall asleep. Then, as the sensors controlling the all-wall screen recognised that he was asleep, they bit by bit reduced the sound and the picture until it was just a ghost of the scene on the screen til it finally disappeared.

Next morning, Mark responded to a door bell chime and he opened his bedroom door to find John there, dextrously supporting, on its finger tips a tray laden with coffee, toast, a pot of marmalade and a bowl of porridge. "Your breakfast, Commander," he said cheerfully. "Talk about being unable to organise a booze up in a brewery, as you would describe it," he said. "I opened the frozen larders at three am this morning to find them stocked full of Ongelian food, most of which you will have never heard of." He placed the tray on the breakfast table. Mark looked the tray over.

"How have you been able to produce a very English looking breakfast then?" Mark enquired.

"With great difficulty," John chuckled, "just producing the toast had the fire control robots at the door because the smoke had triggered a remote alarm at their fire station. We had to get through to Vivienne on Earth and wake her up because it was after midnight in Bermuda. She was luckily able to find a twenty-four-hour supermarket open and she sent all the necessary ingredients post-haste via a DMT dart together with instructions on how to cook and prepare them. I had mastered it by 6 am this morning after I had made my first two batches of porridge which set suspiciously like cement." Mark almost lost his balance laughing as he reached for the spoon to try the porridge.

"Not bad at all; perhaps a little less salt next time," after which he praised the toast, marmalade. and coffee as being spot on. "I think we could find you a job in a cafe on Earth, John," he joked, but John looked falsely serious.

"That is a very good idea, I could give it more atmosphere, too, by making the seating and the tables out of solid blocks of porridge." He doubled up with mirth. They were both sparking humorously off each other as John slapped his thigh probably hard enough to break his leg if he were human.

There was still more laughing to come as Mark tried on his uniform for the first time. He was glad that he had worked on keeping his weight in check in the

"Quite smart uniform," he observed as he checked himself in a wardrobe mirror. Its colour was light navy and the shirt was sky blue with a matching tie. The jacket was of a wrinkle free material in the style of a sleeveless body warmer but closer fitting. The trousers were drainpipe legged in the same light navy as the jacket with a lighter blue stripe running down the outer seams. Finally, to slide over the jacket's epaulettes were his insignia of rank depicting golden Oak leaves. These prompted Mark to learn more about the history of the insignia. His quest found that it could be traced back to the very beginning of the newer history of the Ongle system of planets.

In those days the Ongle system was known as the Rap Foundation which had surreptitiously spirited away captives from Earth, and they were bred as slaves to serve the Foundation and its empire; but the Raps had conditioned themselves to be over secure. They had no notion of insurrection and, when it came, the descendants of the former slaves overthrew the Raps to subsume their empire. Although the slaves, whilst applying vengeance through the isolation of the more sadistic Raps, had allowed the remainder to go unmolested and had integrated them into their society. Indeed, Raps did now occupy positions in the Ongle System Of Planets government. But today, you did not see the Raps very often. Being an amphibious race and with their responsibility diminished, they had sought the coastal regions of the continents. This allowed them relative freedom from human contact and to exploit their natural abiity to roam the seas at leisure. Of course, they were still sought after as employees for marine projects for which they were so well adapted. Albeit earlier Rap escapees of the insurrection, in time, had formed a symbiotic relationship with the robots of the planet Terrabot. Whereafter, they had conspired with Terrabot to attack the planet Earth. Their defeat was history, with many people believing, by its manner to have been a devine intervention. One story, Mark found woven through an earlier part of Ongle's history was about a captured Earth man whose duty was to care for livestock being transported aboard a ship to the British colonies.

Just before he was captured by the Raps he had found two large acorns in the pig feed and he retained tthem to incorporate into a scrimshaw that he was making. Now a slave, he could no longer pursue his hobby and he healed the two acorns into the soil of the Rap Federation planet on which he was held captive. The acorns had approved the climate and soil so they flourished. The Raps, recognising the quality of the wood from the oak tree, spread them far and wide throughout their Foundation. More lately the inhabitants of the AMC planets had also grown to appreciate oak furniture and the mighty oak was being spread by deliberate means to all of the planets of AmOn. Thus the oak leaf had become symbolic and known for its origin on Earth, with its leaves becoming an AmOn national symbol denoting strength, history, wisdom and triumph over adversity.

"It is not a colour that I would have chosen for myself," Mark said thoughtfully, "as a rule I avoid navy because it shows every fleck of dust it picks up from the environment." John gazed at it for a brief second, then said "It looks fine and your grey hair gives it distinction. Don't worry about fluff, the material it is made of inhibits things sticking to it." Any further conversation between the pair of them was curtailed by an announcement over Mark's hucom that a robot had arrived at the main entrance and was waiting to escort Mark to his new office. "How does 'T' bone steak, chips, peas and a brandy trifle to follow sound for your dinner this evening?" John asked via his hucom as he left.

"Sounds wholesome," Mark smiled. "Can you do it?

If not a ready meal will do.

"No guarantees," John replied. "It might be a burnt offering, with wooden chips and hard peas. I expect my culinary skills with Earth food will improve with time." He sounded unconvinced.

The approach to his new offices took Mark and his robot guide along narrow passages which tended to twist and turn haphazardly, the reason for this having been explained to him by Anita yesterday, and he saw that it would, indeed, take a great deal of precision for an infiltrating hostile craft to materialise safely. Certainly no craft of an appropriate size and able to carry an attacking force would ever manage it in once piece. Here and there along the route they passed military revetments which had been hollowed out in the rock face beside the passages. "They are manned by men and women of the Territorial Consolidation Force, which, in turn, are an off shoot of the military establishment," the house robot told him conversationally. "They are probably pleased to be here because their real purpose is to hold, secure, and police conquered territory after our victorious solders have passed through it. The last time that they were properly employed was many years ago when they were called upon to consolidate the planet Terrabot after the Rap-Terrabot war. So they are a bit of an anachronism really because it is so long since the Ongle System of Planets waged a land war on anybody. The Territorial Consolidation Force has, since then, become a force employed almost entirely for ceremonial duties which is a bone of contention for 'Hu' tax payers."

"Hu tax payers?" Mark asked.

"Human and humanoid tax payers," the house robot explained.

"Ah ha," Mark rejoined, "do humans and humanoids have a special name for robots?"

"Yes, they call us bots or botties." Mark laughed,

"Are those names derogatory in any way. I have to be careful not to make mistakes?"

"Certainly not by the bots. We recognise that without human money and enterprise there would be no robots at all, so 'long live Hu tax payers' are our thoughts on the matter!"

"Well said," Mark sounded surprised, "I had half expected there would be resentment and accusations of enslavement! Thank you for that explanation Mr. Bot."

As they neared the office block, Mark saw that it was essentially a cave cut back into the rock with a brick outer wall facing the passage. Anita was already there waiting and surrounded by a wall of body guards. As Mark drew near she slipped through her ring of guards and came forward to meet him. Now, within her immediate proximity, he caught the scent of the perfume she was wearing which gave memories of freshness and summer meadows.

"Good morning, Commander," she offered her hand to shake. "Welcome to your new home. I am afraid it is not quite ready yet, we only started on it yesterday. We are converting what was, until yesterday, a repository for tunnelling plant. At the moment, we have an army of robots inside to make it shipshape for occupation by Clench. The work should be completed within the next twenty-four hours," she took his elbow and urged him gently towards the door of the building.

Inside Mark could see that 'an army of robots' was perhaps a small exaggeration but there were at least two-hundred of them. Chaos appeared to be everywhere, from stacked wall paneling to electric cables, boxed furniture, as well as the sound and smell of wood being cut. Most of all he was impressed by the speed at which the robots could work. "They only measure once and cut once, digital exactitude we call it, but they are tireless and usually work at roughly five times the speed of a human being." Anita's comment was emphasised by his observation as Mark watched a robot searching through a pile of timbers possibly for a suitable matching grain for something already under construction. The scantings of wood it was searching were in constant turmoil as if alive with movement until the robot found the piece it was looking for. Then, javelin like, it hurled the selected scanting to another robot working at a cutting bench, which reached up and caught it one handed, and slammed it down, then cut it to length. Fluidly passed it through an electric plane, then drilled it with bolt holes, passing it on to another robot that bolted it into place in a console it was building. The entire activity took perhaps thirty seconds, Mark would have guessed. Likewise similar events could be seen the length and breadth of the hanger- like space. "Wow, I have got to have some of these guys. I see a life of ease ahead of me," he sighed.

"I am afraid not," Anita cautioned playfully, "we like our police Commanders to be active people," she laughed. "Mind you, if you can solve the present enigma we have to hand, I could well see our grateful government being quite generous." She raised both hands above her head with her crossed fingers.

"Come" she said, "let's speak to the superintending robot and find out what their plans are." They found the superintendent he was wearing a yellow hat for visual recognition and it showed them around, stopping in places to unroll the blue prints for them to examine.

"Your office will be over there." It pointed to a wall-less cavity. "The walls, carpeting and electrics will be fitted late tonight after they have run wiring and air conditioning to it. You will be able to move in by approximately 10 am tomorrow morning. The other senior staff will have low walled cubicles in the main hall. Each will have second desk for a cheribot. The Officer will sit at a console which is connected to a designated planet in AmOn and it will also have direct connection to the console in your office. You, yourself, will have direct connection to the head of governments of AmOn and the AMC."

Mark could have made the journey back to his quarters from memory now, but his attempts to dismiss the robot were refused point blank and it was then that he came to understand that the robot would be with him wherever he went for a day or two. When he questioned Anita about the necessity he learned that this individual robot had a covert mission to protect him for a day or two in case of a snatch raid while they reorganised. Thereafter he would be watched over by the TCF, should a snatch raid be mounted to capture him "I must advise you," Anita said, "if you are attacked do try to keep out of the robot's line of fire because four of its fingers conceal barrels for poenillium mini pistols that fire automatic bursts. Finally, its brain and its primary eyes are in its torso, not in its head as one would expect. Strategically, that part of its body rather gruesomely implodes, which brings internal isotopes together and they combine to cause them to emit an electromagnetic pulse (EMP) which is powerful enough to render local unprotected electrical devices inoperable. That includes, by the way, weapons which are reliant upon electrical stimulation to operate. The robot is a military top-secret prototype, so its capabilities are unknown as far as the DES personnel are concerned. You will have to keep that a secret, but it is right you should know just in case you are singled out, by the nefarious, as a target to be kidnapped."

"Imploding heads, fingers that are the barrels of ray guns; what kind of world have I joined?" Marks voice was teasing.

"Welcome to the year four-thousand two hundred and fifty" Anita laughed.

Despite John's misgivings over being able to cook a dinner, he had excelled his expectations and marked thanked him. John seemed pleased. "Some humans never thank a robot at all." He sounded saddened.

"I am sorry to hear that." Mark felt a little awkward consoling a robot which, hitherto, he had only regarded as a talkative, interactive, programmed machine. He had never contemplated that they may have feelings. "Tell me," He inquired, "what exactly do you gain personally from praise?"

"Words of praise are all totted up by the computers at Robot Central," John explained. "When it comes to allocating assignments, they are taken into account in allocating the most challenging tasks to the robots that have the highest praise rating. A challenge to a robot is probably akin to giving a child an ice lolly. We love them."

"You may regret telling me that, John. I will look through the cook books to find the most challenging recipes for you to make up and cook. It could be a fun game to play." John nodded, "You call 'em, I'll cook 'em."

When Mark arrived ar the Clench offices at 10 am the next day, the transformation was amazing. The chaos of yesterday had entirely disappeared. In its place was a spanking new and very modern looking carpeted work space, with the smell of paint and new carpets lingering in the atmosphere. His office, which was a cave yesterday, had morphed into a smart new executive suite. He was startled to see an attractive woman sitting at a computer, looking into a compact mirror as she combed her hair. She was equally surprised, quickly snapping the compact shut then putting it away in a desk drawer. In the corner of the office he also saw, who he later came to recognise as Earnest, bent over and making some last-minute connections to a wiring loom with a soldering iron. Both of them stood politely as he continued his progress to take up his chair.

Mark was brief with just the words 'Good Morning' as he sat down and Mavis came over to his desk to await instructions, if any. When they spoke again, he welcomed her to Clench and told her that he knew very little about office procedures in AmOn, so perhaps she could explain for a day or two a little of what she was doing, for him to learn. "It will be a pleasure, Mr Gelder," she assured him.

"One thing I might add, Mavis, is this. I have learned by experience that any type of investigation is heavily assisted by a fully indexed and cross-referenced file system even down to what may seem to be very trivial items. Sometimes these snippets reveal a hidden pattern or a particular event or location that is often repeated, and that can lead to clues. Is that, ok?" He looked towards her.

"Yes, that is fine,"she said, "I will start on that right way, we have the reports and the eye witness accounts of the three incidents we are interested in. I will give them to you to see first. When you have read them, I will file them as you asked."

"Good start;" he gave her a thumbs up.

Next, he turned to Earnest. "I would like you to brief me on all the specialised equipment we use and give me the hands-on experience to operate them.''

"Of course," Earnest replied. "I will guide you through the operating procedures although you will find that they are really self-evident. We can start right away with a practical demonstration if you like?" Mark nodded.

"Go ahead!"

"Look at your computer screen," Earnest pointed. "Now think 'switch on this computer screen'." Mark did as request and the screen flickered once then settled for 'on'.

"Now'." Earnest briefed him. "Out in the hall there are ten low walled offices, they are numbered from one to ten. Inside each open office there is a very senior policeman from one of the AmOn planets. Just think 'connect me to office number five' and he added 'well done' when the picture shifted to looking at the empty chair of office number five.

Chapter 4

CLENCH

With these very basics in place, Mark was now able to commence his first day in command of Clench and he did this by calling the police chiefs to his spacious office and dismissing the two robots for the period of the conference. As his staff arrived one by one, he shook hands with them and grinned inwardly when he learned that the person, he was shaking hands with was the deputy commissioner for police for AMC planet 'Wump' and yet another was from the planet 'Sticky'.

Once they were all seated, he welcomed them collectively and introduced them to each other then he briefly ran through the reports and eyewitness accounts yet again, which they would have seen them many times already. He told them that this case had absolute priority and anything, such as inter departmental rivalry, would be bulldozed out of the away if necessary. Any person or object could be investigated if it was thought bona fide by Clench to do so. He then went on to tell them that unless they had specific instructions from him they were to work independently on their own theories and incorporate any new hard evidence that may become available later. They were to attend his office each morning for his briefing and, in turn, they were to brief each other the direction their enquiries were taking. If any of their lines of inquiry seemed to be promising he would put all of them on the same project and they would go through it line by line together.

Mark stood by the door as they filed through it to their work places. There was banter which he enjoyed because he had many years of experience of people working for him. This, together with his own experiences as a junior policeman on the beat many years ago, had taught him to be approachable because being too austere and remote, in office, made the work less enjoyable for those beneath him.

The feedback screech of a klaxon coming to life had everybody alert as it commenced to issue words of warning. 'We are under attack, take arms, repel intruders.' It continued to issue the warning at five second intervals. There was a rattle at the main entrance doorway and from the direction of the outer wall windows as steel shutters descended over them. 'Attention all biologicals' the klaxon had changed its message. 'Stay down,' the operatives of the Territorial Consolidation Force (TCF) have the situation under control.'

It didn't sound much controlled to Mark because around the steel shutters one could see the flickering flashes of energy weapon discharges. Sometimes the bolts emitted an angry buzz as they ricocheted off solid objects. Mark had, by now, got to his knees and was fumbling in a draw of his desk to find the poenillium pistol that he had been told by Mavis was there. The pistol was motion sensitive with a small embedded screen on the top of the weapon and lit up with a central button which said 'press to arm 'and when he pressed it the word 'kill' steadily illuminated on the screen. The commotion was abating outside so Mark got cautiously to his feet with the intention of checking that his workforce was unharmed. His hand was poised on the door handle to his office when there was an almighty crash behind him and, turning, he saw bits of the ceiling scattered around and writhing on the floor with its jaws snapping was a giant worm-like metalic creature. It was fully a metre and a half broad at the head and at least five metres long and it squirmed towards him, snapping its metal teeth.

There was no doubt in Mark that this was a life-or-death moment as he brought his pistol up and fired at the creature's head but the bolt, he fired hit its teeth; bounced off them and exited his office through a wall, leaving a smoking hole behind it. Momentarily the creature halted its advance when the energy bolt had hit it but it was on the move again and he nimbly dodged it and ran behind his desk to get in a better protected position to take a clear shot. The adversary twisted round, dodged then lunged forward, its scissor like teeth snapped down, removing a bite size chunk of the desk top as the movement slammed the heavy desk up against Mark and he found himself pinned against the wall, unable to move his legs. He fired in haste at the creature and missed.

From the amount of material removed from the desk with its first bite he knew he was two more bites from the monster's mouth and he would be the third. This time he steeled himself as the beast, open jawed, lunged again. Mark did not miss and the bolt from his pistol disappeared down the open throat and came out of its body three metres further on. The mechanical creature immediately collapsed with internal sparks and flashes visible down its open mouth and throat and there was a strong smell of burning insulation. The chaos was exacerbated by the office smoke alarm because the creature was on fire. For a moment afterward its tail end thrashed, then it was still, with columns of smoke and flames rising out of its mouth and from the hole where Mark's earlier energy bolt had exited its body. At this moment the door to his office was thrown open abruptly and some of his staff members came in and looked aghast at the now burning creature. In the meantime Earnest had found a fire extinguisher and was dousing down the flames. "What in heaven's name is it?" One of the staff asked. But there was no immediate reply from Mark because he was intently studying what he later described to Anita as the creature from hell.

"Is anybody hurt?" An Officer and three TCF soldiers came to the door.

"Shaken and stirred but no injuries." Mark assured him again that there had been no injuries reported but he considered it wise they check the main hall. With that advice the Officer detailed his escort to go and check, but he remained

"What is it, is it one of ours?" Mark solicited.

"Most certainly not," the Officer replied. "We have destroyed twelve of them and we have no idea if there are any more. They are tunnelling machines. They have been tunnelling down to the facility but one of them must have got too close to a weak spot in the cavern roof and it dropped through in front of one of my men who didn't know quite what to make of it. Regrettably he wasted valuable time checking it out with control and in that time it attacked him and bit him in half. He was speaking to control when it happened so they were quick to despatch a fighting team and they finished it off but then others came in at all angles. Like this one they are all tough skinned, armoured machines designed for burrowing and grinding solid rock down to small particles with their teeth. The type of weapons that we have down here were designed for close quarter fighting not destroying metal machines." He glanced at the machine that Mark had destroyed. "You seem to have found one of weak points and we have discovered at the point of the turn when the creature squirms its interlocking plates, at the very outward point of the squirm. exposes a transitory gap between the outer plates and their underbody; that makes them very vulnerable to laser type fire; but you have to be quick, the window of opportunity is milliseconds."

Best sit down," Mark motioned towards a chair, "we had better get a record of this while it is still hot in your memory. I have your earlier comments filed by hucom but it is expedient to ask you any questions that come to mind, the answers to which may speed us on our way. You say they are tunnelling machines, what supports that?" To which the Officer told him that they had used a ladder to look at one of the bore holes that a machine had come out of and they found it was perfectly formed, dead straight and shiny walled. "A professional job," was his comment.

"They would have to get rid of the debris from the excavations. How do you imagine that they did that?" Mark had slipped subconsciously into his interview mode.

"There can only be one answer to that question that we can think of. They must have had assistance to remove the rubble and cart it away but where to we don't know. We don't even know where they initially penetrated the planet crust yet." The Officer held up a hand to stop Mark from asking any more questions and pointed to his hucom to indicate that he was receiving an incoming transmission. When it was over he smiled and said "A robo - copter has located the entrance point, it is through a cave at the base of a cliff about three kilometres away from here. They have sent a robot into the entrance and it sent back pictures. Within a short distance the cave entrance tunnel terminated in a vast natural cavern and the debris from the tunnelling is at the bottom of it in a deep layer of pea sized particles of rock. There were also some circular 'scuttles,' they are calling them. They appear to move in the bore holes using compressed air to ripple their skin in waves. We are pretty certain that those must have been the means of getting the rock out of the tunnels. Our robot has examned one of them; it reported smoke was issuing from what would appear to have been the scuttle's computer nodules. We believe they may have self destructed." The Officer showed his delight at being able to impart such up to date information.

"That is progress," Mark excaimed, "I will get that full report later, so let's go back to when the first machine crashed through the roof and what happened. Do you think it was an error ?"

"Yes, it all points to being an error because it suddenly crashed through with slabs of rock all around it then, as I have told you, it attacked and killed one of my men but the machine was not equipped with offensive weaponry, other than its bite and brute strength."

"This is all interesting," Mark said thoughtfully, "but then I wonder why it attacked you, when apart from its jaws. it does not seem to be equipped to wage war. ?"

"I think it was a case of attack to defend," the Officer replied. "Monitors say that at the very point it launched its attack it sent out a rapid signal just three quick pips repeated at two second intervals. Before long more drawn, we assume to be responses, were detected from various points in the surrounding rock. I beieve it was sending a general distress call. My feeling it something like I have broken down' or similar. Perhaps the others were responding when they dropped in through the rock face, ostensibly intending to render assistance, but their actions were seen as aggressive so the were engaged by my men for defensive reasons,"

"As good a theory as any that I can think of," Mark smiled. "Possibly they came through the rock face individually. Once they were engaged by you they sent out distress calls and in time all of them had responded. So do you think that they were drilling entrance points to our location or just generally mining?" The TCF Officer was in no doubt as he replied.

"Almost certainly unfriendly. The tunnels they bored were all headed for this facility but although formidable those machines are not designed for war. Strategically I believe the drilling devices were probably tasked to drill to get as close as they could get to these caverns, without breaking through, when that had been accomplished an attacking force would have been inserted in propelled canisters. As they would have been arriving at different points we would have been hard put to mount a coordinated dfence, especially because we would not have known from which area the main attack was to be mounted. In effect, it would have spread our force too thinly trying to cover every aspect. Because, of course, we would not know at the time how many more buried drilling machines. there were."

"Yes, I can see your difficulty," Mark replied. "What is the military's intention for defence now?" The Officer was in conversation via his military hucom and he pointed to it so Mark nodded and waited for the call to end.

"Right," Officer resumed, "they are going to plug the holes from the top with a thick rubbery non setting gunge. Their reasoning is that the machines ingest rock and grind it into small particles and eject it through their tails into scuttles which carry it away. If fresh machines were to attempt to rebore the holes they would seize up because the injected material would be too sticky for their in internal rock transport systems. In medical terms constipated," he laughed. "The military are also going to bury vibration sensors in the rock which should detect any further attempts to drill down to us."

"Congratulations," Mark praised him, "you have certainly moved fast, but what do you surmise was the objective of the attack?" "We cannot be certain but the vice Chief Minister of the Ongle System of planets sleeps here, so she may have been the target, but we see it more from the point of view that their intention was the destruction of life and the reduction of this facility. If we are correct the target would have been you and the rest of

Clench."

"In that case I am glad you were here." Mark summerised, many thanks to you and the rest of your people; I will certainly convey those feelings to the Vice Chief Minister when I next meet her."

Almost, As if choreographed, immediately after the TCF Officer left him, a picture of Anita came through to him via his hucom and she wanted to meet him to discuss events. He was to meet her, topside, in thirty minutes and they would have lunch together in the executive suite of the government employees' canteen.

"It is quite an enjoyable place," she added, "I think that you will like it."

It still felt very odd to Mark when he opened the door of the lift to find himself in the middle of a manicured lawn and it was hard to believe that despite the physics he had learned on Earth he had just travelled through thousands of metres of solid rock. Even after he had left the lift and he looked back it appeared to be incongruously abandoned in the middle of the lawn but he guessed there would be a facility for its automatic retrieval. In front of him a savuwalk robotic vehicle edged shyly around a corner of the DES building, its canopy raised high on extending rods. The savuwak it stopped before him, voicing 'please be seated mister

Gelder,' and when he did, the canopy was lowered protectively over him. "DES dining room," he probably unnecessarily directed the savuwalk which moved evenly over the immaculate lawn. As they approached the building he could see that Anita stood there awaiting his arrival.

"I thought it better that I came to meet you to forestall any over zealous security procedure," she said as she smiled her greeting and held out her hand towards him. "In the present circumstances of security lockdown, even though you may be expected, they would still view you as an outlander and be quite stringent with their security examinations. From their hair to the soles of their shoes, is a term that they use in their security procedure lectures to raw recruits," she laughed. That special laugh again, he had noticed it before. Was it the trickle of a brook or was it crystal wind chimes stirred gently by a breeze. He had yet to decide before he had heard it more often.

"We can't blame them for getting it right," he flustered a little because he realised that he was still holding Anita's hand but she had made no move to withdraw it. "Sorry." He fumbled with the word because of his embarrassment.

"Don't be," she rejoined, "it was keeping me warm." She gave him the thumbs up. "The canteen is this way," she pointed.

The canteen was quite close to the main entrance where they entered it through the employee restaurant. There were several employees seated and at times Anita stopped to exchange words with some of them. "Normally," she explained, "if there are no important matters to discuss with leaders of the Ongle system or with representatives of AMC, I have my lunch in here. It can be pretty solitary dining alone in the Executive Suite," she turned her eyes skywards, "but we have matters of delicacy to discuss, so I have opted to have lunch in here," she turned into a doorway. It was pretty much as he had expected it to be, a wood panelled room with large oil paintings hung on the walls and dimpled leather seating. "The furniture for this room was one of the first things that we imported from Earth. It is not real leather but a good copy and it is something that we do not have here on Qee."

Once they were seated Anita explained the menu to him and said. "The planet Qee is a vegetarian planet, as are most planets in the Ongle system. I would recommend that you opt for the flame grilled arctic bean burger, it is quite tasty and it is our equivalent of your roast chicken. It would be interesting to see if you can taste the difference." To which Mark laughed.

"I am sure I can try; is it marks out of ten? But John cooks my meals which include meat. Where does he get the steak and bacon from?"

"It is specially imported for you," she looked earnestly at him, "we didn't know quite what else to do."

"Well, I have tasted your artic bean burger now," he indicated it with the fork in his hand, "it is very good," he looked directly into her eyes, "so you can stop importing food from Earth just for me and I will go along with what you are eating provided it is not toxic to me," and she looked relieved.

"I would guess this is exactly the same type of food eaten by our enslaved forefathers. It has certainly proved itself by trial and error not to be poisonous to human beings; but thank you for not wanting to eat only Earth food. Your diet has caused discussion in some quarters with regard to ethics versus tact. I know that a lot of people will be very relieved and, of course, if you really feel in need of a slap-up Earth dinner, we could always make a DMT craft available so you could pop back there."

"Unbelievable, the times we live in," Mark was amused. "I wonder how many light years that would be, just to eat steak, chips and peas," and Anita giggled with him but the laughter faded from her lips.

"It is time to discuss why I have asked you to come here, to ask if Clench have any leads or ideas about who is behind it and what is going on?"

"So," Marks response was drawn out, "it is early days yet but the most obvious thing is that they, who ever they are, did not happen upon Clench by accident. They knew precisely where and at what depth to look, so espionage is the immediate conclusion to that one. The enigma that we have to unravel now is to find out who they are and, from that lead, we will learn more about the people they work for."

"Yes, I agree with that," she nodded, "anything more?"

"Just a small clue," he replied. "We have taken a second look at any sensors that we have down there which would be capable of recording vibrations in the rock. At first there was nothing specific to look at until it was recalled that there was a seismograph in a container in one of the corridors; it is there to warn of potential earthquakes."

"And?" She brightened.

"And yes!" He smiled at her. "There was something detected, there were perfectly spaced vibrations in groups of three, each repeated three times. Each group of three were spaced apart by exactly one second, then there was a pause for five seconds followed by one heavier vibration"

"Mmm, that is interesting," Anita was sitting near the edge of her seat. "What then?"

"The single heavier vibration, during the five second gaps between the lighter ones on the seismograph, also showed a discernible and very precise pattern on its screen, so they are unlikely to be a natural event. We showed them to the chief geologist of the tunnel maintenance staff and he looked at them and said that to him it appeared to be a mechanical signal and a response to it. He thought that the single heavier vibration between the lighter peaks on the graph was probably due to its source being closer to the seismograph. Knowing now what happened it was suggested that it could be an alignment signal for the boring machines to home in on."

"Would that not have given the game away. It is not every day that somebody stands banging rhythmically on a rock face unnoticed?" she was teasing him.

"Indeed that is so," he responded gravely, "and we have checked all cameras and questioned personnel and nothing was heard, seen, or noted but one surveillance camera blacked out about half an hour before the seismograph started its recordings. When we centred upon the seismograph directional sensor it pointed towards a short-abandoned tunnel that had been blocked up with debris. We discovered that the debris had been disturbed recently. When we removed the blockage to reveal the uncompleted tunnel it was ten metres long and contained one discarded, very heavy hammer and an electric stethoscope." He looked at Anita to see if she reacted to what he had just told her.

"The plot thickens," she said, "but please go on."

"Indeed, it does," Mark smiled. "We think now that it was an inside job. Assuming the hammer was used to respond to the signals coming through the rock, we turned again to the seismograph readings. We analysed them very closely. The three beats every five seconds were absolutely mathematically which was only possible for a machine. So, we reanalysed the single beat between them and that was not quite so precise in its timing but still very close to it. We do not believe that a biological life form using a very unwieldy, very heavy hammer, could have maintained the timing with such accuracy. That should not be taken to mean that a biological life form was not controlling it of course. Those aspects are presently the main feature of our investigations because we feel that if we can solve these questions, we may be able to connect up the threads, who and why!" Anita was nodding her head as she took in what he had just told her.

"Now that is interesting," she looked him straight in the eye and held his gaze for just a milli second longer than would be considered correct and he briefly held her gaze, too, and he looked for a hidden meaning in it but she composed herself quickly as if it had never happened, then said; -

"I have something to tell you from topside," she laughed. "Two days before this incident our electromagnetic echo sounding, EMES, you would call it radar, picked up a large meteorite above the position where we have discovered the cave entry point for the mechanical worms that invaded you. The meteorite disappeared and it was thought to have dispersed. In the light of recent events, percieved wisdom has changed and it is postured that it could have been something else, a space ship for example, employing a stealth approach using EMES warping to conceal its presence. This, I add, is pure conjecture, but short of any other answer it is as good as any other explanation!"

"EMES Warping?" he asked.

"Technical term," she replied. "In essence, it is possible to falsify EMES reflections. If an EMS reflection can be delayed, for even a second or two, it would make an object it is scanning appear to be further away.

Alternatively, if an object does not wish to be scanned it is possible to cause the EMES pulse to go past it and not be reflected. The EMES signal then continues on, out into space, so the object would not appear to be there at all. It would be construed, of course, that there was nothing there to detect. In reality that is very rare because there is always a backdrop of bits of meteorites, space rocks or man-made objects floating, especially in orbit around a technically advanced planet. These anticipated near space orbital objects are already factored into the EMES's computer which then sees them, notes them, but disregards them for the area being scanned. But if it was, as it was thought to be, a disbursed meteorite then they could have expected to see a residual trail left by it. That trail would have blotted out the space debris in that area which the associated computer would normally expect to see at that date and time. So the assumption they made was that there had been no meteorite there and the original trace was likely due to an equipment malfunction. Technicians are still rechecking the space backdrop and the reflections that the EMES reported at that specific time."

"Wow! Complex," Mark replied. "It is at least a point for an investigation to start from; perhaps you could ask them to let Clench have the results of their studies.

They may be very relevant."

"Yes, I agree with you and I will put that in place, at once," she said.

Anita accompanied Mark to the lawn and in answer to his call a DMT lift materialised out of thin air. He was surprised and inwardly delighted when they came to shake hands to say goodbye for, she grasped his hand in both of her's and leaned forward and gave him a fleeting butterfly kiss on his cheek. "We are so glad to have you here, you have a formidable reputation for solving criminal enigmas on Earth. In the Ongle system, policing is somewhat different to that on Earth, we lack the skill of your painstaking appproach," she remarked. "I am sure that we will get to the bottom of this soon.

"Once in the lift Mark hesitated a moment before he directed it. Anita was different he decided. She didn't have the false laugh and guarded language that you would excpect of a politician on Earth, yet at this very moment she was the acting head of government for nine inhabited planets with a population many times in excess of the entire population of Earth. Yet, she came over so normal and approachable.

Mark was about to go but stepped outside of the lift and called to Anita who turned and he hurried up to her. "I am thinking deception. If the EMES scanner did not see something that it was expected to see, such as the missing trail of a burned-out meteorite, would it have any effect upon its operation?"

"I don't know," she said." Wait, I will ask," and he waited as she walked up and down obviously in contact with EMES experts somewhere afield, and she returned to him. "Yes, it would because the EMES would be automatically obliged to carry out a detailed rescan of the void area and it would do that up to three times."

"Would it narrow its field of search to do that. Please ask them."

"Yes, indeed it would." She re-quoted the experts reply. "I see what you are getting at Mark, an event was staged to slip something in while the EMES had taken its eye off the ball. I will leave that one with you to investigate. Well done," she said and with a wave she turned to leave.

Chapter 5

NETWORK OF SPIES

Mark was still mentally sifting over his conversation with Anita and he was almost unaware that he had arrived at Clench before he had been reminded verbally for a second time that he had arrived at his destination. He shook his head as if to clear it and made his way back to his quarters to change and brush up before he headed for his offices. John greeted him and asked about his trip and, unrequested, produced a good size glass of red wine and suggested he sat down for a breather before he headed back to the treadmill. "A good idea," Mark agreed and he was fumbling in his top jacket pocket for the key to his brief case then he called John. "Have you seen my brief case key anywhere?" he asked. "I didn't take the case with me top-side but I usually keep the key for it in my top pocket."

"No," John responded, "you did leave it once by the kitchen sink and I gave it to you. Perhaps it is there again. I will take a look," and he disappeared only to return a moment later. "Sorry, it is not there." He was glancing round as he spoke. "Ah, there it is," he bent down and picked it up from behind Mark's chair. "It must have come out of your pocket with your glasses."

"Thanks John, I don't know what I would do without you." Mark took the key.

There were only a couple of hours of normal business left of the day when Mark returned to his office where he spent the time briefing the senior officers about his meeting, earlier, with the Deputy Chief Minister of the Ongle System of Planets. He was also able to ascertain that no progress had been made with respect to the mystery hammer signals, although the heavy hammer was still being inspected for finger prints or minute fibres stuck to it.

The day after, Mark glanced at his brief case before opening it and he realised that it had been moved during the night. He knew this because tt was a peculiar habit of his to always carry or to put the case down with lock positioned so that he didn't have to turn the case around to put the key into the lock. It is a bit fastidious; he would admit to himself. The habit only applied to his brief case. He now picked it up and walked to his office and as he did so a TCF soldier fell in step with him by his side and informed him and the accompanying house robot. "It is a new policy." VIPs, if seen, are to be escorted as far as practical." "These are indeed troubled times," Mark replied and thanked him.

For the remainder of the day Clench was sifting through the findings of the forensic labourites testing the burrowing machines but so far, they had turned up little of interest. The integral parts of the machines were barren with no part numbers or detail or manufacturing references upon them. The only unusual thing they had found was a hair clip normally used by women but, in this case, it had been repurposed to keep a wire away from its neighbour where there was evidence of a previous short circuit between them. One of the investigators ventured that at least the enemy were probably not hermaphrodites, but that found very little favour as a conclusive observation.

There folowed a flurry of data from Anita's office to the effect that they had found the presumed landing for the craft that had clandestinely brought the burrowing machines. From the indentations and flattened scrub, they had learned, it was probably about one-hundred metres long and about twenty-five metres across. There were no tracks that would indicate that the burrowing machines had made their own way independently to the cave entrance so they had probably been carried over in parts and assembled in the cave. Very few people visit that area but there was one witness who had reported that she saw a large flattish craft in that position and it was there all day but it had disappeared by the next morning. The people near it were helmeted and dressed alike so she assumed it was a military exercise and passed it by.

I think we can now say that the EMES was 'tricked,' as per our conversation yesterday, he typed his reply.

Mark was in a pensive mood as he made his way back to his quarters and he was thinking about his wife's untimely death due to cancer. That had been a few years ago now but there were moments when it all came back very vividly. It had been a good marriage and they were both well suited to each other. She had a great interest in the outdoors and she was an accomplished artist. Everybody who knew her found her to be attractive in looks with an outstanding personality and indeed that summed her up. He smiled secretly to himself when he recalled that she was far better at solving crosswords than he could ever hope to be.

His thoughts led him to wonder if she could have been saved if they had lived here on Qee, and he asked his escorting TCF soldier where the medical facilities were because he had never been briefed about them. "There are a few hospitals mostly concerned with regrowing limbs or correcting deformities," he was told, "but for most accidents or other medical matters, a team of medical robots, called physimeds, would be despatched and they would create an operating theatre and treat medical emergencies on the spot."

"All medical emergencies!" Mark was astounded.

"All normal ones," the soldier replied, "but if they cannot handle it they send the patient on to an appropriate hospital by DMT. That could mean to a hospital on another planet."

"Well, tell me what would be a case they had to pass on to a hospital," he was on a learning curve. "Could they cure cancer out here in the field, for instance?"

"Of course, sir," the soldier replied. "Most cancers only need a simple injection. The only case I have personally witnessed where they couldn't cope in the field was when one of our number suffered a massive heart attack and the medical robots sent him straight on to a specialist hospital on the planet Sticky. He told me afterwards that they had actually removed his heart from his body, cleaned it up, fixed the plumbing and put it back in his body. He was only there for two days and he came back to us as right as rain and was back on duty within another two days."

"Gosh," Mark was impressed and saddened, because Earth was such a medical backwater and his beloved wife Janet, along with millions of other people, had died because more was spent on armaments than on health by Earth's tribal governments.

John welcomed Mark warmly when he entered his quarters and informed him that he had now been told that Mark had requested that he would eat everyday Ongle food from now on, so he had prepared him several traditional Qee dishes to see which ones he liked. Several was an understatement because John started to scurry backwards and forwards bringing small sample dishes for him to taste. Some Mark found to be delicious and others were decidedly strange tasting. All in all, before the survey had finished, Mark had eaten a full meal but in individual spoonfuls from twenty dishes. "That will do to start with," John laughed as he cleared the dishes away. "We can try others on different days but I now have a good idea of what you like and dislike." Mark thanked him and retired to his bedroom to study the various documents that he had received during the day, then he tore a scrap of paper off the bottom corner of page 51 and folded it loosely to use as a book mark over the head of page 30. Then he locked the brief case and took it to the hallway so that he could just grab it when he left for work the following morning. He left the key in his trouser pocket and the trousers hanging on the door knob of his bedroom from where John would collect and iron them.

Mark arrived a little earlier in his office the following day and he dealt with the most pressing questions and responses until mid-morning; then he placed his brief case centrally on his desk and opened it. Noticeably the paper he had used to act as a book mark for page 30 was not in place and he had to delve down into the document to find the torn off piece of paper between pages. It had obviously been dislodged and it had fallen, unnoticed, off of page 30 when somebody had interfered with the file. In the event, as Mark had expected to happen, a logical attempt had been made to match up the jagged torn pice of page 51. The torn corner had then been dropped on top of that page and the papers had been replaced in their original order. Mark carefully closed the case and pressed a button to call his chief of staff, Petan Maggf, who was seconded to Clench from AMC planet Andfrell. While waiting for him to arrive Mark placed the brief case in a bin bag and addressed it to the forensic facility on Qee. He would tell them later why he had sent it by alternative means rather than use the same courier service.

Petan arrived in due course. He was a little more squat in stature than an Ongolian, which was due to the higher gravity of his home world; he also had the faintly blue complexion endemic to the population of Andfrell where he had been born. Mark motioned for him to sit down then he asked his robot support staff, Earnest and Mavis, to go together 'topside' and deliver the wrapped brief case to the chief scientist of the Ongle government forensic laboratory. He waited for them to go before he turned to Petan and explained what had transpired. Petan listened carefully, observing that official papers would be of little interest to a robot personally but they would be all important if they were to be repeat them to a third party. "I agree with that," Mark put both of his thumbs up. "Robots have no concept of reward, so they neither gain nor lose by having access to secret data."

"True," Petan confirmed. "Robots only conduct their affairs according to their programming, so it is the programmer we need to find. They have no emotional interest but they do like new experiences to add to their skill base, that is the only one-up-man-ship anomaly they suffer i.e bragging to each other what they can do!" which casused Mark to laugh.

"The prime suspect and I would say the only suspect I have, is John. He seems affable enough but I suppose being a robot he is only following what his processors are telling him to do. However, he did demonstrate what I believe was a deliberate deception when he fooled me into thinking that the key to my brief case had come out of my pocket and had fallen to the floor where he found it. I could be wrong, of course, but my instinct, together with this latest event, inclines me towards suspicion. What I would like you to do is to gather all available facts about John and keep a check on the facility surveillance cameras to build up a picture of his activities and contacts he makes when I am not in my quarters. Find out where he was made, for whom he has worked in the past, and whether he has any special modifications to his circuitry or programmes. What I would like to do, also, is to have security diagnostics done on all of the robots that we employ. Give that a fancy title to obscure the fact that we really are checking they are kosher."

"The word kosher does not translate on my hucom," Petan spread his hands to invite an explanation.

"Oh sorry, it is a word that had an original meaning but it has now been stretched to describe a genuine article. I'm afraid these odd words will crop up from time to time. Anyway, if you could get that underway, just rope the robots in at random but make sure that John is high up but not at the top of the list. I'll leave that with you then."

Mark rose, as did Petan, to shake hands before he departed. Then Mark opened the new brief case supplied to him by Clench from the Stores Department and he put some selected but not very critical papers in it. Enough to be interesting but not revealing enough to do any harm if they fell into the wrong hands.

Petan was in contact with Mark via hucom. "The new branch I have created is to be called Robot Quality Assessment. Under that disguise I will issue instructions that all Clench robots are to be called to attend a computer clinic to ascertain that they were operating at their full capacity which will involve some internal inspection." Mark meantime had briefed Anita who was concerned but she wished him well.

Two days later, Mark received a classified hucom link from Petan:- 'We have uncovered something of the history of your robot called John. Apparently, he was once a fleet robot and was on the Ongle ship, the Daffodil, which was destroyed by enemy fire during the Rap-Terrabot war to annihilate the planet Earth. The Daffodil was literally torn apart when it got caught inbetween two enemy cruisers outside the main combat area. Outgunned, she was taken on from both sides. After the 'Hands of God' incident, we sent ships to gather up the remnants of the battle to prevent accidental discovery by Earth astronauts. Robot designator Daf326 was found intact and adrift in space. Its primary purpose was as a chef and restaurant worker on the Daffodil. Daf326 was fully functional when it was recovered so they sent it back to stores for reissue. After they had constructed the underground redoubt below the DES, they indented for various specialised robots and Daf326 was renamed John and it was received here just before you arrived and was assigned to the quarters which you now occupy.'

That night when Mark went home, he deliberately left the key to the new brief case by the sink in the kitchen and John handed it to him the next day with a mild rebuke for not looking after his keys. "As long as you are here, John," Mark replied, "they will certainly never get lost." But Mark had not been in his office long before Petan called him.

"I have some bad news for you," he sounded a bit breathless. It concerns your robot, John. A smoke alarm in your quarters went off half an hour ago and when the fire team attended, they could get no response from the house robot, John, so they used an emergency override code to gain access. When they entered, they found the robot slumped on the floor with smoke issuing from a hole in its torso. A preliminary on the spot report by the fire crew is that they are of the opinion that it appears to be a deliberate act on the part of the robot to totally incapacitate itself. It seems that it had removed its own breast plate and then connected an extension lead from the house main electricity supply across its processors and memory bin. The result is a molten mass in that functional area and it will need an entirely new computer reinstallation before it will ever become reusable. Clearly the intention must have been to deny any attempt to recover its stored memory."

"Yoiks!" Mark said explosively. "Poor John, he seemed almost like a friend. It had to end, of course, but I was thinking in terms of him being reprogrammed."

"I am just arranging that," Petan advised, "stores will issue you with another robot. I have already asked them for you; but we can now say we have definitely found the miscreant.

"I'm still shocked, but are you thinking what I am thinking, that the robot knew that he was under suspicion?" Mark asked.

"Yes, I am probably thinking on exactly the same lines, but how could it have known. I have not yet sent out the recall notices for robot quality assessment so it would not have known about that officially, so it suggests a tipoff because

I am sure you did not tell him." Petan's statement contained the question.

"Certainly not," Mark was quick to answer. "Nor did I make any record of our earlier conversation, nor write anything down. The only thing I can think of is that our earlier conversation re investigating John was somehow relayed to him and he made the ultimate sacrifice to protect his mission. There are two possibilities that spring to mind, the first being that your check up on the origins of robot John may have got back to him or you have made a recording or written it down?"

"Most certainly written down" Petan responded. "I hand keyed it into my computer but that has some pretty sophisticated government high level security protection; it is considered to be an unbreakable code."

That evening, when Mark returned to his quarters, he found a new robot waiting for him outside the entrance door, it introduced itself as Joshua and told him that he had been asked to explain that he was hitherto employed as a mechanic but a house robot programme had been installed in him so the transition should be seamless. Later he was surprised to answer the door to find Anita there and she told him that she had just dropped by on her way back to her residence. She knew about the demise of his previous house robot and she had heard that a new one had just been pressed into service so she took it upon herself to give Joshua detailed instructions about his new duties. The robot dutifully followed her from room to room as she explained what needed doing every day and she seemed to enjoy her self-appointed task. When Mark did hear parts of the conversation, she was having with his house robot, it appeared to him that she was able to slip into and out of the role of being the most powerful person in this star system, yet able to subordinate all that to discuss mundane household matters with a robot.

She did pause at times as if listening to something in the distance and he guessed that important government messages were flowing backwards and forwards via her hucom. Then, when she finished, she instructed Joshua to bring tea and biscuits. Afterwards, she came to sit down with Mark by a coffee table. "Please repeat the story," she said, asking him to repeat everything again in fine detail, together with any leads emerging from the investigation, which he did. But then the conversation turned more personal.

Anita seemed to want to talk and she asked him about his life on Earth and if he had been married and he told her of the death of his wife and that he had never really contemplated a relationship with anybody else. He was surprised to learn that much the same applied to her because her husband had been a military Commander who in his spare time was an ardent cave explorer. He had met his death as a result of a rock fall whilst pursing his hobby; and she told of how devastated she had been. To compensate she had thrown herself into her work with the result she had garnered expertise and praise. She had not expected it but immediately after their last general election she had been called upon by the Chief Minister of the new government of the Ongle System of Planets to take up the post of Vice Chief Minister, thus second in position only to himself. Her position presently was acting Chief Minister in the absence of the elected Minister. She was, he decided, quite vivacious, but at times she had held up her hand to kill their conversation as unheard messages came to her hucom. But on occasion when this had happened, she would roll her eyes or raise them upwards towards the ceiling and alternately smile at him to indicate that she was beset by a tedious caller or a vexatious subject, which would make him laugh. Plainly they were enjoying each other's company as they discussed their jobs. She also questioned him about Earth and any hobbies that he had and they discovered that both of them, work permitting, had found joy in nature and drawing. As the evening drew to a close, Anita asked him if he could cook a traditional Earth style dinner for her. and It was left that he would do this in three days time when the newly appointed acting Vice Chief Minister would be holding the fort to give her a break from official matters. They parted at the doorway to his apartment and outside a savuwalk vehicle with an escort of four other savuwalks manned by armed TCF soldiers awaited her. In the limited distance he also noted other soldiers maintaining a watch over the route that she would take to her residence. Before she left, she placed a delicate hand on his arm and thanked him for a lovely evening and this time it was Mark who leaned forward and brushed her left cheek with a kiss. There was an unintentional linger to his action for which he immediately reproached himself for signalling that he may have conveyed something more meaningful. Then as he watched her leave, he was aware that he had a feeling in the pit of his stomach. It was like a hunger and it was something he had experienced before when he first met his wife, all those years ago. Perhaps Anita had felt something too, he surmised, because as soon as she got home, she came through to him via hucom to thank him once again for a lovely evening and to reconfirm the date for their lunch 'Earth style' in three days time.

When he was back in his office the next day, Mark decided to go out into the main hall to see Petan Maggf to discuss if there had been any new discoveries or theories regarding the death of Mark's housekeeper robot, but he was told there were none. There was nothing to be learned from its memory core either and he was about to leave when he glanced up and saw that there was a high camera looking down straight at him and it followed him as he walked away back to his own office. He said nothing but on return to his own desk he called up Petan on a secure connection to ask about the camera. "It's a security camera," Petan told him, "There are six of them spread around the building."

"The one above your enclave followed me for quite a while after I left you; why would it do that?"

"I really can't say for sure," Petan advised him with a laugh. "My guess is that it gets quite boring in the control room, day in, day out watching for something to happen, but you have a status of some standing, so the operator of the camera was probably just being nosy and following you around for personal entertainment."

Mark laughed with him. "Where is the control room for the surveillance cameras?"

"That would be topside in the penthouse above the DES building. Anybody short of the higher levels of government needs special permission to enter there because of privacy laws concerning eavesdropping on the good citizens of Qee." It followed, of course, that getting permission from Anita to visit the surveillance control room was not a problem.

Mark was met by the director of the surveillance centre who briefed him that they only surveyed areas on request, either because of suspected criminal activity, or for government departments, such as his own, in this case, with an eye to personal security. Until recently, work had been pretty mundane but the abduction of the Chief Minister of the government of the Ongle system and the attack by the mechanical burrowing worms had given them, albeit with some reservations, a reminder of their essential role.

"Yes, I can see that you are doing fine job" Mark reassured, but with your permission I would like to try an experiment. Could you arrange for me to see through my eyes exactly what a robot was watching from here and I will direct it to what to look at?"

"Of course," the director nodded "we could put it on a screen; that would be no problem at all. Tell me what you want."

"Thanks," Mark smiled, "just give me a moment to set it up," and he turned away as he entered a hucom exchange with Petan, then returned his gaze towards the director.

"We are ready now. Could you use your camera, the one that has a figure three painted on it, in the Clench headquarters. I will control it." he asked the direction.

When this was done, they found themselves watching Petan seated at a computer table and at Mark's request he started to type. "You can stop now," Mark said, "we probably have enough." and Petan lifted his fingers from the keyboard. "Now," Mark said to the director,"please rerun the sequence and ask one of your robots to reconstruct what Petan just typed by just watching his fingers on the keys." After a short delay word appeared onscreen. It was headed 'HIGH TEMPERATURE (the Ongle classification of Top Secret). Restricted Distribution. The Government Of The Ongle System of Planets, Directive 117/117/840. Below were the words 'FOR CLENCH EYES ONLY',

"Thanks that's all for now," Mark said loudly," then he nodded to the director's room. Once seated Mark explained to the director what he had been doing. "There has been a serious security breach. I believe that one of our documents has been compromised, normally the only way is by direct communication of the document to somebody else. In this case that is unlikely. The compromised document would have been similar to the one we have just witnessed being typed into a computer. Once it had been typed in, the document would have been encrypted and undecipherable but we have discovered a potential weak point if the pre-encryption activity is being overlooked by a video camera." He opened a notepad and from it he read out the date and exact time when Petan Maggf had started to type the, suspected to be, compromised document into his computer. "From your records," he asked the director, "could you tell me exactly which robot would have had control over camera number 3 situated in Clench at that time?"

"I can, indeed," the director started to type on his computer keyboard. "Yes, I have it," he exclaimed. "It was our robot that goes by the name of Herbert; its official designator is a jumble of figures and numbers, so Herbert is somewhat easier to remember."

"Is Herbert here now?" Mark enquired.

"Of course, that is the beauty, robots don't need time off to sleep, eat or take holidays. They work, as you would say, twenty-four hours all day and every day. The only time one of them would not be working is if it had broken down."

"Sounds a boring job?" Mark's reply carried the inflection of being a question.

"Not really, but I do try to keep them occupied. They all have spare computing capacity so I introduce computer games into their work to make it more interesting for them." Mark laughed not because of the introduction of computer games but because the director had sounded very paternal regarding the welfare of his robots.

"I am afraid that I am going to have to take Herbert away from you for a while." Mark opened his hands.

"I don't know that I can spare him to go with you," the director sounded desperate.

"Afraid needs must," Mark replied. "The authority is the Acting Chief Minister herself." Mark kept his voice monotone to avoid any sound of triumph in his statement. "Look, we will take great care of Herbert but we need to do some security investigations on him and at the end of it he will be returned fully functional to you, that is the deal."

"I was wondering why your colleague typed the document into his computer, though. If he had scanned it in, nobody could have read the key depressions?" the director asked.

"Good question," Mark affirmed. "It has to do with a theory that too much auto copying of High Temperature documents result in mistakes, such as originals left underneath the lid of scanners or residual impressions being recovered of what was last scanned, or simply a blase attitude, such as taking extra copies in case they are needed! In this case the person typing this had received the message via his hucom and was transcribing it onto a special water marked paper which triggers copiers to reject it if somebody tries to recopy it without the necessary safeguards in place. As yet this may not have reached your department where the subject is mainly physical security, but I am sure that it will."

"I suppose we could manage without him for a while," the director was coming round to accepting the inevitable, "when do you wish to remove him?"

"Right now." Mark stopped to confer with the TCF team already stationed outside of the DES building, he continued. "There is a danger because if Herbert is programmed as I think he may be, he may try to self-destruct if he is told any of this. Can you prevent that?"

"I have heard about the housekeeper robot that worked for you in the DES," the director confirmed. "Yes, I can just switch him off. Wait and I will do that." Mark watched from the office doorway as the director made his way over to Herbert and talked to him as he raised his hidden right hand to just above the neckline of the robot and he then plunged his fingers into its hair to press a concealed button. Momentarily Herbert moved to stand up and swing around to resist but it was already done and he slumped in his chair, devoid of motive power. At Mark's call, four members of the TCF arrived and picked up Herbert and placed him on a stretcher and for a second it looked as if the director of the establishment would break down in tears, but stabilised his emotions and asked Mark to keep him updated concerning Herbert. In promising to try to do that, Mark responded, the fate and future of Herbert was now in the hands of the military who woulld attempt to debrief him; but Clench would also be very involved in the procedures.

As it turned out, the military were moving quickly and efficiently and Mark had just finished his evening meal in his quarters when he received a priority update. It turned out that the TCF did not take Herbert direct to a laboratory but they had they commenced doing physical checks on him instead. To this end they directed that he be taken to the safety of their practice weapon ranges and it was there they carried out a comprehensive body search for hidden explosives. Wisely too, he thought, from what they told him. They had decided to ignore the proper access points in the robot's chest and they had created a new access point through the side of its rib structure. Thereafter, they had used a remote viewing fiberoptic probe inserted through the new aperture and straight away the air sampler of the probe reported it had detected the presence of Zylex explosive in the robot's interior. In the more detailed investigation, which followed they found a suspicious container wired to a digital count down meter. The container was also wired to the robot's normal chest inspection cover and it was clear that if they had attempted to remove the cover it would have resulted in an explosion. After that, the TCF team maintained a safer distance from the robot and used an AI linked mechanism to sever every cable that it could detect inside Herbert. Luckily that did the trick and the digital count-down meter ceased its activity. The carcass of Herbert was declared 'safe' and transferred to the laboratories for systematic examination.

Chapter 6

QVO THE REVIVAL

Mark went to bed early that night but almost as soon as he awoke the next day Anita was calling him on a secure channel via his hucom"Good morning Mark, I hope that I didn't wake you up? By way of explanation, there has been significant developments during the night in respect of the late robot, named Herbert, and they are very relevant to your department's research" she paused and he asked her to continue. "To cut a longer story short, they found a mysterious sealed, shiny, oval shaped metal container inside Herbert, and it was wired to a complex interior wire loom, and they have removed it. They have since drilled into the container to see what is inside it and it was discovered to be filled with brain cells, specifically, Rap brain cells! We have only one example in history to compare this with. Some years ago, when Vivienne's father, Geoffrey Holder, was onboard the QvO, he was attacked by a robot that had been secretly infiltrated into the ship's complement. There was a firefight and the robot was killed. The subsquent investigation revealed that an internal Rap brain had a symbiotic relationship with the robot brain. The container they found then, was much the same as the one that they have found in Herbert. After we deeated the Rap-Terrabot armada we had assumed that the remnants, if any, of Terrabot would be scattered across the universe and incapable of ever reorganising or mounting another attack upon Earth or AmOn. It seems we may have been over optimistic.

"Yes, I have read about the exploits of Geoffrey Holder. His story is the most read book on Earth. There are not many children and adults who have not read it. It it led to the point of first contact we had with Ongle, at the old Royal Air Force station, Greenbrook. That is now a major tourist attraction with a space museum, coffee houses and luncheon rooms, planetariums etcetera. But, where do we go from here? There seems to be no doubt that Herbert read the letters being typed by Petan and Herbetrt must alerted have John that he had been rumbled. So now we know of two corrupt robots, I wonder how many more?"

"Indeed, I agree, how many? We have plans to bring them all in and we are to use specially screened robots to examine them," she replied.

"I suppose it is a military matter now?" Mark asked.

"Not necessarily all military," Anita countered, "we must have law and order input as well.

We still have no idea where they are coming from and there may be other civil aspects, so for the time being we will keep Clench fully operational, but you may need to be relocated into space. At the present AmOn are marshalling three-hundred thousand war ships; their job will be to seek out the Rap-Terrabot base and bring them to account. But quite frankly three-hundred thousand ships is not a lot to search even the near universe, so the intention is for them to cruise about in groups to try to pinpoint radio signals which may lead us to them; but if they are based very far away then their planetary radio transmissions may never reach this quadrant in our lifetime, so at best it is a long shot. The unanswered question is how are they getting here. None of our dark matter submerged beacons have given so much as a suggestion that unregistered ships have used DMT within this territory, so they have a trick up their sleeves that we do not yet understand. Anyway," she added, "I am seeing you tomorrow evening for dinner, so we can continue this briefing then. I hope I am not taxing your culinary skills too much?" She laughed.

"Oh, not too much," he replied light heartedly. "I had planned to do a family type lunch with just a few variations. For that I have consulted with Brenda who is one of my female police commissioners back on Earth and at this very moment Vivienne is shopping for the ingredients and she is going to send them to me tonight."

"I'll have to make a note of that," Anita laughed, "using our highly paid ambassador to Earth to do your shopping may make the tax payers of AmOn blink, but I know it is in a good cause."

"Undoubtedly that is true and she is a volunteer, but to confuse and perhaps excite you I have planned upon a starter of bruschetta with cherry tomatoes, main course vegetable lasagne with fresh salad and olives and for dessert, lemon ice cream sprinkled with crushed pecan nuts.

"Sounds delicious, I think," her laugh tinkled. "I will bring a bottle of wine as my contribution; it is from one of the planets which we have nicknamed the Vineyard because they grow little else there but the various berries and fruits that they make their wine from. The Vineyard, on its own, virtually keeps the rest of the Ongle System of planets in wine and they are the real masters of their trade; there are few who could challenge their superiority. Over time, they have even perfected vintages so that they do not leave you with a heavy head and the next day wish that you had not drunk so much the night before."

Mark felt strangely excited as the day wore on, but he was grounded by the lab reports as they came through. It seemed that Herbet's Rap brain cells were, in fact, a fully functioning brain. It was wired into the robot's logic circuits which balanced the input of the robot's digital brain with that of its Rap host which used them as a supplement to its decision-making processes. The bioogical brain was in the sealed container which would preserve its encapsulated contents for as long as they remained in the container and no further nutritional input was required. However, the very act of severing the capsule from its wiring loom had resulted in the organs's deliberate suicide and there was nothing to be gained from any attempt to rewire it. There were no clues to its origin, directly or indirectly, to be obtained from an analysis of the compounds and elements used in the container's construction. Their current opinion was that the robot named Herbert which they were inspecting was not the original Herbert. The original had been replaced with the robot they had on the lab table right now. This was supported because there were minor detectable, off-spec, differences in his computing technology and the traces of unusual compounds in his casing.

Now at home, Mark was even more on edge to see that every-thing was perfect for the evening and he painstakingly went over the details with Joshua. For Anita's surprise he had imported a Belgium lace table cloth and a fine antique tea set from England. However, he could not wait patiently so he darted from place to place to adjust a faint crease in the table cloth or to line up a piece of cutlery or table furniture, although it was already perfection and nothing actually needed to be adjusted. Thankfully his agitation was brought to a stop by the sound of the TCF coming to attention as Anita dismounted from her savuwalk and he went speedily to open the door. His eyes widened to see she was wearing the Ongle formal dress for women, a long ankle length dress, tight at the bodice but flowing from the waist down and had large white flower heads sewn in around the neckline. On her head she wore a matching white cap at a cocky angle. Mark took a deep breath because she looked absolutely gorgeous.

"Are you going to let me in?" she said, which jogged his mind. With a laugh, he recalled instantly that he was supposed to do something other than stare at her and he stepped aside.

"You look very presentable," she pointed towards him, "I like the style, is that a national dress?"

"Sort of," he replied. "It's called mess dress and is usually worn at official dinners. I have it because as the Global Police Chief I get invited to all sorts of functions back on Earth and all the males attending them wear much about the same."

"And the ladies, what do they wear?" she cocked her head to one side inquisitively.

"Gowns, mostly," he smiled. "You would be just fine as you are."

"Good," she said, taking his arm, "now please lead me to the best table in the house" and he guided her to the tea table. Joshua hovered attentively nearby and then went to the kitchen to bring a large pot of green tea, imported from Earth.

"Beautiful crockery and table cloth." Her eyes were alight.

"Joshua will prepare dinner and we will have tea here first. We can then move on to the dining room," Mark explained. In an interval of time, Joshua reappeared in the lounge to announce that dinner was ready to be served and Anita and Mark rose to walk arm in arm to the dining room as Joshua opened the door to admit them. Anita gave a gasp as she saw that the room was brightly lit with candellabra.

"Where did these come from?" she asked.

"Straight up from Earth this afternoon. I didn't order them but Vivienne thought it would be a nice touch and she included them along with her shopping for the ingredients of the dinner."

"Ouch!" Anita withdrew her hand quickly from experimenting with the flame of a candle.

"Careful," Mark exclaimed, "as you have found out it is a real flame. Luckily, they are the smokeless, odourless candles that we use today. In days gone by, the older style candles would have quickly developed a blanket of smog. Clearly, Anita was enjoying the meal immensely and almost child-like she enthusiastically described each mouthful, although she was initially suspicious of the baby tomatoes which she thought were the eggs of an Earth creature; but he assured her that they were not and she found them delicious. She was wondering, aloud, about saving the seeds and trying to grow them on Qee. Then corrected her thoughts by saying that sadly it would not be legal but she would ask her Minister for Agriculture to import the seeds from Earth who could grow and test them in a controlled environment to to rule out any possible cross contamination.

As the evening wore on, they became deeply engaged in conversation about their past and their childhood, learning, to their astonishment, that they had grown up on farms, so details of animal husbandry, ploughing and crops became a major topic. In many ways Earth methods and Ongle methods of farming virtually ran on parallel lines. But the freed human slaves of the Rap empire were several thousand years ahead in terms of agriculture. Oddly, they had entirely missed the age of steam. So, whereas, on Earth, robots had only just begun to embrace farming and to take on the role of agricultural workers, on Ongle they had a historic role in agriculture. They also touched on the subject of the politics of Earth. Anita reiterated that AmOn would not even contemplate allowing Earth into space outside of their solar system because they were so divided by notional barriers. "If only it didn't have such serious implications," she said, "it is terrifying that on Eath they can draw a line on a paper map with a pen and claim that the people either side of it are culturally different."

"Put like that it does sound a little strange," Mark agreed. "I suppose it really has to do with power and the control of minds. To achieve control, you have to convince the people on your side of a line, drawn on a map with a pen, that they are superior in some way to the people the other side of the line. In some cases the actual distance between the two populations may be just metres."

"Exactly,'Anita responded. "As it stands, America would probably claim the moon as American territory; it will be a toss-up whether China or Russia claim Mars, but if they do that it will be hotly contested by Europe and India and they might even go to war in space over their claims. We simply cannot have that in space; and we could even prevent Earth from ever going to the moon again if they do not get their act together to become a one nation planet; but thankfully the signs we have today give us rise for optimism."

"Yes, still the highest hurdle, for Earth, are the religious groups," Mark upheld, "Under what religion would a new planet be populated but this is weakening after the first contact with Ongle. Of now public pressure is becoming overwhelming for Earth to go out to explore space. They are aware, too, as recorded in the book Dark Matter Transit 2, of the very powerful weapons available to AmOn. Those weapons stopped World War three in its tracks and brushed aside Earth's nuclear weapons and ballistic weapons as if they were toys. Earth people are beginning to feel they would be safer under the protection of AmOn, especially now that they know, for certain, that Earth is not alone in space, but there is a bit further still to go yet."

"Yes, a bit further yet," Anita agreed. "Really a lot depends on the newer generations and dyed in the wool attitudes fading away."

"Not in my life time, I think," Mark smiled, "but the next fifty-years will probably bring about the big change in attitudes that will be needed." He rubbed his chin reflectively and then changed the subject abruptly. "Whew, that wine you brought is really first class and quite strong; you did say it doesn't give you a hangover?"

"We only drink it in spoon size amounts, but you must have had the equivalent of eight spoonfuls in your glass; best take it easy." She reached over and patted the back of his hand playfully as reassurance. "Now I have news to tell you that has just come in via my hucom. The boffins taking Herbert apart have failed to find anything in its construction which would point a finger towards any part of the known galaxy, save for one item. They think it is a capacitor but it is encased. The laboratory doesn't want to break it open just yet, but the casing has a number rather like a manufacturing number or a stores reference number." She was also in hucom touch with Joshua in the kitchen and he emerged from there with a scrap of paper in a hand with a number written on it. Anita took it and gave it to Mark. "It means nothing in AmOn, so over to you Mr policeman," and Mark took the paper and looked at it.

"I can't say that it yields a lot to me either at the moment," Mark screwed his eyes up in thought. "At least I have representatives in Clench from most of the planets of AmOn," he said. "I will get them to investigate each planet, to check their stores manifests and manufacturing marks across the board; but tell me, are the numbers pressed into the cover of the capacitor or are they on the surface?"Anita held up a hand for him to wait as she posed that question via her hucom.

"They are pressed into the metal of the cover, is that significant?"

"Possibly it could be," he responded. "To be pressed into the metal or as a fixed plate on the metal suggests they have to be hard wearing and not prone to getting rubbed out. It is almost insignificant but it does give a very small pointer to the manufacturer because in a robot that would not be important because the capacitor would be installed in a protected place. So this item was manufactured for multiple purposes and all eventualities, with some not always known to the people who made it. A very small clue perhaps, but a criminal investigation often starts with just a minute clue and it builds and builds and expands and expands and suddenly you have the whole picture. Also having a part number eliminates it having been made as a one-off in a workshop for a specific purpose. The second more important clue is that as none of the other robot's parts are stamped with a number, so this was possibly an emergency repair which was done in a situation where the standard parts were not available. But having a part number means that it has been catalogued somewhere and that may lead us to who the part was sold to. We are on a roll."

"On a roll?" she asked.

"Sorry, it's an Earthly informal expression, in this context it means successful."

"I will try that phrase out on some of my colleagues. It may inspire them to greater things," she smiled, "but now I must go. Thank you for a wonderful evening; the dinner was absolutely brilliant. I can see that I will have to arrange more official visits to Earth if only for the dinners." She took his arm as they walked to the door and she turned to kiss him on his right cheek but clasped him firmly so that their bodies touched as she did so Then as they parted, she said "By the way, I was thinking that we could meet up one lunch time soon and do some painting. The DES building has a lovely garden out the back, even with a stream running through; it is an artist's dream. I couldn't spend a lot of time, of course, but say in a lunch hour maybe?"

"Wonderful idea," his voice was slightly more husky than normal and he watched her walk to her savuwalk and until she and her military entourage disappeared around a bend in a tunnel.

When Mark introduced his theory to the rest of the the senior officers of Clench, they agreed with his deductions explaining his faint but plausible reason why the robot had one numbered part among thousands of unnumbered parts in its construction. Nevertheless, he said, "It was a pretty tall order when faced with the realities because there were twenty-one inhabited planets in AmOn so he judged the chances of finding the stock number akin to looking for the proverbial needle in a haystack. Regardless of the risk of failure, they would still apply their best endeavours to it. They would bear in mind, too, that it could not be automatically assumed that the part had been manufactured in AmOn territory at all." Mark nodded. Then also asked his clerical robot to send the part number onto to Earth's World Police Headquarters.

Days later, Mark was seated in his office in Clench Headquarters when the final report regarding the mysterious robot part number from the last remaining AmOn planet came in. 'Another nil return' he muttered as he ran this last one off and speared it onto a spike file on the corner of his desk. Then he gave his report to Anita via a classified hucom link through which they were often in touch briefly during the day and this time she had something new to impart. "Our military advisers have decided that Clench is in danger because of the work it is doing. It is believed that it is too vulnerable to retain it in a fixed location so they want the Clench offices and personnel to be moved to the QvO. Because it is a space ship it can make itself elusive by constantly readjusting its flight pattern, speed, and incursions into dark matter. That makes it very difficult to lock on to by somebody who might intend to board it il legally. At the moment the QvO is being recommissioned and a few modern additions are being incorporated. That should take about a week and the entire Clench team will be transferred to it. She is to be the nominated capital ship of the AmOn fleet."

Mark was listening and thinking, the QvO was simply colossal and its statistics well known by everyone on Earth. She was the largest space ship ever built by Qee. Her deck space, if ever it were placed side by side, would be larger than most of Earth's nations. It had been built that large because it was the first spaceship the Ongle System of Planets had ever built after the Earth slaves had usurped the Rap Foundation and had renamed their prize the Ongle System of planets. They had wanted something very special to mark that point in their history. The planet Qee had, under the Rap Foundation, been the core constructor of large spaceships; they had something to celebrate in those days and naturally Qee was the obvious choice to build a state of the art, show the flag, vessel. The QvO did not have a metal skin as most space ships did, because she was fashioned from meteorites towed in from space and reformed by rock flow methods into the magnificent ship that she was. Inside, she was so cavernous that great swathes of the ship were mothballed and only cleaned by robots once a year. The accommodation for families and married couples was in ethnic villages; sculptured from observation of Earth's television programmes or from the collective memory passed down through the generations, during their years of slavery to the Raps. Another, not oft spoken, reason for her sheer size was that Dark Matter Transit was in its infancy in those days. There are storms in dark matter and if you transferred through it and got mixed up in a DM storm your ship could be hurled billions of kilometres off course and sometimes even in the wrong direction. So, in those bygone days, an exploration ship, such as the QvO, might have to wait it out for months or even years, living off its stored resources and farm produce. The rule was that before transit, their monitors had to show that DM had been settled for three consecutive months before it was deemed safe to attempt a voyage within it. The QvO was historic, as well, because its crew had discovered the Ambrocognian-Mundi Colligation of Planets which had led to the eventual formation of AmOn that a few years ago, was united into a single entity of the governments of the Ongle System of Planets and those of the Ambrocognia Mundi Colligate (AMC). Thereafter the QvO had been pensioned off as aged and uneconomical to run.

Their discovery of and the friendship with Ambrocognia Mundi had led to Ongle receiving the technology how to construct DM navigational beacons these forwarded information concerning DM storms. With this technology it was now possible to travel, at will in the firmament.

The Qvo now lanquished at the centre of the Ongle System and was used inter alia, as a school for space cadets and a hotel. Now Mark, was to be stationed in this historic space ship, but a little pang in the pit of his stomach reminded him that he would probably not see Anita while he was there; but his unease was quelled for the time and disappeared entirely when she added in a less official tone. "If you could come up topside at lunch time today you could bring your pencils, paints, canvas and easel, et cetera. The weather forecast is good and we could go into the DES garden at the back. It would be good to see you because you could be away on the QvO for some time."

"I would be delighted to do that" he enthused. "It would be a most welcome break and a chance to see you notwithstanding, on occasion, one feels to be something of a mole in a hole down here. See you soon."

"I will look forward to that," she replied."

"The atmosphere outback of the DES was curiously hushed, radiating a sense of security and beauty in its carefully manicured gardens as they set up their easels in front of a bench overlooking a clear but slow-moving stream. "As good as it gets," observed Mark as he came to sit beside her.

"I often come here for a breather," Anita said quietly. "It is a heavenly break from the burden of office."

"Yes, I could well imagine that,"Mark was sympathetic. "Quite frankly, I admire you immensely. You have the most demanding job in the Ongle System, you have none of personal support that you could expect from a partner at home, but despite that you are always serene and balanced. I find you quite amazing."

"Thank you for the praise," she turned to look at him straight in the eyes. "If you could see some of the undercurrents going on you may not have said that. It can be very difficult at times and a partner would be a great help. "In truth, my outward demeanour is really part nature, part act and part developed ability to delegate." She laughed and Mark laughed with her.

"There is a saying on Earth, 'the art of good management is delegation,' and that is a tactic which I have honed to my advantage over the years," he grinned.

With that last revelation they crossed the line and Anita was no longer just the Acting Chief Minister of The Ongle System of Planets and Mark was no longer just the Chief of the Police of the Global Police Force and the Commander of Clench. They had become friends and were able to freely discuss personal subjects as well as the affairs of State as their hands were resting near to each other on the bench they were sitting. Mark moved his hand fractionally so that his fingers touched Anita's fingers gently and neither of them pulled away. Very soon they were touching and responding to each other's touch and their fingers were caressing each other's hands. Waves of reciprocal joy and tenderness swept through their bodies and they could feel their increased heart beats racing with anticipation because they knew it would lead to all out love.

"Gosh," Anita took her hand away. "Look how late it is, I have to get back," she said as she swept up her easel and drawing pencils. As he stood up she leaned forward and for the first time their lips met. Then with a backward wave she hurried towards the entrance to her offices in the DES building leaving Mark watching her until the DES door closed after her and he could no longer see her. He stood for a while, his thoughts churning with chaos, but he knew and dearly wanted that they become lovers in the not-too-distant future, but already Anita was in contact by hucom and thanking him for the lovely time they had spent in the garden together.

He was still standing there lost in thought but he jumped when a light brown creature dashed out from underneath the bench that they had been sitting on and the animal hopped away into the undergrowth but not before he had seen its white scut. He blinked and took a closer look. "Anita" he called urgently "I think that I have just seen an Earth type rabbit. What is it doing here?"

"Oh, right" she replied sounding very concerned. "I didn't think that you had that much to drink?"

"Nothing at all" he responded, "you know I haven't and I know a rabbit when I see one."

"This sounds very serious," she said evenly.

"What did it say to you?"

"Rabbits don't talk," he was exasperated.

"Hang on, I'll get a physimed (robot doctor) to you, don't go away."

"I don't want medical attention; I need an explanation?" But Anita was beside herself laughing. "Oh dear," she exclaimed as she struggled to stop laughing.

"Yes, we do have rabbits all over the whole Ongle system. The Raps brought them here as curios in one of their slaves runs, they are all over the place and are a bit of a pest with their habit of digging up lawns. We have caught as many as we can and transported them to huge fenced in reservations but some always manage to evade our attempts to round them up."

"Hah," Mark was amused, "just wait. I'll get my own back for that one day," he laughed, "there is a side to you that I had not expected and it sounds like fun; but who would have thought that the humble rabbit would beat the rest of the Earth creatures into space." He was still amused by Anita's leg pull when he reached his underground offices at Clench. True it was a diversification but very important and he was secretly pleased because it showed that Anita, in the right setting, could easily switch from dealing with matters of great importance and would be apt to even tease on occasion. If anyone had been nearby and close enough to have heard him, they may have wondered why the Commander of Clench was laughing aloud when there was nobody else present.

Chapter 7

TRANSLOCATION

As the move to the QvO drew closer, things were becoming hectic at Clench and a small fleet of robotic luggage carts were formed up with digital exactness on the Clench forecourt. Inside Clench, all except the most strategic operational equipment was being dismantled for shipment and as each load became ready an empty cart trundled in through the doorway to be loaded by general duties robots, before it moved off to a designated position in the forecourt. The operation was going to plan and sometime previously the QvO had moved into a near orbit to Qee, from where it could be seen as an extra star in the night sky. The real purpose of the move was to shorten the radio time lag between the QvO and Clench because hucoms used radio frequencies to interact with each other. Both Mark and Anita were very busy at this time but Anita did manage to establish a video link to wish him bon voyage and then it was back to work. It was Mark's chief of staff, Petan Maggf, who was to lead the advance party and set up a skeleton network of communications aboard the QvO. Finally, it was done, with everything packed, indexed and in a convoy which made its way to the DMT lifts which materialised, with there loads inside the transit craft.

The legend only become real when one approached the passive looking QvO lying motionless as if anchored in heaven. At first seeming insignificant against the backdrop of space, it grew into the colossus documented so often in stories of its many adventures and encounters in the cosmos. In close up it overwhelmed the senses to know that it was constructed and not a natural feature of space. It was while they were traversing the QvO's length towards the hanger deck that Mark noticed two parallel metal humps running out of sight like a hoop around the hull and he guessed that this was the, spoken of, floating belt which extended from the hull to become a robotically manned bombard to deter would be aggressor ships from launching an attack below the deflection angle of the ship's main armaments. Then there was a burst of light emanating from the interior of the ship as the giant doors fell away to reveal a maw the size of a village. Seconds later they had entered a new world.

Although it swamped the mind to come aboard this historic vessel, its internal layout had already been documented many times by television companies whose cameras had pried its corridors and activity centres. Thus, one could rarely observe any aspects yet unknown to them; but the cameras with their fixed viewpoint could never fully capture the sheer size and the awe it engendered. The Captain of the ship, Anda Anjar, was indigenous to the AMC, but now serving in the forces of AmOn. He came over via hucom to Mark to welcome him aboard.

"Your offices are to be located in the empty quarter of the ship," he told him. "Essentially you are here as single men and women so we have taken a reserve military barracks, including dining halls, out of moth balls and we intend to accommodate you all there That also relieves your team of having to buy food and prepare and cook it as well as all the other domestic chores associated with living in a normal house."

"I can't say that I would disagree with that Captain," Mark agreed.

"Your unique nonmilitary status on board entitles you to call me by my first name, Anda, and I will refer to you as Mark,"the Captain responded.

"That has got things off to a fine start, Anda," Mark acknowledged. "I will endeavour to not use or abuse that privilege in the presence of crew members."

"Thanks for that," Anda responded, "that would be helpful. I will let you get unpacked and your offices up and running, then I will pay you a visit. Meantime, any problems encountered or questions to ask, contact me or the first officer if I am not on duty."

"I estimate that we should be wired in and up and up to speed in about three days time,"Mark replied.

"Good." Anda came back. "Oh, I forgot to mention that the Clench status on board is that of being lodgers, so you have to go where the ship goes but if you have any special voyages in mind, it is best for you to put your requests through DES. They may send this vessel or allocate a different vessel for you to use. I will call you back in four days time." And the hucom image of an iris in Mark's mind closed to indicate that this contact had been discontinued.

The barracks which Clench was to occupy were tidily laid out with green lawns and avenues, albeit the trees and the grass were artificial. It still had a feeling of gentle order rather than the alternative which would have been block paving or large concrete slabs. Above it an artificial sun carved its way high above the barracks and backlit clouds drifted by. Occasionally, with prior warning, it rained, mainly one imagined to keep the dust down and to ground any airborne pollutants. The new activity centre for Clench was in the existing military style operations centre where its installation was going ahead apace and would be fully operational quite quickly. Then a tremble felt through the soles of their shoes, told crew and passengers that the QvO was underway using its conventional poenillium thrust engines and Mark took a window of opportunity to call Anda on his hucom to discuss data exchange between Clench and the DES. Anda replied that they were already out of effective radio range of DES, henceforth communication with them would be via DMT messenger darts to a varying schedule, except for emergencies wherein they would be sent immediately. The objective of a varying despatch time for the darts, he explained, was to negate an analysis of the entry point of the darts into the DM thus disclosing the whereabouts of the QvO. In consequence the darts were despatched when the ship was on the move and they were sent out at varied times each day. For their return a rendezvous point was encoded in them giving the precise coordinates for them to intersect the QvO's daily movements.

Mid-morning the next day, the Clench teams were still working on the installation of their equipment, but they stopped their activities and looked towards a broadcast loud speaker which had started to wail a warbling sound followed by a voice which announced 'Ship Alert Wolf One.' The Clench workforce switched its united gaze to Mark in askance and Mark turned to his gekobot robot, Earnest, and asked him to find out what Alert State Wolf One was all about. Shortly after, Earnest was able to inform him that Wolf One was a fairly low-grade security alert but as with all security alerts everybody onboard was obliged to check the nearest person to them to see if they recognised them. If they did not, they had to send a hucom still picture of the unrecognised person to the security computer and action, if necessary, would be initiated by the computer. In general, Wolf One concerned matters in the ship's loading areas. The incident, however, served to remind the Clench operatives this was a warship. Thus, Mark allowed things to settle down on the bridge before he put in a call to ask if the recent alert was of specific interest to clench.

When he made the call Anda greeted him and told him that he was just about to call him now the panic had died down. "Indeed, I believe that this is something that Clench may well wish to investigate. I will give you a word picture of events as they unfold on the bridge; you take it from there," he paused to zip his thoughts together. "Before we started to use our DMT messenger darts, we decided to run a security check in the form of a dummy run on the system. With that objective in mind, we released a flock of messenger darts back to AMC and to Ongle. Among the flock there were two specially rigged messenger darts which we despatched, one each to Ongle and AMC, the two rigged darts were fitted with anti-tamper devices which would give no outward indication that a secret trigger had been activated if they had been violated by someone not using the approved key to open them. All of the message darts arrived back safely, save the specially rigged one that had returned from AMC bearing a discrete indication of having been trespassed.

"Were there any indications such as a delayed treturn ranmission time?" Mark inquired.

"Indeed yes,"Anda confirmed, "but we cannot be certain of its accuracy because that facility was never intended to be fool proof and whoever opened it could reset the internal clock to a time of their choosing. The turnaround was expected to be five minutes, but this one took ten."

"You have certainly given me quite a lot of useful info to commence an investigation," Mark confirmed. "It does give rise to suspicions with regard to how it was handled at AMC, so I think we had better take a closer look there. At this point we cannot trust the darts with classified information so I will have to go there myself, but first I must ask DES to approval a shuttle for my use."

"No, don't do that," Anda cut in. "We had better not use DMT devices to summon up transport for you. I will use my Captain's prerogative to authorise one of the QvO shuttles."

"Thanks for that," Mark responded gratefully, "that would speed up things considerably. I will be taking the chief of police for Andfrell who is currently on my Clench team."

"Consider it done, "Anda replied.

Mark knew the force of gravity on AMC was stronger than it was on Ongle or Earth but he was still not quite ready for the crushing force he felt as his ship materialised out of the DM on the robocopter landing pad to the front of AMC Defence Ministry building. Understandably it caused surprise and consternation to military guards on duty that a shuttle had landed there without filing a flight plan. Hence the view outside shuttle was of a heavily armed, robot infantry training their weapons upon the ship. Caution turned to curiosity when the landed craft's stairway dropped down to reveal to the identity profiling, scanner cameras the instantly recognisable Andfrell police chief, Petan Maggf, standing on the ramp, accompanied by the Commander of Clench. Both then approached a sentry point where Mark handed over a letter. It requested that the bearers be given an instant audience with the Secretary of State for Defence and the military head of security. The guard took the letter and scanned it over to the guardroom who called them both in. There Mark had to explain to them that his mission was urgent and very secret and he could not reveal it for security reasons; and they were satisfied with that and no further questions were asked.

Thus, it was with haste that Mark and Petan were sped to the appropriated government building to be ushered into the friendly furnished office of the Secretary of State for Defence who rose from his chair to shake hands and at the same time the head of military security entered the office. The Secretary of State asked them all to sit down and he said no further word but he looked questioningly at Mark as a cue for him to explain his presence, so Mark started to relate their reason for being there which were also their excuse for not sending a prior warning by a messenger dart. They were astounded when they did learn the reason for their visit as Mark revealed it to them. "Effectively no government communication is safe then!" the military head of security summed up the information they had just learned. "Up to now, we have always sent sensitive documents in combination locked mini safes."

"I am afraid not any more, I would advise," Mark told him. "But let us work through this first; an abrupt halt would alert any mole in the network, so I suggest just sending low grade material in the interim."

"What do you want us to do?" the Secretary of State leaned forward in his seat to ask and Mark nodded to his colleague to step in with their Clench suggestions. Petan rose from his chair to outline the plan and ask the pertinent questions.

"Our plan of action is relatively simple." They gave him their full attention. "It seems fairly obvious to us the documents are being compromised somewhere in the chain of receipt and despatch in AMC and our focus is on the handling staff engaged in the receipt and despatch of the official messenger darts.

"It is a robot," the military head of security explained.

"That is a good start," Petan nodded. "In that case Could you tell me which robot was employed doing the despatch of the messenger darts at this date and time?" He handed the head of security a slip of paper which he took and held up his hand while he consulted via hucom.

"Yes, we would know, there was only one on duty at that time. They used to have two but the Robot Resources Department took one of them away because there was not enough work for two robots." They waited again while he consulted elsewhere, afterwards telling them. "Apparently the request to reduce the number of robots for the government came from the DMT Messenger Service. But when asked the DMT messaging staff said that they had sent no such request. We didn't think a lot about it, and we concluded desipte denial it really must have orignated with the Messenger Service, so we agreed to try it."

"Ok," Mark came back into the conversation. "We can deal with who did what later but this is really crystallising our suspicions. We would like to conduct a very discrete surveillance of that particular robot without raising its suspicions. Our experience so far is that as soon as they realise they are under suspicion a rogue robot commits digital suicide, but we want to capture one intact." He then outlined their plan. "For two days we will watch it carefully to see if it has any other contacts then we will, literally, move in for the kill. With your permission, what we hope to do is to erect a metal arch inside the walkway into the despatch centre. The arch will in fact be the disguised antenna of a very powerful electromagnetic field. Our experts tell us that any robot passing through the arch would suffer interference to its internal networks, enough to render it inoperable. Thereafter, we will move in to shut it down for good then we plan to take the carcass back to our laboratories on the QvO for examination. In the meantime, just to check our theories, the QvO is going to down load a single DM messenger dart at 8pm this evening. It will be addressed to the Secretary of State for defence, AmOn. Thus, it would be reasonable to assume that the document carried by the dart was of some importance indeed, it will appear to be when one gets to look at it because it will give away the entire dispositions of the AmOn fleet, except in reality it will be pure bunkum. It is the very sort of document that would be highly prized in the world of espionage."

That night at 8pm they met again in the Secretary of State's office where they gathered before a screen showing the DMT messenger arrival cradles. Exactly as timed, a single dart appeared in the otherwise empty receipts cradle. The dispatcher robot stepped forward and examined its address, then it promptly disappeared with it into a nearby store room, emerging five minutes later with the dart's inner strong box which it gave to a courier to deliver. "Is there any special equipment in there it would need to open the dart?" Mark asked. 'Not at all,' he was told 'but there is a combination safe within it which would certainly present problems to open.' "So, there is no reason to take the dart into the side room?" "That should be unncessary," The Secretary of State took it upon himself to answer.

"I think that we have got our man then," Petan was all smiles as he said it. By the second night of observation, they knew that the robot disappeared into the side room with selected darts as they arrived. On the third night they were again, gathered before a screen to watch the target robot at work and an operative was sitting with them, his hand on the paddle lever which activated the electromagnetic arch through which the suspect robot must enter and leave the building. From there they saw their prepared message on their screen as it was transmitted to the robot. 'Robot 3571AZ/OP8 report to the entrance of the service tunnel to assist to unload a consignment of DM messenger darts.' The robot stopped what it was doing and jerked its head uncertainly and then it set off for the service tunnel. Just after it entered the tunnel the operator pushed the paddle switch down and 3571/ AZ/OP8 halted as if turned to ice. What followed was brutal to watch but necessarily decisive to prevent itself destructing. Armed TCF personnel entered the tunnel with laser pistols and severed the head from the robot's body. Other lasers were used to take off its arms and legs. Finally, they cut the torso in two and the remains lay scattered in seven pieces.

"Ug! what are you going to do with it?" the Secretary of State for Defence asked. "Is it not useless to you now?"

"Not at all," Petan replied. "We can soon connect up the wiring again but we won't put the body back in one piece; it is likely to be spread around on a work bench with control wires connected all over the place while we run tests on it. The only thing we have to do now is to locate and remove the storage batteries in its legs and short out any major circuits in the body that may still retain a charge. Only then will it be regarded as truly deactivated." Later, following Petan's request, a party of general duties robots arrived. Showing no concern for their fallen comrade, they gathered up the parts and put them in the most convenient containers to hand which was a coffin taken from a pile of them in a nearby loading bay. "Very appropriate," the Secretary of Defence uttered.

The next day, Mark, Petan, plus the cargo of a coffin returned to the QvO. The coffin was emblazoned as 'High Temperature' with a caveat of 'Government Eyes Only.' It was embarrassing to Mark that he could not even divulge the contents of the coffin to Captain Anjar but he apologised and told him that as soon as he was allowed, he would be told all. It was a difficult situation because, normally, a Captain of a ship has the right to know everything concerning his ship and its cargo. But AmOn security were adamant, it was designated 'Government Eyes Only.' To placate the Captain though, he was able to tell him that the messenger dart security test that he had devised had proved invaluable and it had uncovered an exploitable weakness in the DM messenger dart procedures which had now been plugged AmOn wide. Anda was in line to receive a letter of appreciation and a medal for outstanding service to AmOn when he returned from this mission.

Robot 3571/AZ/OP8, shortened originally by the lab staff to OP8, and later to a more familiar sounding Opy, lay in parts strewn across a laboratory test bench and connected up wire for wire so that it could digitally, but not physically, function. Like Herbert who had died before him an examination of his body yielded no clues to his origin but it was revealing becaus, as with Herbert, OPY was found to incorporate a sealed container of Rap brain cells wired to its processor. Efforts had been made to communicate with the brain but they were not a great success. Preliminary investigation, however, showed that it was a fully functioning brain which had belonged to a Rap whose name was Dapper. That was as far as the interrogation of it was able to go because it refused to cooperate any further. Ethics crept into the picture and the argument ran that it was a living sentient organ; there was no automatic right to kill it nor threaten it with death as a means to induce it to cooperate. In any event, you could not torture a brain because it was incapable of feeling pain. The method adopted was to show it kindness and they had given it a pair of digital eyes and the brain sat in a dish under a glass dome watching the lab technicians silently and disconcertingly until one of the technicians, not wishing to be watched any more, propped an open magazine up against the glass to shield its gaze. Then the problem was more permanently addressed by putting a video screen in front of its covering dome and all day long it was shown videos and films but on day five the brain shrivelled and died. 'Thank heaven for that' was whispered from bench to bench in the laboratory.

Opy was 'singing like a canary' now, as the saying goes and they were downloading masses of information from it. They also caught glimpses of the inside of Rap- Terrabot ships that were manned completely by robots. Another discovery revealed an independent digital camera inside Opy which could take pictures down its nose. The camera also contained a radio transmitter and was probably used to transmit the pictures it had taken of documents to a receiver elsewhere. But as the picture was to be sent by radio it implied that the receiving equipment would not be very far away and presumably aboard a Terrabot ship.

The security implication of the likelihood of a masked hostile ship somewhere in AMC space could not be discounted. Therefore, Captain Anjar was included in the Clench staff meetings held to discuss Opy and the threat posed by it. Mark told them they were now able to decode Opy's memory and it contained a stored, yet unsent message. Under controlled conditions they were going to get it to send that message and then monitor radio frequencies for a reply, which would enable them to map-pin its source. Captain Anja was asked to task his radio engineering branch to provide the necessary tracking. It was soon discovered the radio return came from within the sasteroid belt that accompanied AMC in orbit around its home star. The dart they sent, to reconnoitre the area, surprised them all because it incongruously revealed a garden shed and not the high-tech structure they had expected to see. Clearly it was obviously just a forwarding point for information so the eventual destination was not evident to them. The shed, as they were now calling it, was expected to be protected by a force field to trigger the structure to self-destruct if it were violated.

"Right," Mark summed it up. "May I suggest the following. We will cause Opy to send another dart to the shed in the asteroid belt so we can trace where it goes from there." He looked at Captain Anjar for a reply. "Relatively simple," the Captain smiled. "Give us fifteen minutes to, also, set a couple of DMT beacons near the shed." He laughed. "Then if your dart is relayed on again through DM, we can monitor the track it takes, but then what?" he looked back at Mark.

"Sounds efficient," Mark praised him. "I propose to blow the shed up to deny it to them and serve as a warning that we are onto their ruse and they will hopefully withdraw their other clandestine networks of a like nature."

"I can't just blow something up in AMC space," the Captain cautioned. "I would need authority from at least The Vice Julate to explode something in his domain. Julate's tend to get a bit tetchy about that sort of thing."

"Leave that with me," Mark replied. "I'll get onto that." Forty minutes later the QvO was in position near the shed and Mark asked the Captain when he was ready to obliterate it. "Mind you," he added "I would prefer something to blow it apart rather than something that dismantled its atomic structure. That way, we may be able to gather up the bits to learn something from them."

Mark was on the bridge twenty minutes later as the QvO approached the discordant garden shed nestled in the AMC asteroid belt. "We have now learned from OPYs dart the coordiinates for the next stage in the relay for his DMT darts," Anda briefed Mark.

"Good Mark replied, so there is there nothing more needed from this one may I suggest take it out?"

"I agree with that," Anda turned to face his control desk and said "Lay in the preset target. Engage and destroy, fire!" The explosive tracer shell could be seen streaking its way to the shed to explode with a bright orange flash inside it. As Mark had hoped the blast dismantled the shed making it possible to send out robot teams with jet packs to recover as much as possible of the remains.

Chapter 8

GATHERING EVIDENCE

The Clench team which had received the pieces of the alien shed were now trying to fit them together like a jigsaw puzzle. Already they had most of the outer walls, less a few pieces, and their reconstruction slouched drunkenly and swayed to one side on the point of imminent collapse. But an enterprising robot used its machine strength to brace it while another robot pushed a heavy wooden packing crate across the floor to shore it up. Now stable, Mark arrived to take a look at the inside of the shed but there was, as yet, nothing for him to see. In time the contents that had been blasted into space were mostly recovered and were spread across a military parade ground in the empty quarter. A glance would show small parties of robots and humans wandering among the debris, stopping occasionally when they saw something which they thought they knew the purpose of and they would take it to one of the randomly growing piles of like bits and pieces.

On the bridge of the QvO they were on full alert because they were in the process of initiating yet another DMT jump to the coordinates which they had down loaded from OPY's messenger dart. Their objective was to discover the ultimate destination for the data that Opy had misappropriated. In the meantime, a breakthrough had occurred. A female scientist sifting through the remains of the shed had come across a metal plate which was attached to a circuit breaker. From the robust wiring on the other side of the plate she deduced that it was intended to deal with very high current, suggesting that it was a master circuit breaker for the shed. From there she had reasoned it was affixed to the outer hull so it could be the isolation switch to facilitate entry and exit to the shed. With alacrity Mark passed that information and photographs of it to the bridge where its arrival resulted in a reappraisal of their current plan which had been to simply destroy the structure on arrival

The primary mission of their amended plan was now 'to gain accesses to the shed and a small team of specialists were assembled, equipped with jet packs and personal side arms, together with a team of robots who were to accompany them. The Clench scientist who originally found the circuit breaker was rushed in to meet them and to show them the isolation switch.

She was also able to tell them, following the reconstruction of the shed, that the circuit breaker had been positively identified as located underneath its floor immediately beneath the doorway. Soon after the whole crew of the QvO were glued to monitor screens watching the party jetting their way over to the shed. There was no wasted bravado as the jet pack party headed over to the nodule and they saw them circle the shed looking for the isolation switch. When it was found, a robot carefully edged its hand towards it but as its hand neared the switch a glow flicked around it which increased in intensity the closer the hand came to the switch. It was evident it was a warning signal. and there would undoubtedly be a point, if the robot had continued, where any closer proximity to the switch would have triggered a defensive response.

"It could be that the robot's arm is metal," the Clench scientist on the bridge ventured by radio to the away team. "If anyone is brave enough, they could try their hand instead!" With those words, a human member of the away team took off his glove and gingerly approached the isolation switch. This time the glow was decidedly angry and it flickered alarmingly causing the away team to back off.

"If we can't get what we need from it, we may have to blow it up where it is," the Captain said to Mark on a closed Channel.

"I agree with you there," Mark affirmed "but if we can get access, it may be best to leave it unsullied so as not to arouse suspicion. We can come back for the coup de grace later after we have no further use for it," and they both agreed to that.

It, it was a deometic robot that finally that solved the problem when it disappeared into a broom cupboard and came back with a wooden mop handle in its hands. "Try this,wood is not something you do not expect to encounter in space so it is likely it will produce no reaction." When the Captain saw it, he immediately issued orders to a jet pack equipped robot. When it was tried out, the mop handle solution worked perfectly, producing no reaction from the shed's sensors when it was used to trip the isolator. "Ingenious," Mark told him.

With the isolator inactive, the shed door was easily opened manually and it was discovered that the isolator switches only deactivated the shield, leaving the internal circuitry unaffected. "The mission," Mark told them by hucom, "was to analyse, photograph and download its programmes to memory sticks. Above all, to find out where the next link in the Terrabot message dart chain was located in their star charts and how to address that link with an explosive messenger dart if needed. Once we have everything we need, ensure there is no sign that we have visited, then close it and switch the protective screen back on. We are going to leave it where it is. Then we will proceed to the next link in the chain."

In all, they stayed there for a week observing, recording, and eventually they had successfully extracted all of the other DM locations used by the messenger dart relays. Once these had been transcribed to AmOn star charts they then become a part of the ship's database. Thereafter, if needs be, the QvO could navigate to any of those locations if it was required to do. Their current findings, thus far, had confirmed that there was, yet, a further onward hub in the chain which was given the name 'the conduit' because it was actively serving eight tails which included the one, they were following.

Captain Anjar and Mark had habitually fallen into the routine, most afternoons, of having coffee in a coffee bar not far from the bridge. In this relaxed atmosphere they briefed each other on events of the day and their expectations for tomorrow. "So what's the next move?" the Captain inquired.

"Therein lays the problem," Mark sighed "We cannot trust our messenger darts at present, but I have to go back to speak with the acting Chief Minister of Ongle; she also acts on behalf of AmOn as the overall political

Commander of Clench. I will be away for tonight and back about midday in three days time."

"Mmm," the Captain mouthed the sound. "We will first have to move away from this spot under poenillium thrusters. If we DMT out we may leave a trace that we have been here. Pity I didn't think of that when we came," he wrapped his forehead with his fingers to jokingly stir his brain to action. "Still, we have been here a whole week now, they have had plenty of time to attack us, so we seem to have got away with it. It will take roughly four hours to get far enough away to safely engage DMT." The distant rumbling sound indicated that the ship was already under way. "Why are you are going to the Department of Earth Studies," the Captain was slightly perplexed. "The DES, to me, does not seem a very appropriate place to discuss a war with Rap-Terrabot?" Mark placed a finger to infer 'Shsssh,' and cleared his throat.

"I think it was an oversight that you were not told, so I am going to take it on my own back and tell you, but it is very hush. The DES is, of course, a cover story. Clench has nothing to do with the DES, but that title sounds innocuous enough to arouse no suspicion that it may have a hidden purpose. After the kidnappings, the government of AmOn created Clench to track down and bring to justice the perpetrators of those crimes. The DES has deep underground caverns that are reasonably bomb proof and it also has modern facilities installed down there. The government of AmOn killed two birds with one stone. They needed personal protection for the acting Chief Minister of the Ongle System plus a home for the Clench setup. Since she was on the spot, she was also made the overall Commander of Clench and there you have it. Most people in the DES think that we are just a local police investigation to inquire into the disappearance of the Chief Minister of the Ongle system, but it is, of course, a much wider investigation."

"We're here,"Anda spoke in Mark's mind, "and incidentally one of the other tails of the alien DM messenger relay is also near here; it lays about two-hundred thousand kilometres off our port bow. While you are down there, please ask them if they want us to take it out?"

"I will certainly do that," Mark chuckled, "but not before I get back to you; a policeman does not normally get to see that sort of thing."

"I can do better than that," Anda rejoined, "I'll even let you push the button."

"Wow!" Mark joked back. "What with that and the new train set I intend to buy when I am down there, can life get any better?"

"Be reminded then," Anda was up for a tease, "it is a Captain's duty to ensure the safety of his ship at all times. I will have to check out the train set!"

"Shan't!" Mark said stubbornly.

"Shall!" Anda raised his voice and they parted mirthfully.

The shuttle put down on the DES lawn and Mark was escorted to the committee room of the Cabinet of the Government of the Ongle System of Planets, which was presently given over to a combined AmOn strategic operations task force. He took his place on the chair indicated to him at the committee long table, with Anita the other side of it and centrally seated. She looked up and smiled and held his glance. Slowly he inclined his head very slightly and winked at her and he was inwardly amused to see her shyly glance around for reassurance that nobody else had seen him wink. Apparently, no one had. So, her gaze averted, she shuffled her papers absently and then welcomed Mark to the meeting.

Mark was accorded centre stage to outline the events of how they had trapped the rogue robot then used its circuitry to find the first part of the alien DM messenger relay and how they had followed it on from there. With their permission the next part of their quest would be to find the major conduit, which was difficult because it was in uncharted space about ten light-years distance. He and the Captain of the QvO were, therefore, seeking guidance from the committee on how to proceed once they had found the conduit. Some members of the committee were looking decidedly worried at this new piece of information, no doubt thinking about the possibility of a war, but they agreed that they would discuss it and then consult the AmOn government to seek their agreement.

Having left the committee to debate their approach to AmOn, Mark found himself at a loose end and eventually he entered a small shop which claimed to sell Earth memorabilia and he purchased two items as presents before returning to his previous apartment, sub ground, in the DES complex. There was no welcoming robot to greet him this time and the apartment lacked a lived-in feel, but early into the evening Anita called to say that she was working late that night but she could meet him tomorrow evening and she would bring at takeaway.

Then she said the words that he had longed to hear, but she disguised them by using a matter-of-fact overtone which one would normally use to say good morning. "I have missed you," she said." Despite his racing heart he told her in a similar casual voice.

"I have missed you as well, Anita." Those words, although also heavily shrouded to appear as matter of fact, were very significant indeed and an obstacle to saying more meaningful words in the future had been easily vaulted.

When Anita did arrive the next evening, she was clutching two silver heat retaining boxes the contents of which turned out to be an oddly flavoured but acceptable copy of an Earth pizza. "I chose this because it was the closest thing that I could find that would make you feel at home" she smiled; and he decided there and then that it was a beautiful smile. It carried warmth and generosity, above all it was an honest smile, he decided, with a personality so genuine that it stunned him. The following desert was cold and it heavily featured 'spangey' which was a fruit, remarkable because it left a flavour that endured long after the last morsel had been swallowed.

To please Anita, Mark had asked Vivienne back on Earth to hunt out the old film South Pacific and they sat side by side on a settee to watch it. He was conscious that he wanted her in his arms but there was no way that he could do that uninvited; but then she did a surprising, unexpected thing. She turned herself lengthwise on the settee and draped her legs over his knees. Initially he didn't know quite what to make of her move, it was so very trusting and friendly, as if she thought nothing of it.

To test if there were another meaning he took her hand in his and stroked the back of it, marvelling how small and delicate it was. 'Made in Dresden' hands he told her. She didn't know that Dresden, on Earth, made renowned, exquisite, fine and delicate china but she guesed he was being complimentary.

With great gentleness he slowly moved to brush her wrist and now her lower arm with his fingers and she sighed and settled deeper into the settee as he lifted his hand to smooth down and stroke her hair, his movement becoming ever more sensual as his fingers brushed behind her ears and down the side of her neck; and then he cupped her beautiful face and framed it in his hands and they were looking deeply and movingly into each other's eyes. Briefly he touched her lips with his and soon he was kissing her neck, her lips, her hair, behind her ears and down and along her throat and at times she moved her head slightly to assist him. She responded to his kisses by returning them or pressing herself forward to receive them. They both knew, within them, a tiger had been unleashed and they were on the cusp of an overpowering, deep, sensitive and exquisite love. A love in which they both mattered and it would endure to never go away. With him, she knew, love making would be a shared experience in which they would give and receive love. But it was not to be because an urgent recall message came through for her to return to her office because the AmOn government had reached a decision which they wanted to discuss with her. "I am sorry," she laughed.

"They seem to lack a sense of timing," he grinned.

"You certainly have them rightly summed up," she laughed again as Mark escorted her to the doorway where, before they parted, they stole yet one more kiss.

Chapter 9

JUST IN TIME

Mark Anita did not meet again the next day because Anita had been up for most of the night, but before she had left, he had given her one of the two gifts he had picked up during his visit to the Earth memorabilia shop. It was a broach depicting a bird in flight, its plumage picked out with coloured stones and she really did appreciate it. "I like the colours and I like the thought behind it. I will wear it in your absence." Their parting kiss was long and searching with neither wishing to let the other go. For both of them, they knew as they parted this was it, that hunger for each other would never go away. Now back on his own, Mark was recalling the soapy smelling freshness of her hair as he kissed her head then spontaneously in his day dream, he blurted out "I love you," but he became embarrassed because he had spoken the words aloud, though very relieved to see that he was still alone.

The QvO shuttle phased into being on the same lawn where he had arrived three days ago but today, he realised that Qee had today morphed in his mind from a temporary place of work to a much deeper attachment. Anita hailed him briskly to wish him a safe journey. In his hand was a hand written note from her expressing her sorrow for her untimely departure the night before, 'I would have like to have stayed longer,' she said. He marvelled inwardly that in the space of three hours yesterday evening everything had changed and fractures had been riven to his previously staid lifestyle and it was all good! But his heart was leaden as he boarded the shuttle and took a seat within it. In his hand was a brown paper envelope with the logo of AmOn on its cover. He opened it and was still reading it when the craft announced that they had arrived at their destination. He stayed seated for a moment more to digest the letter. It was not written in official jargonese, on headed paper, but the simple note placed the QvO at his disposal to carry out their instructions as herein. In essence, it read: - 'The QvO with two escorting cruisers are to proceed to the coordinates of the alien DM conduit. Their prime directive is to destroy it but if circumstances permit, they are urged to first study it, provided that does not jeopardise the completion of the mission. Once it is destroyed the three ships are to linger discretely some distance from the former conduit's coordinates to observe, monitor, and learn from any Terrabot investigative activity in the vicinity. Then with caution they are to try to capture an alien vessel and bring it to Qee.'

The letter ended wishing them God's speed and protection and it was signed for and on behalf of the government of AmOn. "Over to you," Mark said, on arrival, as he passed the AmOn letter to Anda. "It seems straight forward enough," the Captain said as he read and handed the letter back to Mark, glancing at the screen in front of him. "The two ships to escort us are the Endeavour and the Wellig; this tells me that they are at separate planets engaged in resupply and they will be with us shortly."

"Ah," Mark smiled, "that reminds me," he opened his brief case from where he took out a cardboard box. "I picked this up at the Earth memorabilia shop on Qee. As Captain Anjar looked at the box and saw the picture of the Flying Scotsman steam train with smoke pouring from its funnel and the words 'working model with real steam' in big letters inscribed beneath the train and he burst out laughing. "There you have your own train to play with now,"Mark grinned. "But you will have to get workshops to make the rails for you," he said and they both cuffed each other in fun.

On return to the Clench offices, Mark called for a progress meeting with his staff to brief them on the forthcoming mission. "Its slow but progress has been made," he reassured them. "From knowing nothing just a week or two ago, we now know the hostile force is Rap-Terrabot. We don't know where they are based but we do know that they have an active, quite sophisticated intelligence gathering network which evidence suggests has at least eight field agents. As yet we have no idea what their motive is unless it is revenge for the defeat, they suffered at the hands of the combined fleets of Ongle and AMC in our pre federation days. We have destroyed a part of their espionage network and we have learned much from OPY about their method of espionage and communication and, we believe, it has now probably revealed all that we can glean from it. Of course, it was only operating to a programme; it had no motive or political allegiance. One interesting, overlooked fact is how OPY came to be employed in the messenger loading and distribution bay. It seems that a robot employed there inexplicably walked in front of a fast-moving vehicle; it was thought to be due to inattention at the time. But now we have reopened the case and AMC police are trawling the scrap yards to try to find the memory core of the vehicle that was in the collision with the robot. That is important because of the possibility it was a deliberate act to create a vacancy for an agent robot in a critical area. There is every likelihood that their search will be unsuccessful because that specific memory core might, by now, have been sold, scrapped or repurposed. AmOn want to reconstruct OPY and put him back into the DM government messenger service, where it worked before. It will retain its previous alien communication ability but it will also be covertly programmed to observe and report to AMC any unusual suspicious activity in the loading bay. Conversely, because of its dual role, that means that it will also report its own suspicious activities too and a titter of aughter ran through the group.

The heavy cruisers, the Endeavour plus the Wellig, had arrived on station and the three Captains met aboard the Wellig to discuss the mission and to make 'what if' plans should things not go exactly to plan. The QvO would be in the centre of the formation and emerge from DM to be the closest ship to the conduit. The two cruisers would protect its flanks. They decided on a long count down, of twenty seconds before they translocated, this to give their crews time to nervously check and recheck their readiness as the seconds laboriously fell away.

"DMT jump imminent," Captain Anja's voice informed his crew and passengers through their hucoms and public address speakers. To an onlooker the three ships shimmered for a second then apparently winked out of existence. In reality, they had reemerged light years away into maelstrom. Clearly, they had been outguessed by the Rap-Terrabot fleet because there were three hundred of Terrabot warships, with their fighters already deployed, laying in wait for them, thus giving them a clear weapons platform advantage. The QvO was the prime target for them but it was simply too large to be destroyed by a single fighter but they could inflict damage which if compounded by many would end up in her total destruction. Already the QvO's exterior view cameras were showing globules of molten rock, like droplets of life blood, splashing from her hull. The enemy fighters were pounding her mercilessly but the floating cannonade ring was expanding from the QvO's hull and it began to rotate at an alarming speed around the ship. Then, like a tetchy demon awakened, it poured out counterforce from the barrels of the canons of the robots manning them on the expanded ring. Very soon, many Terrabot fighters were sent cartwheeling away through space with pieces breaking off them as they passed the QvO but there were too many of them.

Over to their right, the Wellig was in trouble and there was an opening in her metal hull, revealing fires burning inside her. Noticeably her return rate of fire had dropped to a trickle. Then she disappeared into DM to lick her wounds. On the left, the Endeavour was putting up what looked like a searchlight display but the beams one could see were its deadly poenillium cannons and laser beams. It also could be seen that there were bright orange explosions against her hull which denoted that Terrabot was also finding their target.

In the ferocity of the fire fight, the enemy fighters had discovered a defence weakness of the floating cannonade ring of the QvO. Its cannon was designed primarily to fire horizontally along the hull and up to a forty-five-degree angle above it, meaning the vertical defence was thinner centrally above the ring. The Terrabot fighters had learned that by coming in, in a nose dive directly above the ring, they could evade much of the flak and this tactic was beginning to tell. Despite her sheer size, the ship shuddered as a huge part of the floating ring was shot away and it peeled off, writhing like a snake, as it hurtled through the heavens. The loss of a section of the ring unbalanced the remaining part of it which wobbled as a collapsing top. Another long piece broke off at one end and flayed around the ship, in the process smashing two enemy fighters to pieces. To save the ship from further damage, they cut the power to the ring, leaving them very little protection below the deflection capabilities of the barrels of the main defensive armament. Captain Anjar made what he believed would probably be the last organised offensive move his ship would ever undertake when he ordered the main laser weapons to target the shed like DM conduit which they had come to see. At his command laser beams blazed out from the QvO towards the shed which promptly exploded, leaving an explanding cloud of dust where it had once been

The QvO was now in dire trouble. There were pools of red molten rock upon its surface and the remains of the defensive cannonade ring was strewn on its hull or in orbit around it. Over on the Endeavour they could perhaps last for just another ten minutes of combat. Both ships had lost large parts of their embedded DM mesh, so they couldn't DMT out of their situation because to do so would result in parts of their ships disappearing into DM with other parts remaining where they were. The future looked very grim and they had already witnessed the enemy fighters shooting up the escape pods released by Wellig when it had feared its imminent demise. For the remaining crew of the Wellig, their new experimental virtual DMT mesh a had saved them from being reduced to an angrily glowing red wreck, billions of kilometres from home.

Mark joked afterwards that he had heard the bugles of the United States Cavalry because, thereafter, the AmOn fleet started to arrive. First, one or two seemingly cautious ships materialised, but within minutes thousands of warships came out of dark matter until they reached the proportion of being the overwhelming force in the field. The QvO, with retreat now out of contention, launched its five-hundred fighters, then the newly arrived AmOn force added its own fighters to the vengeful flocks, seeking to hunt down and destroy the Rap-Terrabot fleet. With increasing effectiveness, the Terrabot fleet was being badly mauled and it was on the cusp of defeat when it retreated into the DM.

"Thank heaven we now bury the DM meshes in the hull these days," the Captain said to Mark. "In the old days it would have taken months to repair our mesh but our forecast now is only three weeks." The repairs did go to schedule and they were even able to recover most of the detached sections of the cannonade ring which were refabricated together and adjustments were made to the hull cannons, too, to enable them, in future, to also defend the space immediately above the ring. Of course, Anita was one of the first to learn about the recent battle and she sent a flurry of concerned messages to him and he answered them cheerfully to buoy her spirits. Then she told him that she had once been given a bottle of wine by the AMC Julate; it was reputed to be two-thousand years of age and she had been saving it for a very special occasion. That occasion would be when he returned safely to Qee, she informed him.

When the repairs had been completed, they received new instructions from AmOn, via Anita, revealing that AmOn had modified its opinion. To now, they had been thinking of Rap-Terrabot as a territory, but what if it was not? The Rap brains cohabitated inside the Terrabots, thus Terrabot had no need for agriculture to grow food for them. All Terrabot needed were the resources to make new warships and new robots. At a personal level a Terrabot's only constant need was a reliable electricity supply. They could easily obtain the resources needed from dead planets of which there were countless numbers in every galaxy. The new thinking was that the Rap-Terrabot entity were nomads and they existed only where their fleet was. Perhaps the hunt for them ought really to be aimed at deep space rather than the star systems as hitherto was the case. But it did mean if Terrabot had no home world to invest, then a treaty could not be made with them and any battle against them would need to be one hundred percent decisive, leaving none to regroup or rebuild their strength to attack again at a later date.

Now that Clench was based upon the QvO, AmOn edicts started to flow. and the three Captains of the QvO flotilla were to be taken into the full confidence of Clench with immediate effect. The latest edict decreed that the QvO along with the Endeavour and the Willig, were all seconded to assist the operations of Clench, allthough in times of need in uncharted territories, they could call upon fleet reserve craft to back up their undertakings. AmOn had also granted Clench a semi-autonomous role, provided that they kept AmOn in the picture with regard to their intentions and why their actions were felt to be necessary.

At the next Clench committee meeting, a debate arose over what do with the Terrabot DMT messenger relays which had been orphaned when the QvO had destroyed the conduit through which they had communicated. It was decided that they would pay each one of them a visit and secrete a DM beacon in their near space. Necessary, because it needed to be explained how the Terrabot ship that had originally placed them had managed to infiltrate the AmOn sensitive defence zone without being detected. The question then arose at the meeting of how could this have been accomplished. "That is precisely my question, too," Mark said. "I put it to the members present to look for a solution," but only one hand belonging to one of the Clench technicians was raised and he stood up to say.

"I have a theory but it is not derived from any direct observations," his voice tailed off uncertainly, "please bear with me."

"As it happens, we are a little short of theories," Mark smiled at him, "so I welcome yours, please go ahead and explain it."

The technician looked relieved when he said "As you know, our DM beacons have two functions, the first one is to record any turmoil in DM and to factor that into rendering safe navigational predictions which it will only transmit in response to a secret interrogation code. That aspect is absolutely essential because without that information a ship transiting DM could end up anywhere in the universe. The second function concerns security because a beacon is able to monitor ship movements in DM up to five light years distant; it sends this information direct to the Defence Ministry which plots them. However, spaceship detection in DM is pretty crude; but it is the present state of the art, there is nothing better. In effect the beacons can only register DM movements up a limited distantance. This is as much as we really require because to extend the ability much beyond that would mean that we would be receiving DM transit information for every ship in every galaxy of the universe." He paused to take a glass of water and he continued, "As far as we know, it would be impossible to interfere with the operation of a beacon because one would have to remove it from DM to make any changes. Moreover, none of our beacons have reported any technical problems of late. There is a weak point because, as you know, we cannot transmit radio signals in DM. To get around that we use what is termed a'floating antenna,' so named because, for want of a better explanation, it literally rides above the DM. For explanation our antennas are in real space but connected to beacons which are in dark matter. My thoughts are that the antennas are the most accessible part of a beacon to interfere with. My proposal is that we pay them a visit!"

Mark thought for a while, then nodded. "Agreed, and well done", he added. "We cannot work properly in the DM so we will have to haul them out into physical space." And when they did, they found that an unexpected nodule had been added to the base of the floating antenna; the nodule contained a nano motor which artificially disconnected the transmitter from the aerial wire to the beacon by pushing it apart for two minutes before closing the gap again. During those two minutes the beacon would still be transmitting data about DMT movements but with no antenna in place the signals were going nowhere. They found also that the nano motor opened and closed the contacts with predictable time lapses and it was realised that if they inserted a new DM beacon nearby, it they would be able to obtain a true picture of any DMT transits that occurred during the enforced 'off air' lapses of the original beacon. 'Just a lapse of two minutes, here and there would be sufficient to slip a whole amarda through the gap,' Mark was told.

In the follow up, Mark had contacted Anita, and afterwards he asked his second in command, Petan Maggf and both agreed with him; the plan should go ahead to install a second beacon near the first one. The additional beacon would only be active when the existing beacon was unable to communicate, as a fall back they would also add additional circuitry to the first beacon to enable it to store and repeat its transmissions on demand. Thereafter, once the modification had been made to the original beacon, it was returned to DM along with another stand-by beacon. When they were both operational, they, only then. came to realise that occasionally there were quite large movements in DM during the periods when the original beacon's antenna was artificially interrupted.

"What they are up to, we have no idea." Mark made an open hand gesture to Petan and their discussion moved on to the next part of their operation which was to visit the DM message dart relays which had been orphaned when the OvO had destroyed the conduit during their recent battle with the Terrabot fleet. There were, they had already discovered, eight Terrabot message dart relays widely distributed in the vicinity of the AmOn planets. But when they arrived at their coordinates, they could only find one and they assumed that Terrabot had removed them, but why leave one? Cautiously a space-suited individual jet-packed over to the shed shaped structure, only to discover that it was a lure because it promptly dematerialised as it was approached; but there were two, what appeared to be, bundles of rags left floating where the shed had been.

"Caution," the warning went out from the QvO bridge, "it looks suspiciously like a booby trap from here. We will send a general-purpose robot over to take a closer look at them."

When they did get to look more closely at the bundles, it was to learn that they were the frozen bodies of two men and Mark ordered that they be brought over and sent to the ship's hospital. A moment or two after the bodies had arrived Mark tore his hucom from his head and stared at it. The bodies, he had been informed, had been visually identified as the Earth President of the United World Government and the other was the President of the Ongle System of Planets and there was nothing that they could do for them, so they were now passing them on to the forensic labs. The labs confirmed to him soon afterwards that it would take a full twenty-four hours to defrost the bodies at normal ambient temperature. A day later the forensic lab came through to him via his hucom. "We have come across something unexpected and mysterious," an unhurried voice told him, "We think that you ought to be here immediately."

"Right, I'm on my way!" Mark would have to descend three hundred floors and then catch a tube and then, from the final tube station, call a savuwalk to take him to the Forensic laboratories. The Ongle efficiency and timing was perfect with everything dovetailed exactly as required to assist his journey. As a policeman, Mark was used to seeing bodies, some of which had been quite badly smashed, and a cursory glance as he approached them revealed that they were pretty much intact albeit naked for the overall examination.

"Come look at this," a masked and shielded operative beckoned him but as Mark came over even his police training had not prepared him for this one; the body next to him had a three-centimetre bloodied hole in its skull, just above the ear.

"Whew!" Mark gulped, "what has done that, some kind of specialised animal?"

"More like a specialised brutal robot," the operative informed him. "The evidence suggests it was done while the victim was still alive and most of its brain has been sucked out through the hole; the other guy is just the same."

"Sheeeow," Mark blew the air from his lungs, "why would they have done that so brutally?"

"We can only guess but it was done by Terrabots, but because they are robots they would hardly have bothered to invent or obtain a comfort gas or liquid to operate on two biological life forms. Screams of pain mean absolutely nothing to a Terrabot which utilises machine law which does not encompass the notion of pain or sentiment. If they did regard it at all they would probably have put it down to a humanoid ritual and as they were going to die anyway what was there to make a fuss about!"

"So," said Mark speculatively, "do you think that they are attempting to use these brain cells in the same way as they use Rap brain cells to introduce a biological input to their own digital brains?"

"That seems the most likely answer." The operative replied "there is hardly any other use that I can think of for a grey sludge, which is what it would be, after they had extracted it through a three-centimetre hole."

"I was thinking, why would they take powerful planetary leaders? But perhaps I can understand that one myself" Mark opined. "A computer would probably assume that to become a leader you would have risen to the top of the majority by dint of possession of the most dominant mental ability. They still have a lot to learn," he sighed.

Later that day, Mark had asked that the QvO be moved closer to Qee where it was now in orbit around it and they were in direct radio contact with the DES. The DES had now dropped its pretence of being a liaison and research organisation whose purpose was to foster relationships between the Earth and AmOn and to prepare Earth for union with them. It was now recognised by many to be a front for other serious matters. From Mark's point of view, the near proximity to Qee enabled him to make encrypted radio telephone calls with Anita and, when they did, the titles of Madam Chief Minister and Clench Commander were dropped from their conversation and supplanted by Anita and Mark and sometimes just darling! But they were still unable to meet because the small flotilla to which the QvO belonged was required to be at the immediate disposal of AmOn.

Anita, throughout the dramatic news of learning that the two world leaders had been murdered, had to appear rational and enigmatic in the public eye. To the media she made announcements to the effect that AmOn would track down those who had perpetrated these crimes and when they were caught, they would be brought to justice before the Courts. Privately, to Mark, she was in floods of tears over the deaths and the barbaric way in which they had been carried out. Understandably she sometimes expressed a more human response of 'shoot them on sight.

"Indeed, that would be a very satisfactory solution," he agreed.

Chapter 10

WAR IS INEVITABLE

With matters now discussed between Mark and Anita, the QvO and its escort cruisers retired from AmOn territorial space to form a small picquet line three light years distant from AMC. Mark was surprised to receive, almost as soon as they arrived, a High Temperature message dart from the DES. It had been sent by Anita whose name was on the transit label attached to it. He suffered a little confusion because he thought that they had just two hours ago covered events past, present and the DES intentions for the future so it didn't seem that there was much more to discuss. The likely importance of this communication, he guessed, would be significant, when he broke the security seal on the container, he found a furled document within it.

What he was to read was akin to a nuclear delivery in the pursuit of his enquiries. It was almost a personal letter from Anita who hoped that he had a safe journey. They had finally identified the part number of the nodule recovered from the rogue robot Herbert. It had been traced to Earth. "Earth?" he exploded incredulously as he read, that the part had originated from a manufacturing company in Norfolk, Nebraska, and had been used in their American Airforce Volcano aircraft. When that aircraft had been superseded by a newer generation of fighter aircraft the manufacturing company's store of spare parts for it was sold off as job lots.

The relevant job lot had fallen into the hands of an international buyer from the Near East, who had broken it down in smaller lots and sold them on again. The specific item then turned up in Manchester in England as part of an even smaller sublot which was, again, sold on. Records recorded it had beem purchased with cash and the copy of the receipt showed it was purchased by Wormford Dale Industries Ltd. They had managed to track down the sales representative who sold it. She recalls that the person who made the purchase was unsmiling and seemed to have a flawless face which displayed no emotion and she remembered him in particular because he had spent such a long time examining the lot and it was not before she had told him that they were closing the store in five minutes time that he made the purchase. Immobile facial features could indicate it was a robot, Mark noted later in his repy to Anita He also tabled a letter to Vivienne in Bermuda to ask the Global Police Force if they could get a photo-fit copy of the person who made the purchase and he also requested that they gave this subject their top priority because any lead they uncovered, no matter how small, could lead to signifiant progress. Mark added in a side note to Vivienne that Earth had a very effective police force but assistance if they required it was available. Indeed, privately he knew that Earth's unified police forces were highly respected in AmOn and the history of police forces on earth was often comparable, and in some cases longer than some of the AmOn planets. but he also knew although the people of Earth were aware of the 'Hands of God' war in which Rap-Terrabot had sought to threaten the destruction of the Earth in order to draw the then separate forces of Ambrocognia-Mundi Coligate the Ongle System of Planets into a fight to the finish which; conversely, had led to the defeat of the Rap-Terrabot fleet instead. They had not, however, been told the full nature of the Terrabot renaissance but they had now been told that their president had died, but the manner of his death was still a closely guarded secret on Earth.

Anita had now messaged Mark and told him to go down to Earth to brief their new President on recent events and also that war with Terrabot seemed inevitable.

But before he left, there was more worrying news and it was that two scientists had been abducted from their homes in AMC territory. Both of their homes had already been fitted with surveillance cameras as part of new security procedures to protect persons of intellectual interest to Terrabot. But there were thousands of just such individuals in society and not all of the safety features were yet in place. Indeed, it would be many months before they would be. In these two incidents, the abductors had arrived out of DM in a small craft and as before they used smoke to conceal their identities; but there was a fresh wind at one of the locations which blew the smoke away to reveal to the surveillance camera that the assailants were robots.

After Instructing the QvO to remain in the picquet line, Mark called his second in command, Petan Maggf, and briefed him on the latest message from Anita and told him about his forthcoming visit to Earth. Then he rose from his chair and invited Petan to take over immediately; and he smiled as he glanced back to see that Petan was already engaged in rearranging the desk top. Mark had already sent a message to Vivienne to ask her to arrange a dinner for him with the President of the United World Government, the Earth Chief of Security and the acting head of the Global Police Force. Additionally, he would bring with him four TCF soldiers to act as close quarter body guards for their protection. He explained that new AmOn rules dictated that body guards were required for all higher government officials. The soldiers would have signed AmOn's Official Secrets Act because they were never to more than three metres away from the person who they had been tasked to protect. From such close quarters they would overhear matters of great sensitivity. Nevertheless, that would be the position which they would adopt throughout the meeting. On duty, the soldiers poenillium small arms were always set to kill. Earth was invited to send its own bodyguards, too, but they were warned if a firefight developed, they would be in danger of being shot with weapons for which they had no defence.

"We are now at L.F. Wade Airport," a monotone voice announced as the door of the DMT shuttle opened to reveal a blue sky flecked with puffed white clouds and the smell of the ocean wafted in. It was, indeed, instantly refreshing compared to the canned air of the QvO that he had been breathing recently and from the door of the shuttle, before he disembarked, he glimpsed the famous pink beaches of Bermuda. Yes, he had missed all this, he thought, but his body guard had already dismounted and they formed a square around him, maintaining that formation step for step with him as he walked towards the vehicle and escorts that were waiting to take him to a hotel.

Dinner was not scheduled until 7 P.M. that evening and Mark found a shady spot on the beach opposite the hotel where he was later joined by Vivienne and they shared a take-away lunch before bathing in the sea together, but always under the watchful eye of the TCF soldiers. Then he was off to pay a courtesy call upon his former colleagues at the World Police Force headquarters where he was received warmly by all, as a long-lost friend; and eventually he ended up in his old office now filled by his deputy. It was not long before they both got down to yarning about police actions and outcomes in the past and, as always. about the mistakes which sometimes did happen. These raised their loudest laughs, like when, as a junior police constable, Mark had been given a wrong address and he had entered a flat through an unlocked door and had arrested a seventy-five-year-old man in his bath and had bundled him into his dressing gown and taken him like that to the station in handcuffs for questioning. "I received quite a stiff telling off for that; I should have cross checked because the person did not seem to fit the word picture of the dangerous felon that I had been given to believe he was. Also, a wigging for going in alone and not waiting for backup," Mark laughed. Inevitably the subject of tonight's meeting arose and his deputy tried to press him to explain why the late

President of the United World Government had been found drifting in space with his brains sucked out. Clearly, he entertained the thought that AmOn must be involved when he remarked, pointedly, that the chances of finding a body, which they were not even looking for, in space would be pretty unusual. "Were they using very large fishing nets?" he asked pointedly, but Mark would not give any explanation other than to say that all would be revealed at tonight's meeting.

At Mark's hotel the government security agents had decided that it would be in a 'closed to the public' conservatory overlooking the sea. There was one long dining table in the middle of the conservatory and the TCF guards, leaving nothing to chance, had placed chairs spaced out from each corner upon on which two of them sat facing the occupants of the table and two facing outwards from the table. Initially the conversation began in fits and starts and Mark explained that he wanted them to get to know each other before he would tell them the purpose of his visit. Wine had flowed freely during the lunch and everyone was more relaxed as he prepared to relate the story to them. When he did start to explain, it was in the form of a situation report regarding the disquieting matters affecting AmOn. He began with the burrowing worm attack on Clench headquarters and the rogue robots. Then he moved onto how the destruction of one of them had resulted in an investigation which led them to finding a component part of a robot with a stock or user reference number on it. That number had been traced to the USA and thence to Manchester in England. Thus, at least one Terrabot had visited Earth to buy the part. They had also ceased calling them Rap-Terrabots now, he explained, because the Terrabot element was the dominant partner in the symbiotic relationship. Clench's latest observation was that the Terrabots had also perfected alterations to their physique which enabled them to pass themselves off as human beings and there could be others living apparently normal human lives out there among the population. He went on to tell them about the surreptitiously planted robot found on AmOn and its clandestine activities. He explained to them how they were lured into space to the location of the two dead bodies and they were already sitting on the edge of their chairs when he told them of the inconclusive battle that had been recently fought with the Terrabot fleet and how the latter were moving assets around in dark matter. He repeated Anita's prediction that a war with Terrabot was now inevitable. On behalf of the Government of AmOn he also sought their permission to re-atmosphere the planet Mars and use it as a base for several thousand of their fighter aircraft to help protect Earth against attack.

Those present were shocked, of course, by the revelations that they had just heard, especially the news that there would probably be a war with Terrabot in the near future and they had no defence against the sophisticated weapons used by civilisations who regarded space as their own backyard. It was now 10.00 p. m. and they were still discussing what he had told them when the chandelier, above the dining table where they were seated, started to flicker and then drip white hot sparks like rain upon them. The remaining cutlery on the table took off horizontally to crash against a far wall where it remained suspended against it.

Elsewhere, around the frame of the entrance door to the conservatory, a blue light flickered momentarily. Then the door, with its hinges and locks severed, crashed inwards as six all black metal Terrabots raced in towards Mark and his guests, but this time they were up against professionals. The TCF were alert and the leading three robots staggered as TCF poenillium beams hit them and a bright purple spot of light appeared on each robot where each beam had struck. The purple spots glowed on the surface of the stricken robots and were expaning rapidly lit by the tell-tale sparkle, described in weapon-user-,manuals as being like thousands of sun lit diamonds. It also confirmed unquestionably that their fight was over for keeps. Two more robots had been hit and went down, legs; arms kicking and waving as their internal processors tried vainly to rationalise the unintelligible inputs that they were receiving from their host's atomically decaying bodies.

The remaining robot had reached Vivienne and it scooped her up and held her up as a shield defying the TCF to fire for fear of killing her. This was a situation that the TCF had practiced and they knew how to handle it. One of them nodded to the other who nodded his agreement and he adjusted his pistol to stun, then levelled the weapon at Vivienne and shot her. She collapsed immediately. Her unexpected transition from standing to becoming a dead weight in the arms of the robot caught it by surprise and she slipped down to the ground. When the robot bent down to retrieve her, the practiced choreography of the two TCF soldiers paid off and a bolt from the poenillium pistol, on full power in the hands of the other TCF operative, took the head clean off the robot.

There was a moment's silence and Vivienne was groggily getting to her knees, helped to her feet by a member of the TCF. Above them the chandelier started to flicker again and the previously cutlery held magetically fast to the end wall crashed to the ground. "Drat!" Mark exclaimed, "they have gone, we could have done with a look at that machine."

In the aftermath, congratulations flowed freely from the group to the TCF party for the professionalism they had displayed; and Mark was able to tell them that this was the first time that one of these raiding parties had been defeated. Certainly, he would be reporting to AmOn of their cool and heroic action. Mark also asked them to stay put for the time being to protect the technical debris strewn about the conservatory. As the others left, Mark asked the President of The United World Government to stay because there were matters of delicacy to discuss. As they sat down again, he pointed out to the President that they were surrounded by technology that was many years in advance of anything Earth was capable of producing and AmOn would be loath to let them keep it. An argument developed over what constituted technological evolution. Did it mean that evolution could only be advanced step by step or did it also include evolution by acquisition, and they sought advice on this from AmOn. Even though Mark was from Earth he had to agree with AmOn's reply when they reported as follows:

The planet Earth has not yet defeated nationalism and religious rivalry and weapons of this nature in the wrong hands could lead to an imbalance of power. As long as Earth's people still thought of themselves primarily as Russian, European, American, Chinese, Christian,

Muslim or Hindu, the consequence of fast forwarding them four- thousand years could be dangerous. AmOn continued;

they had also taken a note with respect to the table cutlery which had been suspended against a wall by a powerful magnetic force on the other side of it. This was something that despite their technology they had overlooked because it had not been envisaged that these raids would ever take place. Although DMT itself is instantaneous, they said, it still takes up to five-seconds for a ship to fully phase out of DMT when it arrives at its destination. But its magnetic presence would already be evident before it had fully materialised. With this in mind AmOn could build detectors which would offer a klaxon or a visual warning of a DMT craft emerging within the sensitivity range of a detector. Certainly, that would be enough time for security personnel to clear their pistols from their holsters and take up a defensive posture. They estimated that they would require an initial run of five billion of these early warning detectors and more to follow as they also intended to equip their space ships, internally, with them. The detection devices required no specialist equipment to manufacture. So as a gesture of goodwill, if Earth would release the carcasses and the weaponry arising from the recent abduction attempt, AmOn would award the contract for the manufacture of the detection devices to Earth. It would be the first very largest, in scale, contract ever conducted between them; there would be others to follow. The President didn't think long about it and he agreed, subject to his government's support, but it was plain to see that he was delighted and it would be an eyeopener for Earth industry for them to understand just how large the contracts could be between whole star systems.

Vivienne came with Mark to the AmOn DMT departure bay on Bermuda and she stood with him as the flight technicians made ready the craft for its DM jump to the QvO. Vivienne nudged him with her elbow "Thanks for dinner," she said laughingly, "I am still a bit shaky and achy from the after-dinner entertainment. I hope all your dinners do not end like that?" She looked at him straight in the eye.

"Good Lord, no," Mark looked unflinchingly back. "Usually, they are much more boisterous. If you like, I will invite you to another when I next visit Earth?"

"Thank you, but I have a feeling that I may have one of my headaches and be obliged to refuse," she smiled.

"I am astonished." Mark laughed. "Your father would never have refused such an invitation!"

"Oh Dad," she giggled. "He is now more concerned with growing very large carrots in his garden on Marina; and he enters them into the Ongle gardening competitions. That does not give him a lot of time for posh dinners. Mum is no better; she dotes on her Marina roses."

"Well, I think you don't know what you would be missing!" he nodded.

"Yes, I do," she nodded back affirmatively and they shook hands before he boarded the shuttle.

A surprise was in store for Mark when he learned, just before he DMT'd, that Anita was on the QvO where she wanted to debrief him on the incident on Earth and she would then go AMC to brief the Julate. He was inwardly delighted that she was to come down to the hanger deck to meet him. There is love and there is love, he thought. The first one is exciting enough, it has mostly to do with the desire for physical contact; but there was another form which almost seems to be genetic attraction. The form of it was as if, hitherto, inadvertently separated genes of one person had accidentally remet and they had an overwhelming desire to reunite. It was an unselfish, all-powerful love. It could be expressed physically but was much deeper than just physical, he sighed. Thus, it was for the cameras and the media in general that he met

Anita with just a formal handshake, but if one had been in a position, able to intercept the eye messages exchanged between them, they could rightly have interpreted a distinct lack of formality in their greeting. Their less formal greeting took place when they took the lift to the Clench offices. Anita already knew that they would be passing through the empty quarter of the ship so she pressed the buttons for several intermediate floors on their way to their destination to delay the lift's progress. She knew it was pretty certain that there would be nobody waiting for the lift at any of the other floors. So, she removed one of her gloves of office and once the lift had started to move, she slipped it over the stalk of the internal safety camera to obscure its lens. When she turned back towards him, she was no longer the Chief Minister of the Ongle System of Planets but plain Anita greeting Mark and she flew into his arms expressing her fears about when she had first heard the news about the alien abduction attempt. The kissing and holding was passionate as they were carried intermittently upwards to the Clench headquarters.

When the lift finally stopped at the correct floor, they both emerged as per protocol, a metre apart, with Mark following behind Anita as befitted her rank and they were ushered straight into the committee room where Mark was surprised and slightly embarrassed to receive a standing clap from the members present.

Anita spoke and she told them, again, of the recent incident on Earth, adding some non-public disclosures about the contract awarded to Earth to produce the new detection devices to warn of an imminent localised materialisation of DMT vessels. She also told them that AmOn had made the decision that every robot, from the semi-intelligent floor mops to tstate of the art specialist and multi-purpose robots, must undergo additional subversion testing. All in all, Anita explained, when one included the robots on spaces ships, domestic service and the industries, nobody quite knew how many robots there were out there, but it must be billions. "We will start with those robots which work in the most sensitive occupations first and spread the net outward from there. This means a rapid extension of Clench which will mastermind the operation and arrangements have been made to transfer five-thousand personnel from government and local government offices to the QvO. They will be housed in the empty quarter in the accommodation normally reserved for military transportation and natural disaster projects." She nodded 'take over' to Mark who stood up and told those assembled that they were to meet in this committee room again in one hour to map out how they were going to handle Clench's massive and rapid expansion. Petan

Maggf asked Anita if Clench could involve the army to assist as they had the manpower on the ground; but she said that was not an option at the moment because of the high state of alert they were on. Ordinarily the military would have handled it completely, she advised, but these were not ordinary times.

"Thank you, just getting that point cleared up," Petan smiled. Several of the committee members were using the lift at the same time as Anita and Mark descended to the hanger deck; some came along to see her off, so there coud be no fond farewell. Nevertheless, Mark and Anita's official handshake lingered just that fraction longer than the standard official goodbye but, nobody would have noticed. But he felt a little bereft as he saw the shuttle door close and then felt a tremble of the hanger floor plates as the shuttle was catapulted into space from where it would engage DMT to its next port of call.

Chapter 11

SPIDER MEN

On the next day, the first of the seconded government employees started to arrive, initially in dribs and drabs but then in a flood of shuttles that had the crew of the main hanger bay stretched to their limit. Clench operatives welcomed them as they arrived and escorted them to their new accommodation and familiarised them with the existing Clench officers. The QvO, according to the rules, had to retain strategic reserves in case of a major deployment so it was not able to supply all the needs for this sudden influx of personnel. Hence the Clench staff were obliged to vigorously track down the additional supplies they required which increased the number of shuttles arriving and departing from the QvO until all the resources and personal had been loaded.

The Clench plan was to create an individual management group for each of the twenty-one planets comprising AmOn. Separate offices were created for each team in the spacious decks of the empty quarter. As with the existing Clench personnel, the newcomers' food requirements would be catered for by restaurants and their additional treats and snacks by small shops. Their mission was classified as 'High Temperature' so they were not permitted to visit other areas of the ship nor to converse with any of the ship's crew without having obtained permission to do so. Special visits would be arranged for Clench groups to visit the lake in the well of the ship and those times would be set aside exclusively for Clench and decided by Captain Anjar. Mark took a direct hand in allocating a combined radio callsign and identity for each Clench away team and it was simple. Each planet of AmOn was allocated a letter from the English alphabet. The planet Sticky was allocated the letter Alpha and its colocated Clench teams became derivatives, such as 'Clench Alpha 1' or 2, or 3 etc. The planet Qee was designated as 'Clench Bravo' and so on. Simple, but Clench's job in hand now was to impart their knowledge and to train their teams for their missions. Once this had been done, they would be despatched individually to one of the inhabited planets administered by AmOn. On arrival there they were to recruit and train others and provide them with job knowhow. Eventually the work force across all of the planets of AmOn would peak upwards of three million operatives, which would then tail off as they worked their way through the massive task ahead. For Clench, it added up to an administrative nightmare because they had been rocketed from being just a group of some fifty individuals to becoming the fourth largest public employer of AmOn, out numbered only by military, government and health services.

At the moment the clerical administration staff for the operation which would include stores, pay, equipment and personal records, was being trained up in AMC where they would remain for the duration of the operation. Each group in the field would answer to its own planet-based headquarters and that headquarters would answer to one of the Clench inner staff on the QvO. It was a daunting task which kept the lights burning until late at Clench. But to some extent, the task was eased by Anita who used her authority as the chief of staff of the whole operation to clear a path through obstacles and sometimes plain obduracy by departments who objected to a new department with a yet unknown purpose that was demanding over-riding priority treatment for their requests.

Of now the field teams were undergoing training on the QvO with many of the classroom lessons aimed at robot studies. They partook in more active exercises too, in the empty quarter where they learned how to disable a robot that had purposely ignored a verbal command to deactivate, through to robots which physically resisted any attempt to access their shutdown switch. In the event, the main tool for the job was what they had come to term 'the pacifier.' This was a silver tubular device which was pointed at a target robot and when its trigger was pushed it created an extremely powerful magnetic field focused towards the robot. The magnetic field interrupted its ability to communicate internally, thus bringing it to a stop. The drawback, however, was that in the majority of cases, the strong magnetic force also wiped clean a robot's memory, thus obviating the main interntion which was to gain intelligence from it. There was another more fun, less high-tech solution, where two people held a stout rope extended between them and they ran towards the robot and encircled it with the rope to pin its arms to its body. The rope handlers would then be in a position to flick off the robot's deactivation switch. Of course, the most certain way was to engage it with a poenillium pistol, set to kill, but this option left little of a robot's torso for analysis. They also practiced their less violent methods of disabling robots on those that locally served the needs of the QvO. For the exercise to be realistic, the robots had to be unaware of what had been planned for them. This resulted in Robot Scheduling asking Mark, curtly, why Clench personnel were playing schoolboy pranks on their robots.

For several days, half metre square cardboard boxes had been arriving addressed to Clench, care of the QvO. Each box had a picture of a spider stamped on two sides of it and the number of boxes arriving was steadily increasing until they were now arriiving in their thousands. To house them Clench had subsequently taken over another large multi-purpose hall in the ship's empty quarter to store the boxes and they had already almost filled the space available, with more arriving by the day. The most popular theory held by the field teams was that the boxes contained uniforms to be worn when they had taken up their duties on AmOn. But this changed when Mark called a meeting of the entire field force in a very large assembly hall. His prior instruction to them was that they were all to wear their hucoms switched to 'Channel C12" which was a very high encryption level, AmOn channel, designated for 'Government Eyes and Ears Only.' By using this facility Mark was able to appear to everybody present as if they were in the front row of seats and the visual demonstrations that were to be presented to the throng would appear likewise to them all.

The audience rose respectfully as Mark, a computer engineer, plus all of the members of the inner Clench committee took their seats on the rostrum. Mark had remained standing as he bid the assembly to be seated. When Mark commenced to address them, it was initially to thank them for their hard work and initiative that they had all displayed during their course of instruction. "Even though none of you were aware precisely what you were training for, you have all set your minds to the task in hand and now it is time to tell you what your mission is." Then he told them about the rogue robots that had been discovered among the robot population of AmOn and how they had been modified to become intelligence agents for Terrabot. He said how difficult it was to detect them. Even when we have managed to unveil them, he told them, they invariably self-destruct rather than be captured. The self-destruction of the robots resulted in a complete loss of data and memory and there was nothing useful that could be extracted from the remains. The rogue, or spiked robots, it was believed, were also fitted with anti-tamper mechanisms that would trigger self-destruct if any of their standard access plates were removed. An attack upon them with energy beam weapons would also be met by their automatic suicide. To counter this threat, Mark told them that AmOn had ordered that every robot, plus all static machines employing artificial intelligence, were to be tested to see that they conformed to their design specifications and that nothing had been added to their specification since they were originally manufactured. "We are speaking about billions of them," he said. "By way of illustration, the QvO alone has seventy-five thousand machines that are governed by artificial intelligence. Of course, not all of them require testing. A tractor ploughing a field did not represent great danger to society but a navigational robot on a star ship, for example, is party to many secrets including the present deployment and the future deployment of the warship.

You, the people in this hall," he told them,"have been specially selected to form the nucleus of the new force. Within the week you are going to be transported to the planets where you are to work. On arrival you are to set up a new headquarters on your planet and disburse the remainder of your group in small parties so that there is at least one party on each continent of the planet that you are assigned to. From there you are to recruit, train, and mastermind Operation Datasave. That name is deliberately innocuous and it is unclassified so that its true purpose cannot be construed from its title; The proper meaning of Datasave is High Temperature and cannot be disclosed. Your mission is to check every AI on AmOn that is employed in affairs of state or is in a position to learn affairs of state, including domestic robots working for government officials. Your status on the planets is autonomous as far as your mission is concerned and you have the right to co-opt police and security forces to assist you should you require them. You will be provided with uniforms," he added, "which are sky blue in colour and they will bear the word Clench in capital letters on the right breast pocket and the badge of a spider embossed below it." A titter could be heard in the centre of the throng when a wag said "Oh, we are spider men, then."

Mark beckoned the nearby computer engineer to take the stand which he did but he never spoke to them. He brought with him one of the boxes printed with a spider on two sides and hefted it up onto a table on the rostrum, then, peeling back the lid, he plunged his hand inside the box. When he withdrew it, the assembly were to see that his hand held three hairy legged spiders. Then he removed the box from the table and pressed the right-hand feeler of one of the spiders between his finger and thumb. Then he set it on the table and it immediately started to crawl over and beneath it. Still in silence, he left the stage and returned with the torso of a robot which he also placed on the table and then showed his left hand which held a square metal object with a black boss on the outer side of it. The item was secured in his hand by a cuff going around his fingers. For a moment he held the black object just below the arm pit of the robot torso and then removed it to reveal a neat round hole in the side of the robot where his hand had been placed. Next, he took the activated spider and placed it at the lip of the hole that he had just made in the robot's sidewall, whereupon, the spider scuttled inside and disappeared from view.

Once again Mark took up the briefing. "The spider is usually referred to as a digispy in written and spoken terms by its users. It is equipped to recognise the internal layout of most of the robots in use today," he said. "We make a hole in the side of the robot's armpit because the robot manufacturers tell us that is the optimum place to make one if you are trying to avoid using normal access plates. The digispy is inserted in the hole and it goes to work crawling through every cavity, including the arms, legs and even the hands and feet of the interior and on its way, it analyses and photographs. Aditionally it can use its legs to electrically bridge the robot's internal circuitry to make the connections necessary to download its host's memory, history and storage. It will, also, seek out a robot's individual serial number which by law is stamped on the main drive shaft of the servo motor. In all, a digispy can spend up to four hours inside a robot and then it will re-emerge through the artificial aperture it had used to enter it. Once clear, the digispy wi-fi's its findings to a Clench computer. Human intervention will be initiated if non-standard alterations have been discovered inside the robot. Each digispy can then be reprogrammed and given a new existence after it has completted a mission. You will all get a chance to practice this procedure before you are posted to your distant work place." Mark reiterated that their new job was of pivotal national importance because recent events had suggested that Terrabot was planning to make war on AmOn and they had already used spiked robots to 'probe our defences.' Then confirming that the objective of the operation was to deny Terrabot access to sensitive or strategic information sources of a quality that might weaken our own position, should they wish to attack us. Lastly, he told them, that their drafting papers would be given to them next week. Also, two identical uniforms had been made for each person and these would be issued during the same period. They would be eligible to receive an absence from home allowance which would boost their salaries by approximately one third. He ended up by wishing them God's blessing and good luck with a cautionary warning not to discuss their mission with anyone. "It would, of course, become obvious to the public in time, but if their real objective was not known then it would generate rumours and speculation. The more diverse these rumours became, the more confusing it would be for Terrabot's intelligence gathering networks." As he left the rostrum the whole gathering rose to applaud him.

In their final work-up the field force, now fully uniformed, armed and equipped, tested their new skills on the robots and AIs of the QvO flotilla. In the process, they discovered two robots had unregistered internal modifications and they deactivated them. Subsequently they were crated and sent off to the DES laboratory to investigate. The third was, indeed, a rogue robot but it had been made suspicious by a clumsily executed approach to apprehend it and it had self-destructed in touching distance of the team that had been intent upon examining it. 'A lesson learned!' was how Mark downplayed the incident in a situation report to Anita.

Chapter 12

DEPLOYMENT

Over the next few days and weeks, the field teams were despatched to their respective planets where they were now in situ. Yet it was to be a further six-weeks of hard work before each group were able to fully create their infrastructure and commence their dual purpose of conducting local operations and training their new recruits. Once the field teams have started their field tasks they had, here and there, detected modified robots and these were immobilised and shipped to the laboratories. The number of detections was not large and after a month it only numbered thirty robots overall and most of those would on investigation be proved not to be spiked but suffering from an electronic debility. But a worrying development had emerged because in the past week three robots had self-destructed as soon as they came into contact with Clench field force personnel. "It would seem," Mark confided to Petan,"they must have an active tip-off system somewhere. I have consulted with experts and their consensus is that the radio instructions to the rogue robots could be embedded in an innocent signal but to do that in AmOn would be difficult because there are regulations which require broadcast stations to filter their transmissions to prevent any possible misuse. So, we have got to think out of the box on this!" But where and how, was presented to them two weeks later when the Clench party, 'Foxtrot,' reported to them that one of their sub groups, callsign Foxtrot-5, on AMC planet Andfrell had, by accident made the breakthrough.

From time-to-time Robot Scheduling issued new tennis balls, randomly and regardless of location to robots. They were used as a simple function test to self-assess the robot's logic and response times. In effect if a robot had a free hand, they were required to carry a tennis ball. A robot carrying a ball on approaching another, at the precise distance of ten-metres, would shout 'catch' and throw the ball at speed towards the other robot who was to catch it and retain it. When the appropriate conditions were right, they would then throw the ball on to another robot. In any area there were always several balls circulating, and on a planet, it would number several thousand. Humans, especially children, joined in and they would often pick up a discarded tennis ball and throw it to a nearby robot. Surprisingly, over the course of a month, where they had been carried aboard space ships, the tennis balls could cover unbelievable distances and were, in consequence, bandied around on other planets. It followed, sooner or later, just about every robot took part in this test. If they failed it twice, they were programmed to report their failure to their planetary Robot Scheduling Department who would then log the robot for a bench test aimed at checking its electro-mechanical fitness. It was an uncomplicated but quite effective rudimentary test that did not require expensive equipment nor a technical person present to perform it. In the case of the Andfrell, the 'Foxtrot-5' party had approached a robot intending to apprehend it for testing. However, when it saw them coming it threw a ball it was holding as far away as it could into nearby undergrowth and then it self-destructed. The unusual action taken by the robot, obliged them, by suspicion, to recover the tennis ball which appeared to be ordinary and not unlike those that could be frequently found where they had been discarded by robots when they had been allocated a new task requiring both hands.

Foxtrot-5 had examined the ball and they found another one; in comparing them they seemed to be identical, even to the length of the nap on their surfaces, but when they weighed them, it was found that they were minutely different in weight. On closer examination they found that the ball which had been thrown away by their suspect had a few very short strands of wire within the nylon nap that were so very fine one could hardly see them. They made a guess that these were conductors which terminated inside the ball and their guess was later proved correct because inside the ball was a microcomputer. They couldn't determine what was in its memory because it was encoded in sophisticated cryptology which only yielded an endless stream of letters and numbers to their technical inquisition. But they could construe that when the metal hand of a rogue robot clasped the ball in its hands it would complete the circuits within the ball and data could be transferred between the robot and the ball's bead sized computer. In time the ball would find its way around but its content would be meaningless to a robot that had not been repurposed to be an agent of Terrabot. "It is a slow method of transferring data," Mark remarked, "there are bound to be gaps in its distribution but it was reasonably secure. Terrabot was just unlucky that this robot was caught in a situation where it could not destroy the evidence. The way forward now is to discover who made the doctored tennis balls and how they are introduced to the robots!"

A structural analysis of the tennis balls came within two days which realised that the electrical component parts within the tennis balls were all manufactured on Amborocognia-Mundi. Thereafter, Clench used its sweeping powers to obtain every commercial statistic available to track down the sellers and the buyers of the specific electrical parts of the assembly; given the official push behind their quest, the results came through quickly enough. The search arrows on their electronic maps were increasingly pointing to a startup company that within its first year of operation had purchased substantial quantities of parts identical to those used in the tennis balls. The company was located in a remote nonfunctional sawmill at the edge of a forest. A day later Mark and a TCF combat group swept in by robocopters, only to find the sawmill was abandoned and the layer of dust upon the floor and sills indicated that it had not been visited for months and they would have to come away empty handed.

Good fortune now lent them a hand when one of the TCF teams carrying out a wider sweep in the forest around the sawmill came across a backwoodsman's hut about half a kilometre away from the mill. The man who occupied the hut had worked at the mill until it had shut shop and he felt a strong attachment to the area so he had built his own hut to live in from an unsold stock pile of sawn timbers which remained after the mill had closed. He was surprised that the mill showed no signs of having had recent visitors because he had witnessed some activity recently in the shape of occasional noise and in the form of strange lights there in the past week. He had intended to visit it soon to see if the mill was going to resume work and. perhaps pick up a job. "Of course," he told them, "I used to work on the watermill drive gear. That's under the main floor of the mill, they cemented that over when they closed down because the machinery in there could be dangerous to vagrants or to unwary kids fooling around!"

"Cemented it over?" Mark asked.

"Standard practice," the backwoodsman replied, "they only discontinued operations because there was a housing slump on AMC and the price of timber dropped to what they said wasn't an economical level. They had every intention of reopening the sawmill when the price was right.

"Could you come with us to describe the layout of the floor space in the engine room? We need that because we intend to DMT through it," Mark told him.

"I can do better than that," the backwoodsman replied, "I have photographs of the layout I could show you," he searched a drawer in a rough plank table. From the draw he produced a memory stick and he plugged it into his computer, so they gathered around the computer screen to watch the photographs that had been taken by the ex-employee of the mill. These they uploaded to their own operations centre to be factored in to assist them to calibrate DMT landing zones, avoiding the static machinery.

For their descent into the engine room, they had provided four TCF, two-man insertion craft, the force commander told Mark. "Those photographs were a great help because they marked out the immoveable hazards but also, we have to confirm them plus any new obstacles by an echo-scan. Where possible, we will try to land at the extremities of the room which, in theory, should put any hostile presence inside it at the disadvantage of being attacked from all sides." For the mission, Mark was to travel in the same vehicle as the TCF field commander of the marauding force. Their insertion was to be launched from a site a kilometre away from the mill but, right now, they stood, stern mannered but keyed up to await the arrival of their craft. "We are going to use shock as a weapon with all four craft arriving at the same time," the TCF commander appraised Mark of the plan, at the same time as he could also hear the monotone countdown to action in the background........." three. two. one. engage."

There was a slight mismatch in the set down calculations and Mark's vessel materialised half a metre above the floor whereupon gravity completed the journey with a spine juddering crash which alerted the six robots working in the engine room. Only four of the robots managed to reach the small arms that were laid on a table nearby and two were cut down before they could lift them. The other two, now armed, took shelter behind one of the mill's massive gear wheels and a shot from one of them killed a member of the TCF. A female member of the TCF took advantage of a lull in the firing to gain access to one of the craft they had arrived in. She reappeared at its' doorway with a poenillium rifle and she took a shot at the gear wheel which disintegrated exposing the two combatant robots behind it. In that pregnable position, lethal TCF beams reached out to them from the four corners of the engine room and terminated their digital existence. The remaining two robots had shown no hostile intent and stood as if bewildered in the middle of the room, not sure what they should do. But when told to, they deactivated themselves at once and remained motionless as TCF soldiers approached them to slip handcuffs over their wrists and shackles around their ankles. A subsequent investigation of them revealed that they were standard AmOn robots that were configured for industrial duties. They had been sold as surplus to requirement to a store which refurbished and recycled robots. Their task for Terrabot was to assist with the construction of the fake tennis balls. They had been legally sold and, since being purchased, they had only been employed on industrial duties. They were unaware of the purpose of the product they were making. The residue of the other robots engaged by the TCF was largely solidified metal droplets created when the multiple energy beams had been directed at them from all sides by the TCF.

Although the two coopted AmOn robots had no ethical difficulties with regard to the programmable tennis balls which they had been constructing for the Terrabots, they did understand that it was a secretive project and there was a good deal of subterfuge concerning their activities. They had learned, through observation, something about the organisation and the distribution network for the finished articles. Also, originally when they had been purchased the two commercial robots were taken by a DMT Terrabot ship to an unknown destination, arriving there in the middle of the night inside a very large cave complex. Here they were programmed and trained to make and test the fake tennis balls.

Training complete, the two robots were transferred to their present location to set up shop beneath the sawmill.

As far as they knew, there were no other robots employed producing the tennis balls. A normal output for the balls was only five-hundred a month. The special balls were packed ten to a box in the centre of boxes which also contained ninety ordinary tennis balls. The boxes were outwardly marked up by the Terrabot supervising staff as containing Robot Toys. Thereafter, they were collected by a Terrabot craft which normally landed outside the mill at night and they were then taken to a warehouse situated on AMC. From there they were despatched via normal freight services. The information gleaned from the two robots was not lost on Mark because it confirmed to him that the distribution of the programmable tennis balls across AmOn began right here on AMC. He immediately set his teams to follow the leads to see who had received them and to assess the recipient's allegiance to Terrabot and to discover who bankrolled their activities. Crucially the investigation centred upon the two captured robots which had been sent to the DES and yet more information about them flowed in from the DES laboratory. One robot had been decoded and although it was was not a Terrabot it had unknowingly acquired some unfiled knowledge from Terrabot security lapses. The objective of infiltrated robots, it had gathered, was to collect information and military intelligence. They could do this by becoming employed by a member of the executive and eavesdropping on their private conversations or by seeking social association with robots that did work for them. Their secondary mission was to keep an eye on the local press in their area regarding impending visits to public meetings or civic extravaganzas by the executive. Cutting ribbons and inaugurating new structures were mentioned as examples.

"So that is it," Mark was addressing his department leaders at their scheduled morning meeting. "We have had people watching the AMC warehouse which was the next link in the chain to where the tennis balls made at the sawmill were despatched. Nothing has happened there in five-days so we can pretty much guess that it has been abandoned. Tonight, a team will force their way into it. We have identified the bank account Terrabot uses to pay their production and distribution running costs. The account is unusually topped up by cash and the bank became concerned about the attache cases full of bank notes that were from time to time paid into that account; but they had no proof of a felony. Therefore, the account was placed 'in-house,' on special watch. Privately they thought that it may be the proceeds of a tax fraud or a money laundering operation so they passed their worries to the AMC Inland Revenue. However, when IR checked their tax return it was in order. It was a company dispersal account, they said, the money placed in it was properly recorded as profits from sales elsewhere in their accounts so the IR expressed no further interest."

Mark beamed at those assembled. "As you have already been made aware, starting at one minute past midnight tonight we are going to forcefully enter their warehouse and the bank account of the company will be frozen. Looking at this altogether, Clench has done a pretty good job. I wish to thank you all. In a relatively short space of time, we not only have teams working on every AmOn planet, Furthermore, we have detected their robot-to-robot communication system and some of their fifth column robots. Now we are on the cusp of breaking-up their command structure." From that point on the meeting relaxed into into reminiscences and not a little verbal back slapping.

That evening Mark had an hour-long call with Anita who was quite jubilant with the successes of Clench, thanking him and asking him to convey her delight to the whole team. "One bad thing out of the way," she observed. "I have to tell you that you are to report to the Defence Ministry at eleven hundred hours tomorrow morning for a briefing. From what I have heard, it sounds like a bit of a boy's day out, so I hope you enjoy yourself."

"Well, you certainly keep me moving." Mark laughed.

"We don't approve of sedentary police officers in AmOn," she giggled, "but I do think that you will enjoy this one. Sorry it's a bit of a rush; without giving too much away I think that they are now of the opinion that they don't want to lose you."

"Delighted to go then," he exclaimed, "nothing motivates better than appreciation, even if it is sometimes misplaced. In my case I am supported by a whole team, you know!"

"Don't go all coy on me," she gently reproved. "It is pretty much accepted on AmOn that you have welded an excellent team together and you have achieved some remarkable results Mr Gelder; so be a good boy and go along and be fawned over and enjoy it."

"It seems ages since anyone fawned over me," he injected a sad note into his voice, "and I also like to do a little fawning myself, but no such luck these days. Are you still busy?"

"I am this week," she gave a mock sigh, "but I could come over next week and we can practice our fawning. Is that in order?" "Indeed, it is, I'll hunt out my fur mittens for the occasion."

"Oooh!" she said, "book me in."

"How many nights, madam?" he asked.

"Oh, two I should think," her giggle was sultry. "Right, I'll tell Jeeves to prepare for your visit then."

"You do overwork that poor robot," she replied, "why not give it a couple of days off, I can manage." They continued to indulge each other for a few more moments until a messenger came to the door of Mark's quarters with an official priority message and when he opened it, he saw it confirmed his next day appointment at the Defence Ministry.

Chapter 13

BUGX

The AMC Defence Ministry was a short walk away from the hotel where Mark had been booked into for the night. Although he was greeted respectfully at the Defence Ministry it was with some curiosity because of his Earthly origins. A colonel who had been assigned to act as his liaison officer accompanied him in a robocopter to a tightly guarded AMC projectile and energy beam weapon's range, concealed in a steep valley in the AMC hinterland. "There are not many projectile weapons used by the forces in this day and age," the colonel confided, "but we retain the 'projectile' description for historic reasons. We have something here of interest to show Clench but it can only be demonstrated in a secure and controlled outdoor environment."

For the test that Mark was to witness, they had placed a robot some one hundred and fifty metres down-range and Mark noted a soldier was standing at the firing point with a cross bow in his hands. "We are ready, please go ahead with the demonstration," the colonel called to the soldier who nodded and lifted the cross bow. Simultaneously, the distant robot came to life and started to run away from them. The soldier lifted the crossbow into the aim position and fired at the fleeing robot. The bolt sped away then, after it had been airborne for a second, an internal rocket motor started automatically and a jet of flame shot out of the tail end of the bolt which redoubled its speed. At a point before impact with the robot, the shaft emitted two streams of intense orange plasma which curled around to encircle the robot's waist. If the robot had been motionless, it would have dropped lifeless to the ground but due to its residual forward motion it did three spectacular cartwheels before subsiding to the grass with the plasma lariat still jostling about its frame. "Wow, what was that?" Mark exclaimed.

"It is still hush hush; its prototype it is caled a Radio Frequency Lariat or RFL in military parlance. The principle is a bit similar to the Taser that I am told are used by your police forces on Earth. In this case it is an electromagnetic force carried by the plasma in the missile's shaft. It is capable of subduing both humans and robots; it has a range of two kilometres," he was told

"Why use a cross bow?" Mark inquired.

"Ah, I guessed you may ask about that because it does seem rather odd, so I have read up about it. The plasma carrier for the lariat is housed in the shaft which makes it too wide to fit any existing military infantry hand held weapon. The use of the cross bow is also silent and it is only fleetingly visual. If we relied only upon a jet for the whole journey it would have to build up an exhaust velocity before it could fly. When it is fired from the bow, however, it will have already flown one-hundred metres silently before the jet kicks in. Once an archer has acquired the target a system housed in the shaft of the arrow works with the bolt's fins to keep it on target. When the bolt achieves a proximity to its target a sensor fires the lariat and any electronic systems in use by the target are overwhelmed, like those of the unfortunate robot laying lifeless on the grass out there. Finally, from a military point of view, cross bows can be easily stowed with their bolts and they can be boxed and transported in quantity. We are very happy with the design," he nodded.

"I can see that," Mark agreed, "but why show it to me?"

"Well, these cross bows are still a few years short of becoming standard issue, but I wanted to demonstrate our new toy. What I have also been told to tell you," The colonel cleared his throat, "is that the government of

AmOn have recognised that Terrabot, by their actions, have apparently designated Clench as a priority target to eliminate. In consequence we have been tasked to assist you with suitable weapons and training. The crossbows are to be issued to Clench and we will provide military personnel to visit your detachments to train your operatives how to use the bow." He smiled and patted Mark on the arm. "Now we are going to our laboratories to learn yet another of our secrets."

"And hopefully as useful to Clench as the secrets I have just learned. Lead on," Mark joked.

The journey by a roco was not long and they landed on the roof of a building set alone in some of the most beautifully manicured countryside Mark had yet seen on AmOn. After they had disembarked the colonel led Mark to an entrance doorway. "Worth it for the ride alone," he laughed as a message announced via his hucom that they were about to enter the Defence Ministry Department of Defensive Medicine, with a warning that it would be on pain of imprisonment if anything seen, heard or learned whilst in the builing were to be conveyed to others without obtaining the authorisnation of the Defence Department. The colonel directed him to a lift and they descended to a floor below. A curiously blacked out floor, he thought, as he was introduced to a charming female dressed overall in white personal protection clothing. She handed them both medical gloves to slip on and face shields to wear, before she led them through a decontamination cell to a door which she told them was the office of the director of the facility. She knocked before leaving them there and the suited man who opened it wore no gloves or mask and he invited Mark in and asked the colonel to wait in the ante room while he spoke to Mark.

"Well, my first Earth visitor" he shook hands. "You can take off the mask and the gloves in here, it is a constantly sterilised office. It has to be because I get so many visitors. You are Mr Gelder, the Chief of Earth's Global Police Force and I am Brian, the director of this establishment; do sit down."

"Oh, call me Mark," he interceded to which Brian nodded and continued.

"I have to tell you that I am slightly familiar with the planet Earth. I find it a very beautiful planet. I am one of the few who is allowed to go there on behalf of AmOn to attend lectures and sometimes give them at your World Health Organisation headquarters. The reason is because all planets have their home-grown diseases and they have generally developed medical remedies for them. So, we wish to keep abreast of developments and be prepared as the races comprising AmOn and Earth combine in the future. You know that even what might be regarded as an inconvenient bug on one planet could be quite life threatening on another, so we have to learn about each other's afflictions. The alternative being we could inadvertently create a catastrophe that would sweep through a whole planetary system. We have been lucky with you, as you are aware, but we insisted upon a full course of antibiotics as soon as you arrived; and that is the procedure for all our outworld visitors."

"Yes, I can understand that," Mark sounded puzzled, "Is that why you asked me here?"

"Oh no, sorry," Brian flustered, "that was background conversation. For two of our killer diseases, we have gone further than antibiotics and we have nurtured a natural germ to predate upon viruses that cause those maladies. But that is as far as we can go because, until recently, it has proved impossible to progress further because there are a host of beneficial bugs carried around in the human body. Until recently, all of our attempts to target our laboratory produced, friendly pathogens at other diseases have failed because our experimental bugs also consumed the beneficial germs and viruses. To cut a long story short we learned of a turtle like creature that lives on Marina in the Ongle system that is said to live for more than one- thousand five hundred years."

"Gosh!" Marked gasped. "What on earth does it find to do in all that time?"

"Part of the answer to that question," Brian replied, "is to manufacture an enzyme, in its stomach, which digests foreign bacterial and viral infections. It ignores the turtles' natural virome and microbiome and we have been able to grow the enzyme in our laboratory. We are now able to reconstruct it after lengthy experimentation so that it works precisely the same way in humans. We have named it BugX. Our field tests are now complete and we are ready to roll it out."

Mark was on the edge of his seat when he heard of the research. "That could mean a life without coughs, colds and worse, for everyone."

"Well not just yet," Brian responded. "For a start the manufacturing process is tricky and very expensive to sequence. Moreover, we would be seeking to vaccinate the populations of twenty-one planets. Given time we expect to simplify the manufacturing process. Of now, we have built up a small stock which brings us to the real reason why you have been asked to come here today. Apparently, you are in a position to frustrate Terrabot's aims. The Secretary of State for Defence has reasoned that the machine law of Terrabot will soon alight upon the fact that biological life forms can be attacked and eliminated biologically. It follows that you will undoubtably become one of their primary targets. Sort of a reversal in which the computers infect humans with viruses," he laughed as he pulled open a drawer in his desk and from it he took a small pill box and handed it to Mark. "Please take the tablet at your earliest covenience. It may give you a tummy up-set but within a few days you will be invulnerable to all our known pathogens. In a few weeks you should receive sufficient quantities of the tablets for all of your staff as well."

"Gosh," Mark said as he thanked Brian, "that certainly makes one feel unassailable like being in a protective bubble in a room full of sneezing and coughing people, I like it; and when I return to Earth, I will be able to socialise even with people who have flu or even Covid 19. I cannot thank you and your team enough. "

Mark, on returning to the QvO, booked himself two days holiday to coincide with Anita's arrival. They had decided upon the QvO because it was a secure environment and equipped with the very latest equipment to detect any DMT ingress to the interior of the ship. The alternative in any other location would have been in the company, night and day, of four burly TCF body guards. "What if I wanted to kiss you," she said,"I can't have a soldier noting it down in his duty log book exactly when and for how long!"

"I understood that you were coming here to cook lunch, you didn't mention kissing" he quipped.

"You have misunderstood something. I was to eat lunch" she laughed.

"Ah yes, I remember now," he sounded assured, "I am reminded that I must get a loaf of bread to make the sandwiches."

"You dare!" That tinkly laugh of hers followed and stayed with him, in memory, for the rest of the day as he returned to the job in hand. There was really nothing that needed doing, his quarters were as perfect as they were possible to be even to the exotic flower arrangement that he had shipped in from light years away.

Come the morning of her arrival, Mark was up earlier than normal and making ineffectual changes. What was mostly being churned through his mind were the words 'My Anita is coming here today.' That does not sound very sophisticated for the Commander of Clench, he chastised himself inwardly, but the language of love has its own idiom that is rarely rational. Then his hucom bleeped that an incoming DMT message had been received for him. "They are just setting the DMT bias on my shuttle at this moment, so we will be outside the QvO in about five minutes and in the hanger deck and secured five minutes after that. Look forward to seeing you there," and another bleep sound told him that she had closed her messenger dart channel. Time was short, he glanced at his wristwatch and hurried to the door, to a waiting savuwalk. He used his authority to demand priority passage. Thus, with flashing blue lights and broadcast radio alerts causing other vehicles to automatically pull off to allow passage, he made it to the hanger in just nine minutes. Well, she is the Chief Minister of a whole planetary system, surely it is a diplomatic necessity, he justified to himself. But, in truth, he knew that was not the real reason.

Chapter 14

THE STAKES ARE RAISED

Captain Anda Anjar was already there together with a group of senior ship's officers when Mark arrived and Anda raised his hand to beckon Mark to join the group. "Nice timing," he grinned. "Just one minute to spare." But any further conversation was cut short by the strident sound of an alarm, broken by a call for all fighter trained crew to man their fighters immediately, and to form 'cordon pattern Juliet' around the ship and to be prepared to engage hostiles.' The message repeated itself twice more. The Captain moved apart from the gathering, his head cocked to one side, as a stream of information uploaded from the ship's bridge versed him through his hucom. Mark could see him silently mouthing his orders, but what he said was suddenly rebroadcast over the public address system. It was to the effect that fighter squadrons Alfa and Charlie were to be ready to engage the space ship off the port bow and to render inoperable its ability to engage dark matter transit. They were not to destroy the ship itself. It became obvious, too, that the Captain had called for a virtual bridge to be set up in the hanger deck. It followed that the party which had originally intended to welcome the Chief Minister to the QvO now found themselves standing in a reprojected image of the bridge of the ship with the Captain at its centre. When the bridge spaceview screens flickered into life the assembled group of people voiced a collective murmur of dismay when they saw a giant warship, alongside of them, there were energy beams flickering between the QvO and the other vessel but they were clearly not on full power, so tperhaps they were deterrent or target ranging beams. The QvO space cameras, at the command of the Captain, refocused and they zoomed-in on the closing hanger doors at the rear of the alien ship where they witnessed an AmOn shuttle craft disappearing inside and the doors of the hanger closed behind it. A moment later the alien ship craft disappeared just before the QvO fighters arrived on station. and all there was left for them to do was to hunt the scattered remnants of the escort fighters which had accompanied the Chief Minister's shuttle on its journey from the DES.

"Was that the Chief Minister's shuttle?" Mark looked dismayed as he asked the Captain.

"Yes, it was, I am sorry," Captain Anjar confirmed. "The alien came out of nowhere as the shuttle approached and its advance fighters dismissed the AmOn escorts in a volley of energy beam weapons; as you can see, they have captured the Chief Minister."

"How come our escort was defeated so easily?" Mark's voice was almost a shout. The Captain frowned fleetingly but noting the anguish on Mark's face he replied evenly.

"We do not know what happened exactly; it was an ambush. We also know where something went wrong though. Normally for this type of escort, five fighter escorts are routinely supplied. The protective posture they use is for three fighters to leave fifteen seconds before the shuttle they are escorting. The remaining two leave at the same time as the shuttle. It is designed so that the advance fighters can ensure that there are no nasty surprises at the shuttle's DMT emergent point. For some reason that did not happen, all of the fighters plus the shuttle arrived at the same time. The aggressive alien arrived perhaps three seconds before the shuttle arrived. They must have been primed and ready to fire which had our force completely wrong-footed and they were decimated on the spot. The Ongle shuttle was piloted by a robot. Apart from the Chief Minister the only other entity aboard was a barista robot to provide for passenger needs. We were categorically told by AmOn security that no special measures needed to be taken at this end. In any case, unfactored obstacles at an emergent point risks collision if we had deployed our fighters to welcome them. Something has gone very wrong with the planning. Personally, I would have thought that given the fraught times we are experiencing, the Chief Minister would, at the very least, rate conveyance by a cruiser, but the decision was not ours to take."

"She could be tortured and have her brain cells removed." Mark was addressing nobody in particular as he spun on heel and walked off, tears pricking at his eyes. He didn't go directly to his quarters but instead went down to the lake in the under belly of the ship and sought out a secluded bench in a leafy dell where a stream rippled through the lush tropical undergrowth. He was still there six hours later with his hucom turned off and laying at his feet, his brain numbs and refusing to even let him think. He might have been there even longer but for a robot which passed by. It stopped, looked back and scanned him, then remained observantly nearby. Shortly after, a security guard arrived and approached him and asked if he was Mark Gelder. When he nodded the guard told him that the whole ship was looking for him. This returned Mark to the reality of the situation and that his status as the commander of Clench could not be relinquished because of a personal set back. The guard sensed Mark's inner turmoil.

"Are you alright sir?"

"Not functioning entirely normally," was Mark's reply. "I had better get back to the office." It was true, he knew, that in his despair he had entirely marginalised the wider implications of the abduction. It was not just his personal loss; because all hell would have broken out over the seizure of the Chief Minister of the Ongle System of Planets, It didn't help to lift the burden he felt. but he knew that Anita would not wish him to mope publicly and he had to get on with the job in hand which was to find Terrabot and destroy it once and for all.

A bell made a discreet tinkle from the pathway near the glade to announce that a savuwalk had arrived and then he addressed the guard and the robot with "Thanks for finding me; I was well hidden too. I'll be off now. Please tell them at my office that I will be there in about fifteen minutes time,"and once more he used his authority to prioritise his journey.

Mark's route at Clench took him through the centre of the Clench's open office 'where the hard work is done' he had told his staff; and the general hubbub died down eerily following his progress until he thankfully gained access to his office. As he closed the door behind him his Chief of Staff, Petan, rose to his feet when he saw who had entered the office.

"Glad we found you," his tone was sincere, "we are inundated with frantic calls and other departments all diving for cover. Some have been trying to lay the blame on us but we have denied blame in the circumstances because the protective weight of a VIP's escort is decided and requisitioned by the sending department, in this case the office of the Chief Minister.

"You are right,' Mark agreed, "I suppose it could be argued that we ought to have sent a welcoming escort but I imagine they would have been pretty huffy if we had done that without asking them. The protocol is to wait until asked. It is also doubtful that we could have prevented it anyway; it only took seconds and once the Chief Minister was in the bandit's transport, we could hardly fire upon them, although I understand that they did use low power lasers to try to disable their DMT initiators. Anything more would have risked blowing it up."

"Aye to that," Petan nodded his agreement, then he glanced directly at Mark and said "Look, I know that you are very fond of the Chief Minister and perhaps more than that. You will be understandably upset on a more personal level than everyone else. The Clench operatives are not aware that you have any special connection with her; it is only that I work very closely with you that I have been in a position to observe your attraction to each other. So, because of that, you need time to grieve. I will happily fill any absences on your part if you want to opt out sometimes. Just tell me to take over without any further explanation and no questions asked." He looked at Mark with solemn sincerity. Mark felt a lump welling up in his throat and sounded somewhat husky as he thanked Petan and he replied.

"I know it is not going to be easy emotionally, Mark replied, "but I am determined that we are going to get her back; but thanks, your words mean much. There is one thing you could do for me which would help, if you would conduct the 'O'group with the staff every morning. I don't think I could really face them at the moment, especially as the main topic each day will be concerned with the conduct of the enquiry into the abduction of Anita," he used her Christian name deliberately to emphasise his status with her.

"Consider it done, until told otherwise," Petan confirmed.

To a large extent the event had now become a military and state security matter with one million warships tasked to scour selected areas of space in an attempt to locate the nomadic Terrabots and to bring them to battle. Clench remained an integral part of the operation and it was constantly consulted especially on aspects of the Machine Law by which Terrabot were governed. Clench remained headquartered on the QvO and they were accompanied, at all times by their escort warships, the Endevour and Wellig. Despite internal torment, Mark remained effective in office but, during quieter times, his mind wandered off to Anita and the hopes and the plans that they had together but also on the more sinister probabilities surrounding her abduction and his mind recoiled in horror that she may be tortured by Terrabot.

On the QvO there was a new mystery to solve because Mark's cheribot secretary, Mavis, had not reported for duty that day; and she had been tracked by sensors engaging a savuwalk to take her to another section of the empty quarter. However, she had not activated any alarm signals there and Robot Scheduling admin monitors which routinely monitored the location of all of its robots had reported 'her location unknown' to them. As of this moment the ships security officers were busy mounting a search of the empty quarter which was the daunting size of the country of Wales. They were making little progress in their quest until, on her own initiative, a member of the search group looked casually into the depths of a large feeder tube used for the air recycling system. In doing so she discovered a wig of the type worn by female robots; and Robot Scheduling duly confirmed, from the serial code tab sewn inside, that it had belonged to Mavis.

The rest of Mavis was happened upon by accident by a crew engaged in outer hull maintenance, in the process of repairing minor meteorite damage to the outer hull of the QvO. They had just ignited their rock flow torches when something fell out of space near them. Conjecture suggested there were other items moving at different speeds in gravitational orbit around the QvO and two of them had collided causing one of them to fall onto the hull of the ship. The object was in fact the left arm previously attached to Mavis. Thereafter, jet pack equipped personnel mounted exhaustive sweeps around the ship's hull and they recovered most of Mavis. The parts were passed to Clench's workshops to put her back together again. Also found was a small lunch pack zipper bag containing the collected broken pieces of Mavis's hard disk and these were sent by Mark to the Electrical Anomalies Workshop who made a magnificent job of reconstructing the disk, albeit with bits missing at its joins and from where flakes had been detached in the attempt to destroy it. The generally adopted theory was that Mavis had been torn apart by force and Clench surmised that her attackers did not have time to spare and it was probably all over for Mavis in a matter of minutes.

Later, Mark with the senior Officers of Clench gathered in the Electrical Anomalies Workshop to hear and see what had been made of the hard disk and they were to learn that some very useful material had been gleaned from it. For a start, when the attack had commenced Mavis's camera was switched on. A fragment of the disk showed that she had met four robots who had directed her to a side room where they had set about dismembering her. From the recovered fragments of her disk, it also became appaent that for most of her working day she had recorded the letters that she had typed and the documents she had seen. Watching it, they agreed that Mavis might well have been terminated for the contents of her disk. By now, her attackers would probably have uploaded it to elsewhere. Then they disposed of her not knowing that state of the art machinery could reconstruct parts of her hard disk which they had broken into fragments. "I don't think that she could have had a lot of information of strategic value," Mark opined. But he was cut short from any further conjecture by Robot Scheduling who came through in a double encrypted hucom exchange to say that from the remnants down loaded from Mavis's hard drive they had identified the four robots involved in the encounter and they all worked as labourer employees of the Refuse Department. A plan had been worked out to lure them one by one to isolated offices where they would be deactivated and then passed to Clench to examine them. The big news was that their own investigation, to discover who was their controller at the time that Mavis disappeared, had zeroed in on Antony 03. This robot, at times, worked in security to implement the AmOn requirements to run loyalty bench test checks on all robots. His objective was to ensure that they had not been clandestinely subverted by implants.

Mysteriously, none of the four now detained Refuse Department robots had undergone these tests. However, 03 had, himself, been subjected quite recently to a human, hands on, loyalty check and it had been given a'fit for purpose' classification by the person who had examined him.

"Umm," Mark mentally conveyed a pre conversational clearing of his throat via his hucom. "Does that mean that our loyalty check procedures have overlooked an aspect?"

"Yes, that is so. We checked our surveillance cameras and we discovered that this had more to do with a special aspect of human behaviour than a technical oversight," he laughed. "Antony 03 was sent down for a loyalty check two weeks ago, so we went into our film archives and retrieved the details of his examination. As it was, the workshops were very pushed for time then and they were working nightshifts." A pictorial view picture zoomed in of 03 layed out on a work bench and a human technician who was to carry out the test was standing nearby. "What we learned from the archive shots was that this technician had a romantic involvement with one of the lady technicians who was on the same night shift. She and the technician we were watching went off to one of the darkened side offices. They reemerged some forty minutes later, hand in hand. He returned to his work bench and made a cursory look at 03 and, presumably to make up the lost time, he signed it off as NFF/FFP (No fault found, fit for purpose) declaration. In view of the camera evidence, when confronted, he could hardly deny that he had made a false declaration in respect of Antony 03. "

"I am both angry and sorry to hear that," Mark responded.

"I know what you mean," the controller replied. "Love hits us all and it is quite the most powerful emotion that most people will ever experience and it is very hard to deny."

"What will happen to the technician? "Mark asked.

"Well, we have to do it," the controller's voice sounded measured, "even if we feel sorry for the guy. He is a member of Space Force and he has committed a military sin. I am afraid he will be returned to AMC to stand a Court Martial for issuing a false document and, thereby, endangering his ship. That sort of indiscretion carries a weighty sentence."

"Oh well," Mark reassured the controller, "it is sometimes tough on the people who have to uphold the rules. It has to be done even though we may feel sorry for him and, as we both know, discipline must be seen to be done, too, but such a shame because it was not for personal financial gain or political idealism or even idleness but for love."

"Agreed," the controller grunted, "but getting back to the subject of my call is that we really want to know what we should do with Antony 03 we have looked inside him and he is most certainly spiked for dual purposes operation. Our investigation revealed that he has two extra communication devices, one for local work and the other for long range external communications which also uses an encoder system. We feel that we have caught a big fish but where do we go from here. Do we terminate 03 or remove the spurious communication devices he carries?"

"First my heartfelt congratulations to you and your team," Mark heaped the praise on, "but I don't think I can make that decision alone. Can you keep 03 dormant while we sort through the options?"

"Fine, but he could be missed by whoever he is reporting to."

"I agree," Mark replied, "we will be as quick as we can but this, I feel, is really something to be decided by AmOn, but we will tack our suggestions to it."

Mark was aware that if he acted alone then all manner of government sensitivities would be triggered so it would be wiser to consult with Martin Fraser who had been sworn in as Chief Minister of the Ongle System planets and that also positioned him to be the political head of Clench. So, it would then be up to Martin to appraise the government of AmOn on the strategy that Mark would outline to him. In essence, the plan was to revive robot Antony 03 and reinstate him in his former position in Robot Scheduling with selective parts of his recent memory erased. It would wake up, unaware of recent events. in the Robot Scheduling workshops. Antony would have no recollection why it was there or why so long. The time lapse would be explained as a battery failure and that workshops had seen it as an opportunist gift to outsource the new improved RX3B battery and put it to the test in Antony 03. If it was as good, as was claimed to be, then it would become the battery of choice for all QvO's robots in the future. Meantime they were discretely going to continue their study of the two foreign radio devices installed in Antony to ascertain the frequencies they broadcast on so they could monitor them. They could only take a hands-off look at his encoder because it was assumed that it would be fitted with a detection tool that would report any unauthorised internal inspection. At least they were in a position to advance a plausible cover story for 03's time in workshops. Coincidental to their investigations they had also discovered a file was queued awaiting encryption in 03's short term memory. Analysis revealed it contained an extract from Mavis's storage disk which was a fleet warning update of the current location of the major AmOn task groups and their piquet lines for the coming week. "Gosh," Mark said in surprise "I don't know how she got that. I'll have to recheck my personal security. I don't recall letting her see the fleet update. I am usually pretty careful with that kind of information."

"Think back," the controller chuckled, "did she ever pass by you when you had it on your desk. She could read at near the speed of light; she could have swept by quite innocently, intent upon retrieving something, but in passing she may have zoomed in on that document on your desk and read it phtographically, all in a milli-second. She may not have intended to read it at all."

"I suppose you could be right," Mark replied ruefully, "I must admit I am still learning about robots and their capabilities. At least it appears that the information had not yet been transmitted to Terrabot. Just the same, I will alert AmOn and they may wish to make changes to their fleet dispositions. Thanks for telling me that. I will tell the Chief Minister right away. In the meantime, leave that information in 03's file, we could possibly put that to good use. He won't know that we know, so Terrabot will be led to believe they can avoid detection by our vessels by passing through the gaps as outlined in Mavis;s dsk or by taking advantage of any shielding offered by space furniture in the areas that we are patrolling. Anyway, leave that with me, I have got to make a call to the Chief Minister,"

Chapter 15

THE ROAD TO WAR

Mark knew, of course, that his initial contact with the Chief Minister would be bound to include several references to Anita. Thus, with the possibility that a hucom slip-up may reveal his personal association with her, he had opted to use a conventional telephone for the call.

"Martin Fraser," his voice sounded brisk when he answered the telephone.

"Good morning, Chief Minister," Mark replied and then ventured. "First let me congratulate you on your appointment to Chief Minister of the Ongle System of Planets," and he felt a sadness well up within as he voiced the standard platitude.

"Thanks for that. I had been hoping to talk with you, but I have only been in the job for a couple of days," he laughed. "Most of that time has been involved with a visit to the President of AmOn and some of the senior members of the united government, then, to the Prime Ministers of each planet of the Ongle system. So, I am really glad that you have called me."

"I can well understand that," Mark replied, "but what I have to discuss is urgent and is a major security problem that we have uncovered and you are the Clench conduit to AmOn government."

"So, it's straight in at the deep end" the Chief Minister gave a mock sigh. "Go ahead."

"Thank you, Chief Minister," Mark started but he was cut short from the other end.

"You are a senior officer of what is essentially really an AmOn government department," Martin said. "I think that we can manage without titles. Mark and Martin will be adequate," he sounded amused.

"That would help no end," Mark replied, "titles tend to stultify conversations, I find. Anyway, what I have to tell you is as follows," and Mark commenced to retell the recent events that had beset Clench on the QvO and Martin listened attentively, just occasionally breaking in to clarify a point.

"You don't think that the cheribot, Mavis, was a part of the conspiracy?" he asked.

"No, we don't think that," Mark was adamant, "our conclusion is that she might have actually resisted passing on information to them which resulted in them curtailing her digital life and trying to hide the evidence. But now you have the story, this is what we would like to do. As I have explained, Antony 03 has a message queued up on his hard drive awaiting encryption. We are of the opinion that we should not tamper with his encoder because that could lead to him shutting down for good. However, we now know the radio frequencies upon which he transmits to his masters and we expect to use him to transmit the message once he has encoded it. In the ordinary sense we could spend months or even years trying to crack a sophisticated code and there are no guarantees that we could do it even then. However, if we knew beforehand the plain text of the message before it encrypted, it would be fairly easy to envisage their coding system, so giving us a head start in decrypting any other messages that we may be able to intercept. The other thing, of course, I might mention, is a bit outside the remit of Clench, by the way. We believe the manner in which Mavis was attacked and dismantled suggests that the information they were seeking was vital, leading to a suspicion that there might have been some urgency to their mission. The present fleet dispersals will change within the week so if they are they planning an attack upon us based upon known fleet dispositions, then it has to be very soon."

It is an important message that I have to convey," Martin was serious, "and I am only three days into becoming the Chief Minister, I wonder what the future holds!" he had put a note of alarm into his reply. "I will call upon the President, Wei, immediately and I will get back to you as soon as I return, sometime this afternoon."

"Probably not the best choice of subject for an opening conversation with your new boss," Mark said ruefully to Petan

"Oh, I don't know; he has something very big to tell Wei, after just two days in office. It could cement their friendship for life," Petan grinned.

As expected, the telephone on Mark's desk rang late that afternoon and it was Martin who took up the conversation at the point where they had left off earlier in the day. "President Wei, has asked me to convey his heartfelt thanks to you and the staff of Clench for the critical information you have provided him with. I could not get back to you earlier because Wei kept me there to answer any questions that may have arisen from the security services after he had imparted your information to them." He deliberately paused his conversation to indicate an emphasis for what he was going to relate. "It has been agreed that robot Antony 03 is to be returned to his former employment with the cover story for his downtime being the search for a RX3B battery. To add realism to the story, 03 is to be tasked to submit daily reports in respect of the battery's performance direct to the research department. The fact that the battery is still listed as experimental will also give you an opportunity of bringing Antony in for examination from time to time." Mark held the phone tighter to his ear and raised his eyebrows at the additional forethought to the subterfuge that had been magically concocted in the space of an afternoon by the Presidential office. "The next point we covered was the anticipated attack by Terrabot. The main fleets are to be thinned out a little but there will be an increased activity of ship movements among the remainder. This will give the appearance, it is hoped, that they are being reinforced by yet more ships. The ships withdrawn will be used to create sub fleets embedded in the major asteroid belts around the planets of AmOn. Additionally, a greater use is to be made of self-intelligent, self-homing, space mines and all this is currently underway." Taking advantage of a natural pause for Martin to collect his thoughts, Mark chipped in.

"You have been busy and all in an afternoon, too."

"Indeed so," laughed Martin. "I arrived for a one-to-one chat with the President and before I left there were two dozen very animated senior military and security people in the office with us. But to resume, the order has gone out that all robots employed on military operations or in sensitive security departments are to have their random action capability switched off. That will not harm them but they simply revert slavishly to their programme leaving a big hole in their social life, albeit to them, afterwwards, it will have never existed. Antony 03, however, is to retain its former cognisance and his spurious radio frequencies are to be monitored night and day by humans. There is an emphasis here. 'No robots or AIs are to be permitted in the interception area.' The messages it sends are, where possible, to be decrypted and to this end a team from the Defence Secretariat Code and Cypher Division, with special equipment, will arrive at the QvO very soon. You are to absorb them into Clench and they are never to form a part of the ship's compliment; and that's it. I must still thank you, again, for the information that you gave me to convey to the President despite my just being in the job. It more or less took me straight into the inner circile, which bodes well for the Ongle System of Planets in its dealings with the central government of AmOn."

"Glad to be of assistance," Mark chuckled.

While Mark cleared up the paperwork on his desk and made the necessary calls to Captain Anja and the other two Captains of their flotilla, Petan busied himself making arrangements with Robot Scheduling for the surveillance of Antony 03 for when he was eventually returned to duty. By the end of the day he had, also, put together an organised radio frequency monitoring extension to Clench's growing empire, to be manned by the two AmOn code and cypher experts from AmOn's Code and Cypher division It would be a closed-door operation and only human beings would be permitted to enter it and outside of Clench that meant only Captain Anjar. Sadly, by virtue of their inbuilt AI, not even an automated vacuum cleaner would be allowed to enter either "They will just have to learn to use a broom and a duster in there," Mark and Petan laughed together. Robot Scheduling came through the next day to tell them that Antony 03 had now been provided with one of the prototype batteries and they had no reason to hold him any more without raising his suspicions. Mid-morning, the next day, they called again to say that Antony 03 had been returned to duties and their initial observations were that he had bedded back in seamlessly. Neither Robot Scheduling nor anybody else for that matter had been told about the frequency monitoring facility because the less people were told about it, the slimmer the chance of its existence being compromised. Mark next visited his new code and cypher cabin to assure himself that there were no snags and he was delighted to find it fully set up and the AmOn code and cypher experts had arrived but they had not yet intercepted any rogue transmissions from the QvO.

A Heads up' came the next day when one of the cypher men called Mark to inform him that they had just intercepted an outgoing message originating from the QvO and it was on one of the known frequencies used by Antony 03. Mark immediately called to see them and once there they played a recording of their intercept to him but it was just a five-minute-long meaningless jumble which sounded rather like a jet of water to Mark or a strong wind perhap. Mark stayed long enough to witness the operatives put the intercepted message into a messenger dart and he took it along to a despatch point on the QvO and stayed there until the green 'dispatched' light signalled that the dart had been sent.

'Commander Clench. EYES ONLY' the black dart was emblazoned when it was handed to Mark the next day by a courier. He opened it by pressing his thumb on an illuminated button and he almost excitedly tore open the envelope. Contained within were two sheets of paper and one of them showed the decryption of a message that sent

03. It repeated the message, giving the fleet dispersals which, they knew was on 03's hard disk when they had returned him to duty. There was a note explaining that 03 had used the water method for encryption. "Water jet encryption?" he later asked the two code and cypher men who looked at each other questioningly, then one of them shrugged his shoulders." Oh well, you are the commander of Clench, in touch with governments at the highest levels," he said. "You will certainly have the necessary security clearance so I will take it upon myself to explain. The water jet system of encryption uses, as one would expect, a jet of water into which the digital version of the hidden message is electrically embedded. This injects billions of variable combinations. Essentially the message is superimposed on the molecules of a jet of water which is then manipulated through, speed, water pressure, gravity, quantity, solubles and turbulence. The principle is that what can be created can be replicated; provided that you have the key and the right equipment, you are then able to emulate the the same conditions and extract the message."

"Whew!" Mark blew the word between his teeth. "I can't imagine how they got that to work, but obviously they did!"

On return to the office Mark briefed Robot Scheduling with regards to Antony 03. "The plan is this. I will send you a copy of the position of the fleets and somehow you have to make it easy for Antony 03 to come across it 'by accident.' In future, we plan to ply 03 with a mixture of selected real information and disinformation. The interlaced real information will be specifically included to maintain his credibility with his masters on Terrabot." He followed up this call to Robot Scheduling with a visit to the Captain Anja from whom he learned that the ship was being tuned for war. The QvO and its small flotilla were under military orders to reposition and take on a military contingent, whereafter it would be designated to become the headquarters of the 21st Space Army, operating in an area termed space sector eight. "Clench will be able to continue its operations onboard the QvO," he paused and looked earnestly at Mark. "I would like you to stay close during the military manoeuvres, if you will. I am the commander of this ship but the problem with being in military command of a ship is that you are the ultimate authority and sometimes you need to test your theories on other people before you put them into practice. One of the pitfalls of command is that you do not always get an opposing point of view from your subordinates. It is more likely that the person asked is telling you what he or she thinks you wish to hear. As a commander of the police forces on Earth and here on Clench, you have an independent view, so it would be nice to run my plans past an impartial observer sometimes." He studied Mark's face for an indication of his reaction.

Mark laughed. "Oh yes, I know it, yes sir, no sir. It is a well understood occurrence on Earth too. One sometimes needs independent council but it has to be from a detached person, otherewise one could be considered indecisive for asking for an opinion. I will be glad to do it but spaceships are not quite my forte." Anda Anjar's face split into a huge grin of relief.

"Thanks for that. As you are outside the chain of command that will make it a whole lot easier because, as you know, the aura of command has to be protected at all times!"

It must be said that Terrabot were a tenacious adversary and a week later the Captains of the ships in the flotilla were reporting a mysterious fatal virus that even the medical science lab on the QvO could not identify. Apparently, it began with all the symptoms of a common cold with a runny nose, sore throat, headaches, fever and pains which did not respond to any of the treatments held on board. Within three days most of the victims of the infection were dead and the virus was spreading. An ad hoc staff meeting was held aboard the QvO at which Captain Anda ordered the crews of all ships in the flotilla to wear chemical and biological warfare suits to work anywhere on their ship, except in their own quarters. It was generally held at the same meeting that this could well be a deliberate attack to debilitate the fighting efficiency of the ships affected and the assembled gaze settled on Mark who understood their inference and told them that Clench would commence an investigation at once.

The investigation by Clench was in full swing within one hour of Mark returning to his work station and they had already learned that in the case of all three ships the first crew members struck down were those working in the Space Environmental Laboratories (SEL) and it had spread out from them. It was true, Clench learned, the three laboratories were in constant contact with each other but this was by electrical means only. It was only very rarely they visited each other and, in any case, it was at least two weeks since anyone had because what SELs did was largely to do with their own ships. In this case, space outside was pretty barren so packages of specimens were not passing to and from AMC and between the ships. Their task had no need of robots either, other than cleaners but these were shared with other departments and there had been no obvious cross infection caused by them, so they, too, could be ruled out. "I'm clutching at straws but could a ship be got at with a biological weapon by drilling a hole from outside?" Mark sounded exasperated to one of the officers of a Clench sub branch but the man took it seriously.

"I can certainly check that out. We will do an interior and exterior check because all SEL labs, through necessity. are situated next to the hulls of their ships." However, what had been a suggestion borne out of frustration, bore fruit because the same officer reported back to him afterwards that, their examination of the outside hull had discovered a source of the pathogen. ingress. Immediately above the laboratories there was a small aperture. It did not duct directly into the ship but at intervals a sticky filter tablet was automatically extended out from it to catch samples of space dust for analysis. The filter was then electronically retracted and passed through an airlock system straight into the laboratory. Because they were in clear vacant space the filters had been building up unchecked in the stack and when they were examined it was found that one of the daily filters was heavily saturated with the virus.

"Eureka!" Mark slapped his thigh when he received the news, but insofar as Clench's detective work had resolved the route for the insertion of the virus, it did not relieve the suffering and loss of life caused by it. Moreover, even the those unaffected by the virus were dead beat because Biological Warfare suits were cumbersome to wear. The gloves they had to wear, too, were cumbersome and they made it difficult to manipulate switches, above all one could lose up to one and a half kilograms of body weight per day just by wearing the suit Mark added at the end of the Clench report to AmOn:- To be a militarily significant attack, the virus would have initially have required a wider internal dispersal to the public areas of the ship which, in the event, would probably have wiped out most of the crew. The method chosen invited the view that the enemy were physically unable to mount an internal distribution of the virus. From that viewpoint there were two readily drawn conclusions. ONE: - They deliberatey chose not use any of their agents that were already aboard the three ships, in order to maintain their cover. TWO: - They had no agents on board any of the ships. Noting the recent additional, recently completed loyalty checks of AIs, then opinion TWO appeared to be the most probable supposition. Comfort could, therefore, be taken that Terrabot was now having difficulty infiltrating its agents into the AmOn fleet.

The increase demand had put a strain on AmOn's sttill slender BugX sproduction facilities but Mark had, been in consultation with the Chief Minister and he had asked him to obtain an emergency shipment of the BugX predatory bacteria that he had been briefed on in the laboratories of the Department of Defensive Medicine. Within hours smart boxes containing thousands of individual packets of the BugX vaccine arrived in the QvO landing bays and they were accompanied with a explanatory note to say that they had contracted a new virus and the delay had been due to the necessity to re-engineer BugX to extend its protection. but it was with relief that they were soon able to take off their heavy, unwieldy, nuclear and biological warfare protection suits

As a follow up, a request was made by the Department of Defence to manipulate Antony 03 to send a report to its terrabot controllers describing the effects of the recent infection. It ensued that Mark made a plan with the ships's Captain for the ship's hospital staff to arrange fake bodies on the beds covered by sheets to give the impression that there was a crises and backlog for the morgue. Antony 03 was sent on an errand to the ship's medical centre to pick up a file. The route they keyed into him was was through a hospital ward and Antony was to collect the file from the ward office indeed, that night the radio detection team locked onto an outgoing transmission from the QvO. Later, Mark learned when he got the decrypt back from AMC that

Antony had reported chaos with signs of death and administrative collapse evident. There were indications, Antony had said, that crew levels had been severely debilitated. In his opinion the vessel was no longer an effective fighting force. Later that night the QvO moved up with her escorts to a more aggressive position, as the lynchpin of a fighting fleet.

War in space was something of interest to Mark, especially the tactics employed and he asked Anda Anjar to explain them to him. From him, he learned that an awful lot had changed since the full-scale war that had been fought against Terrabot in the Solar System. Gone entirely was the concept of front lines instead, it was like a lethal chess game played out across the galaxies. The military referred to it as DMT leapfrog. The intention was to wrong foot your enemy by out guessing them. In the event that you did, you would have just seconds to fire off your salvoes at them before they DMT'd away to reappear elsewhere, perhaps to a new position above or below you. Because they were robots, the Terrabots were very good at chess. To try to pre-empt their moves AmOn employed human master chess players as 'field of battle tacticians.' This, hopefully, would result in an insight into the most likely moves by the enemy and also introduce a human calculated - and unexpected element - into AmOn's counter manoeuvres. Conversely, because the actions of Terrabot were founded on Machine Law, the Terrabots saw no reason to address their on board Rap secondary brains which remained dormant throughout military encounters

'Basically, the advent of DMT tactical war meant that a static defence could always be outflanked and attacked from any direction, so fleets must be able to cover themselves at all angles in their dispositions otherwise they could be trounced,' Anda told Mark. 'The only real opportunity for fleets to slug it out, one to one, was when engagements were undertaken in asteroid belts. In effect, these days, segments of the fleet moved in small groups with their weapons trained fore, aft, up and down, in what was described as the hedgehog formation.' Mark guessed that the term hedgehog was a hucom approximation of an AmOn word because the animal did not exist here. A standard hedgehog was comprised of eight warships. Should one side advantageously manage to weaken an opponent's hedgehog posture they would immediately carry their attack to close quarters by diving straight into their damaged foe's formation to exploit the gap from the inside.

However, it would be a short-lived advantage because the rest of the now vulnerable formation would, as soon as it were able, DMT out of danger, regroup elsewhere and try again. Because of the vastness of space, sometimes hedgehogs could constantly and speculatively move by leapfrogging for days, even months and may never catch sight of the opposing force. Normally, though, the leap frogging procedure would be spread across outer space around the planets that were being defended, with hedge hogs arriving and departing randomly. Closer to the planets that were being defended there would be a conventional home fleet inner defence ring, but even with AmOn and Terrabot possessing very large fleets, the space around a star system is a very large area to cover. So, there were close contact home fleets, too. These were comprised of two- or three-person torpedo ships which hovered in swarms around their planets. The most successful manoeuvre of all, Mark learned, was to accurately predict where enemy hedgehogs were going to materialise and to be in situ laying in wait for them. In that circumstance, when enemy did arrive it would take anything up to twenty seconds for them to scan their surrounds and to lay in their weaponry. During this brief interval they were sitting ducks for a lurking force that was already there and could pour a withering fire at them. There was a secondary advantage for the lurking force, too. If the beleaguered, newly arrived, combatant group subsequently decided it was too hot to remain, it would take them a further twenty seconds to DMT out. It didn't happen often but it was decisive when it did. Nevertheless, it could be seen that a DMT war may last for centuries if no accommodation could be reached between the embattled participants.

Chapter 16

HOSTILITIES

The Amon Defence Ministry seemed to be so very precise in their relocation of the QvO and now, with a new military sector headquarters staff on board, it gave the ship's crew a feeling that the Defence Ministry 'must have its clandestine sources of information. Mark broached that point in conversation with Anda on the subject of the likelihood of AmOn intelligence. "I suppose," Mark said, "it cannot be construed that intelligence gathering is only undertaken by Terrabot. I know from Earth's history, especially during the period of the Cold War, games of spy and counter spy were carried out at nearly every level."

"Oh, how do you think that would work in this situation?"Anda was interested.

"Difficult to say," Mark replied. "Earth used to rely heavily upon sigint and humint. Sigint was gleaned from the messages of the other side. Sigint could show an increase in the density and frequencies of electronics at a specific geographic point thus giving an indication of the massing and the composition of enemy formations. But, of course, that could be a subterfuge by them. It also covered their electronic capabilities and attempts to decrypt their coded messages. Humint concerned direct physical penetration of the political, administrative and military engine. That was carried out by realtime spies. Some of the methods used at the time were quite ingenious. I suppose they would have added 'digint' as well, if it were not for the advent of the one world, one government. By extension, in the case of AmOn and Terrabot, I would anticipate they have been up to Terint," and they both laughed. "Whatever," Mark continued,"they seem to be up to the mark at the Defence Ministry; we have them to thank for BugX. It was forward thinking on their part to engineer a germ that feasted upon other germs and viruses but could be made selective of which ones to consume!"

"I think you are right; they do seem to have more boffins there than there are drones in a bee's nest." Mark looked quizzically at Anda to see if the choice of the word drone was a double entendre, and intended to indicate Anda's personal feelings but seeing no sign of it he decided it was a quirk of translation by his hucom.

The sector of space assigned to fall under the command of the QvO and its flotilla was a very important static position and plum in the middle of the Ongle system of planets. The position was based on the assumption that a Terrabot assault on the planetary system would seek to creep around it and then smash inwards to capture the centre. The QvO flotilla at the centre of the system was in the roll of being a blocking force. It was not a manoeuvre that could be reciprocated by AmOn upon Terrabot because after their last defeat Terrabot had opted to own no homeland and to lead a nomadic existence which was well suited to robots.

By the time the QvO was 'on station,' reports were beginning to trickle in that Hedgehog incursions had been made into AMC territorial space. Not just one here and there but a group of five hedgehogs had materialised in the centre of the AMC and there were similar formations outwith. Their tactic was fortunately guessed to be an attempt to drive a bridgehead to the centre of the AMC and to militarily dominate the system from there. But AMC sector had thrown all but its reserves into eliminating the internal attack which disappeared almost as soon as it arrived. As they were congratulating themselves the Terrabot hedgehogs reappeared again and three more times after that. At the same time, they also changed the positions of their peripheral attacks. Their method became constantly probing to discover or create a weak space in the AMC defence, but they had failed to find one, nor were they able to fashion one. Nevertheless, there was heavy collateral damage on two planets in the system which amounted to death and deprivation of habitat over extensive areas, but Terrabot losses had been severe, too, and they had aready lost twenty-thousand ships, whereas AMC had suffered the total loss of just two and another fifteen damaged.

Thus, alerted against Terrabot's repetative style tactic, the QvO sector fleet had distributed itself to meet them and their ships were ready to hose red hot destruction from their weapons at the first sign of an incursion into AmOn territory. But Terrabot was to prove that they could think outside the box and confound the pundits. A new attack upon the Ongle system began when two hundred small hostile ships blinked in and proceeded not to engage the AmOn capital ships but, instead, they commenced to drop thousands of gravity descent bombs on the Ongle planets. The QvO fleet, to a man, brought their weapons to bear on the free fall bombs. It was at this point the capital ships of the Terrabot fleet arrived whilst the QvO's and its fleet armaments were orientated to deal with the bombers. Thus, they had lost the advantage of being primed and ready for the arrival of more Terrabot hedgehog formations. It ensued that Terrabot were able to loose off the first shots of this engagement and the AmOn fleet suffered some damage before they could realign their weaponry to engage them.

At the special invitation of the Captain, Mark was on the bridge of the QvO with him. He was looking at a screen showing a sector of space and the Endeavour came into view ploughing through space with a two-hundred-metre-long chunk of its hull peeled away, bizarrely revealing empty but still lit offices and private crew quarters still furnished and with pictures on their walls. As she went past, Mark was again reminded of videos that he had seen from the past of giant sea going battleships importantly going into battle, except this one was not billowing smoke from its cannons but, instead, was issuing streaks of red and orange fire as they blazed away. Guided missiles were also erupting from its hull to speed off into the heavens to engage targets that not covered by Mark's viewing screen.

Over in AMC, the Terrabot fleet had been repulsed with vigour but they had obviously decided to try a new tactic and Terrabot returned in force looming briefly out of the dark matter and firing off shots at AMC targets then promptly disappearing again. This was going on over the whole sector. It was not perhaps a well thought out plan because they were vulnerable when they first arrived and the fleet in the AMC were able to come to bear upon them immediately, they appeared. It was wasteful of Terrabot spaceships but it would seem that they were at any cost determined to press on to try to wear down the AMC sector, employing a 'to the last man left standing' battle plan. But that could never be because they had piled most of their assets into a relatively small killing zone. AmOn could do likewise and already they were calling up reserve ships stowed in asteroid belts or from positions close to the corona of stars which had been shielding them from electronic detection. The fighting was awesome if there were eyes to see it all at once. Space was crisscrossed by energy beams and exploding torpedoes and ships bursting asunder as the AmOn and Terrabot constantly leapfrogged around each other in their attempts to out manoeuvre their opponents in a tit for tat quest to dominate the field.

To a lesser extent, the war was not only being fought in the inner space of the two AmOn systems but much further afield where Terrabot hedgehogs were speculatively popping up anywhere in the hope of finding AmOn reserves to engage. The AmOn Defence Ministry had assumed that there must be a launch point from which Terrabot was marshalling its forces and to this end AmOn DMT probes and destroyers were stealthily searching suspect galaxies, asteroid fields and

Magellanic clouds but so far without success. The facts they did know were gleaned from their dark matter beacons and the lack of heavy movements in dark matter suggested that the hedgehogs which were attacking AmOn, from many directions, might have been dispersed around them in a drip-fed fashion so as not to raise undue alarm. It was possible that they could have been there for weeks or even months as Terrabot had built up its forces.

The Terrabot attack upon AMC, if anything, had now increased in ferocity and was clearly intended to sustain loss regardless and they were going to press home their attack on the basis that albeit they were losing more ships than AmOn they were eroding AmOn's resistance. When they had laid waste the number of ships AmOn had at their disposal in this sector, they would probably refocus their attention on Ongle. But, knowing that Terrabot had no personal concern over the loss of life and assets, the Defence Ministry had foreseen their tactic and they had huge fleet reserve of quarter of a million warships that were earmarked for the defence of the AMC. In the run up to employing this tactic, the effectiveness of the AMC sector fleet was deliberately made to appear panic stricken and uncoordinated. The hope being that this would be construed by Terrabot that the prize was theirs for the taking. Just one big push now would seal the fate of AMC. This time Terrabot did not employ hedgehog formations but entered AMC space as a solid armada comprising thousands of ships with a battle plan of 'relentless' and to not to DMT away from adversity. It was their big mistake because to execute such a confrontal approach the ships engaged in it needed to have a unified command structure which could only be exercised through radio links. The AmOn defenders had a trick up their sleeve which they had borrowed from Mark's cold war on Earth recollections. Once AmOn's DM beacons had confirmed that a mass DMT jump had been made, they switched on their radio frequency jammers. Thus, when the Terrabot ships arrived, en masse. they had no working command and control radio links in place. Their Machine law, therefore, dictated that they could only fight in the manner installed by their last programme which was to fight to the finish and they would continue to do just that unless it was countermanded by radio. Their position was impossible without a radio connection, each one of their ships was moving independently through space with the single objective to find an enemy ship to shoot at. Their enemy on the other hand could predict their moves and counter them effectively with tactics and feints, objective to drawing the Terrabot ships into compromising circumstances.

The destruction inflicted upon the Terrabot fleet was horrendous. Without direction they were picking individual fights rather than coordinated strategic engagements. As their fleet was diminished the incoming fire power became concentrated on their remainder. The slaughter had increased to a point where hunter killer groups of AmOn ships roamed freely around, presenting themselves as targets, that albeit represented impossible odds to their victims. Yet, still lone Terrabot ships took the bait because they had no other digital option open to them. Eventually the reduction of Terrabot ships was so evident that their own onboard yes/no electronic flipflop arguments subsumed control and the Terrabot ships began to randomly disappear back into DM.

In the Ongle system the fighting had not been so intense as it had been around AMC, but nevertheless, it had been deadly. The Terrabot ships attacking Ongle had not been programmed for a fight to the finish as they had been at AMC but in a moment, they had vanished, too, leaving the debris of both sides of the battle silently suspended in space and a hazard to shipping. As if to illustrate how chaotic it had been, Mark was looking at a forward screen and he saw, with awe, that a Terrabot ships had obviously popped out of DMT inside a battle debris field where it had simultaneously tried to occupy the space of a derelict Terrabot vessel. Both ships were now blacked out, motionless and permanently fused into a religious looking cross. Anda looked over his shoulder at the scene that Mark was looking at and explained. "It will be a perfect join, no holes or blank spaces around it. The existing wreck being already in existence is the dominant structure so the next vessel will have sacrificed parts of itself in the areas it had attempted to co occupy, those pieces will remain orphaned in dark matter. There may even be Terrabots still active in either of them." He then issued instructions for a spread of neutron cascade bombs to be fired at it. "The bombs are designed to inhibit all robotic activity but leave the ship still available for inspection and intelligence gathering" he clarified those reasons to Mark. Yet still, actions were continuing in deeper space where AmOn ships were still ranging far and wide in a search for the Terrabot control centre from where the attack upon them would have been masterminded.

The news that Terrabot had vanished from AMC territory with their tail between their legs translated into a joyous occasion on the ship. Mark was able to joke with Anda that before the battle had commenced Antony 03 had sent out three encrypted messages. So, he had a word with the ship's water engineers to ask them to cut off the water supply to Robot Scheduling, thus depriving Antony 03 of an encryption medium for any futher messages he may wish to send. He had justified his action by reporting the reason as 'suspected water contamination.'but he wondered if Antony's activities today were the reason why Terrabot seemed to have avoided attacking the QvO. "It's nice to know that we are of value alive, even to Terrabot," the Captain replied humorously The battle for the Ongle sector gradually diminished with less and less hedgehog formations appearing, with their appearances becoming ever further apart until they ceased altogether, but deception was feared and some battle fleets remained 'on station' for several days thereafter.

The conflict itself had shifted further away. The AmOn deep space fleet which was already two galaxies afar had finally made contact with the nomadic Terrabot fleet. The plan was to intercept them and to ram through the element of surprise. Analysis of Terrabot's present tack described a route that would take them between the four outer planets of an emerging star system. The AmOn deep space fleet planned to lurk, shielded from detection, behind the four planets and pounce when the signs were right. They waited patiently as the Terrabot fleet nosed between the planets, unaware of the trap that had been set for them until AmOn launched upon them. In the first five minutes there was a carnage of the Terrabot ships and in a blind panic they opted for the unknown by jumping into dark matter; but it was hurried and space fleet had anticipated just such a move and they had sown DM navigation beacons around them. From these beacons they were able to trace the path of the retreating fleet and allow no time for Terrabot to form a coherent defence strategy before Space Fleet were upon them again. Yet again Terrabot jumped away, only to be followed immediately by Space Fleet. In fact, they did that, all told, for four DM jumps after which the Terrabot fleet, now a shadow of its previous strength, changed tactics. This time the Terrabot ships jumped individually in as many directions as they had ships remaining. Space Fleet demurred from following this move as it would divide their own fleet in the unknown, so they reassembled their ships and headed for home and a hero's welcome.

On the QvO, Mark read of the extended battle leading to the destruction of much of the Terrabot fleet and despite his many years of police training where the cardinal rule was not to display bias, he, just-the-same, inwardly relished the punishment meted out to the robots. "Good riddance," he muttered under his breath. Of late, though, he had been coping better with his anguish over the abduction of Anita, who he had finally resolved in his mind, was dead but still at more fanciful moments he still persuaded himself that she was not. 'Revenge is legal in the appropriate circumstances.'

He imagined a high court judge handing down the sentence to Terrabot.

Chapter 17

TERRABOT NEGOTIATES

Following the Terrabot war the populace of AmOn found they had embarked on anything but a story book peace. The hedgehogs still appeared occasionally, nowhere near as frequently as before and sometimes there were days between events. Consequently, there was no respite, the military requirement for deep space probes and patrols would continue to try to locate the enemy fleet. At any given time AmOn was obliged to maintain a full alert posture against a worst-case scenario where, perhaps, a single hedgehog might appear one day but, on another, numbered in thousands. AmOn could never relax its guard while the possibility of the surprise attack existed and that was a very expensive option in men and materials. For the crews of the ships it meant no home leave could be permitted for them, save for individual family disasters and there was a growing air of mental fatigue evident. Mark could see a change in the crew of the QvO. Nothing was really militarily wrong but there was a host of unsmiling faces in the corridors of the ship and on occasion little things were not done with the precise efficiency which one expected in a military setting. "It is a very clever tactic Terrabot have adopted," Anda told him. "It is a type of warfare which favours machines over biological life forms. Being machines, they could keep this up for a thousand years or more. It will wear us down in the end, I fear. We really need an advance in technology tip the balance in our favour." Mark nodded that he understood the full width and depth of the dilemma into which they had been pitched.

Any further conversation on the subject was cut short because a recall to the bridge was flashed through to Captain Anjar. He rose to go but beckoned Mark to follow him there as an announcement boomed out from the public address system in the corridor 'Gun crews' man your weapons.' They could hear running footsteps in the distance, as they traversed a short passageway to the bridge. The Bridge Officer saluted as the Captain entered and pointed to a ship's side view-screen and they saw that a polished silver ship, having no discernible weapon apertures or markings, had pulled up alongside the QvO. Above it, was a halogram projection of a large white flag realistically fluttering as if it were in a stiff breeze.

"It's Terrabot," the Bridge Officer sounded a little flustered. "They say they wish to discuss peace with us."

"Oh, right," the Captain said calmly. "Signal to them that we cannot discuss peace on behalf of the AmOn government but we would welcome a limited size party of not more than three unarmed robots to come aboard to outline their peace terms. We will relay their terms to AmOn, it is up to AmOn how they wish to respond. Tell our ships in this sector to maintain full security but not to fire on any Terrabot ships within their orbit unless they make a hostile move towards them or toward AmOn assets." Anda put a finger to his lips then glanced at the guard on duty on the deck. "Ask the security chief, in person, to have our visitors discretely scanned for any ionising substances, chemicals, explosives or pathogens when they arrive. They are robots and have no need for air so I will send an uncovered store loading platform to pick them up, but tell the controller to adjust the speed of the platform to 'slow,' when it returns, so that we can get a full scan of its passengers and anything they may be carrying before they get too close. Go now and tell him verbaly what I have said and also tell hime we require more armed guards on the bridge and the bridge approaches, to satisfy the Defence Ministry regulations concerning the necessary standing precautions to be taken when embarking potentially hostile visitors on a spaceship. The same goes for the engineering sector." The guard acknowledged the message, saluted and turned and left the bridge.

The Captain and Mark stood side by side and watched as the loading platform edged up to the robot ship and they saw three figures leave the Terrabot vessel. They were standing on the platform as it made its way slowly towards the QvO. "I am going to conduct this meeting in the conference room," Anda Anjar turned to face Mark.

"Right then, "Mark had misread the message. "I will be off and leave you to conduct this momentous occasion, so I had better let you get on with it. Good luck," he turned to go but the Captain Anjar moved to block his exit.

"Hey, not so hasty," he was quick to respond. "I have a feeling that a pair of police eyes and instincts may not be amiss at this gathering. I would like you to come, too, but take a neutral stance. I will introduce you as my security officer. So the set up will be the political officer to do most of the speaking, my status, as a Captain, is to imply authority and formality for the meeting; and you, are my observer, aka known as the security officer." He opened a console on the bridge and produced a pistol and a belt and holster for it and gave them to Mark. "Please put these on. You do know how to use the pistol, don't you?" Mark laughed.

"It was not so long ago that the Defence Ministry took me to their firing range on AmOn and taught me how to use this weapon," he glanced at it. "They must have had an intuition that this would happen. Just the same, if I do have to use it, I do caution that my friends should lay down on the floor for their own safety." Anda grinned.

"I am sure your aim is not that bad?"

"Nope, just a precaution really. I surprised myself on your firing ranges and did quite well. It is a doddle to use. However, on Earth, we have solicitors ready to sue on behalf of their clients for the slightest failing by a public body, so I added the precaution in case there was a mishap." Anda looked at him seriously for a second to see if Mark was sincere in what he had said, then realised it was in jest and he laughed loudly, and he gave Mark a shove towards the door to the conference room.

The wood panelled conference room at its centre had a long-polished table and the Captain and the political officer sat at one end of it and Mark was to sit off set but facing the middle of the table. From those positions they rose as the door to the conference room opened to admit the Terrabot delegation and they went to meet them. Two of the Terrabots were dressed formerly in suits, shirts and matching ties, outwardly resembling athletically honed humans. The central figure was wearing a toga type cover, heavily woven in gold thread and a golden corona. The most surprising part being that all of it exposed surfaces were coated with shone gold too.

As they approached, they held out their hands for a traditional handshake; Anda told Mark afterwards that the hands he shook were purely metallic. "A lot can be deduced by the handshake" he observed, "but this was cold, mechanical and conveyed nothing at all." With the introductions over, they took their places at opposite ends of the table and Mark looked on impassively from the side. The gilded figure did not rise when it commenced to speak. He, and they all thought of him as male but as Terrabots are sexless he could equally be an 'it', Mark mused, but the question of a title was established when the gelded figure announced that it was the Overseer of Terrabot and explained that he was deliberately engineered for that one purpose. He was enabled with more computing power than a normal Terrabot and he had absolute power to negotiate for all Terrabot. No matter, he explained, all robots were governed logically and he was no different. He apologised for the war which was wasteful but they were only forced to embark upon it because the humanoids had given them no choice because they frequently frustrated Terrabot attempts at acquisition. The political officer broke into the Overseer's delivery to briefly say that some of the acquisitions undertaken by Terrabot were regarded as armed theft and they could not sanction theft by Terrabot or anybody else. They were prepared to trade with Terrabot but to take things just because one desired them was not a friendly act.

It was at this point the differences between the digital and human take on the legality of ownership opened up and the Overseer held up his hand to stop the political officer. Humans, he said, were governed by social laws which often had their roots in religion, whereas robot laws were based upon logic, but who was to say which of those was right? Terrabot had no need for trade or money. Logic suggested that robots were the next evolutionary level above humans because robots possessed faster minds and they had no requirement for comfort, night, day, food, oxygen, sex, housing, schools, religion, recreation, entertainment nor medical facilities. They could exist on almost any planet in the entire universe and their laws, hence concept of ownership, were based purely upon reason.

"Could you explain that?" Captain Anjar interrupted.

"Yes, we can." The explanation he gave was that vide Machine Law, inventions, property, or resources should logically be owned and used by the most appropriate organisation able to derive the most benefit from them. It did not make sense to allow these to remain in the hands of beings or even robots who had only a limited use for them. It was a matter of algorithms, nothing more, nothing less!

"And Terrabot decides the appropriate algorithms to apply?" The political officer queried. "Surely that does not appear to leave a lot of room for negotiations which are usually about compromise. There appears to be no incentive for compromise if you insist on applying your self-generated algorithms?" The political officer laid his hands flat on the table in front of him.

"That may not be the case, in any event it would work in your favour because once the algorithm has been added to the collective minds of Terrabot then an attack upon AmOn by the forces of Terrabot could not happen," the Overseer replied.

"Setting that aside as by no means settled, perhaps you could explain precisely the terms that you have in mind for an agreement between Terrabot and AmOn?" the political officer nodded to the overseer. Mimicking a human gesture, the Overseer leaned slightly forwards towards the political officer and said: -

"As you will be aware, the eariar solar system war between our two forces resulted in our defeat; and the Ongle System of Planets which was then an autonomous system, irradiated our home world. It will probably be another half a million years before the radioactive decay there has died down to the extent where it can be reinhabited. We have wandered as a community ever since that war, seeking a new homeland. During that time, we have continued to expand our population and fleets of ships. Albeit you have had some success recently, we have many more ships in reserve, but war is a waste of time, effort and materials. Our wandering in space is really the result of our attempt to find everything we want in once place to satisfy our needs and thus-far we have been unlucky. Useful looking planets have been found but, on closer examination, all have had unacceptable defects in one way or another, tidal waves, electromagnetic storms, unstable orbits or are subject to meteorite strikes and a limited future, to name just a few. Then there is also a 'what if' factor to process in. If we did decide to set up on a favourable planet but the war between your people and Terrabot has not been resolved, it could be that your future aggressive actions would nullify our attempts to colonise any planet; so, we have decided that we will offer you a chance to end this war here and now."

"Who is responsible for this war is not under discussion here. The purpose of this meeting is for you to submit your requirements for peaceful relations and we will study them," the political officer had sidestepped been drawn into a blame game.

"The terms for ending this war and living in peace with each other," the Overseer sounded schoolmasterly, "is as follows: - The only place that we have thus far discovered that suits all of our needs is the planet Earth." A sudden fit of coughing ensued from Mark and a helper robot rushed a glass of water over to him, after which the the Overseer resumed. "We will guarantee to end all hostilities against you and in the future, we will trade with you for the items that we may require. In exchange for this, you will have to cede the solar system to Terrabot and depopulate planet Earth and relocate it within the populations of AmOn. The alternative is that this war will continue throughout your lifetime and the lifetimes of your sons and daughters during which hundreds of thousands of your people will lose their lives needlessly. There is one other proviso and that is that you will cease to expand your activities in open space. If your space ships are discovered in space, that are not associated with a trade route, those ships will be destroyed."

"Why do you want Earth's whole solar system?" the nonplussed political officer asked.

"They are not using the other planets in their star system so it is an under utilisation of resources. Whereas, on the other hand, we could use most of them. From there we intend to expand and colonise the universe because only we are equipped to take on that job."

"I cannot imagine that the people living on Earth will take to your suggestion kindly," Captain Anjar interceded.

"That is your problem, not ours," the Overseer replied tartly. "You have the power to make them do your bidding. Also look carefully at what an alliance with us will bring. Once we are programmed to accept the agreement that we have outlined to you today, it will be written into our law. Should another distant and yet unknown race in the universe decide to attack you, they will be in the position of possibly usurping our agreement.

In those circumstances the logic for Terrabot would be to defend the agreement against the possibility of change."

"I am now up to speed on what you are proposing." The political officer gave no hint whether he was for or against the plan, although he was pretty sure that it would not find much favour either on Earth or in AmOn. "So let us now discuss the hostages that you have taken. What is to happen to them?"

"The hostages are guests of Terrabot," the Overseer apparently suffered no complications in admitting they had them. "They are to be retained as bargaining chips; they are being cared for at one of our dispersal facilities.' Mark was startled to hear this and, to an observer, he would be seen to briefly look upwards and clasp his hands and his lips moved soundlessly before he resumed his original posture.

"I must advise you that blackmail is not a good bargaining chip," the Captain interjected.

"Unless they are returned immediately it will certainly harden the attitude of the AmOn government towards agreeing to anything because there would be nothing to prevent you releasing these hostages and later capturing another group of hostages to bargain for future concessions if there was disagreement about something Will you release them now?"

"Not now, but certainly when the deal is struck I will; but I must advise you that if we do not reach an agreement on the terms we offer, then the plan is for us to abduct more hostages until you listen to us and this war will go on for eternity. As for myself, I will outlive every one of you and I can assure you that at least up to when I am eventually replaced the war will continue to be waged. So, dwell on the fact, without an agreement the people of AmOn and its space ship crews will live in the fear, day by day and every hour of every day, that they may be the next target."

"Ok," the political officer was on his feet, "I don't think it will help to get into a tit for tat argument. I will forward the video that I have had made of this meeting direct to the Chairman of the AmOn government. He will discuss it with his cabinet and later with his parliament. I cannot preempt their decision but I suspect it will not be long coming."

When the Terrabot delegation left, Mark had remained in the conference room and when Anda returned he was amused to find him on his hands and knees underneath the conference table. "I can see you there he said playfully. I have read that you have woodworms on Earth but I can assure you that there are none here," he laughed but then fell silent when Mark put his fingers to his own lips to indicate that Anda should not make a sound. When he had crawled out, he beckoned Anda to leave the conference room into the corridor outside where he stopped and said.

"From where I was sitting, I had a good vantage position of both ends of the table. I could see that the Terrabot sitting on the Overseer's right was fiddling with something underneath the table. On examination, after they had left, I have found a small black box under there which is glued to the reverse side of a cross member of the table. The most probable explanation is that it is an eaves dropping device. Then, again, it might contain a biological agent because they have already tried that on us once. The standard Earth procedure to check for hidden listening devices is to use a radio sanner which also emits an audible sound. You switch it on in the room where you think your bug is and it captures the audio sound and transmis it as a radio wave and a radio receiver, which is a part of the equipment simultaneously ploughs through the known radio frequencies to try and pick up if the audible sound being rebroadcast on a radio frequency. If it is, they know they are bugged and they start to hunt for the hidden microphone."

"Bugged?" Anda looked confused.

"Purely an Earth term," Mark chuckled. "It means spied on electronically, and to check that aspect out I could do with one of your spectre robots to monitor the radio frequencies plus a standard vacuum cleaner robot. My grand scheme is to start a vacuum cleaner robot up and get it to clean the conference room. Its activities will produce a non-suspicious everyday sound. If there is a bug under the table, it will pick up the sound of the vacuum cleaner and rebroadcast it on a radio frequency which the spectre will be able intercept. Then we will have our answer. I also plan to spread some kind of household powder, salt or sugar will do, on the floor near the suspect bug. When the vacuum cleaner finds its way to the powder it will have to spend a little time gathering it up. The noise in that particular area will, therefore, be quite intense and we will use that as cover for the Forensics Department to take swabs from the surface of the box to tell us if there is a biological hazard present. I am pretty sure it is a bug but we cannot be complacent."

"You have certainly figured this out very quickly and painstakingly detail!" Anda was serious but amused, "it seems to have been a wise decision when they made you the commander of Clench."

"Yes, well, I don't know an awful lot about piloting a monstrous space ship but I did study the Cold War on Earth which helps in these situations," he said.

"I have sent for a vacuum cleaner and a bag of sugar and a Specialist Technician Radio Engineering Robot" Anda confirmed to Mark. Their conversation was followed shortly by a lab technician who came in through the door and Mark briefed him on what was required and of the necessity not to make any audible sounds. The technician nodded that he understood. Then from the medibox he was carrying he selected a packet of soft wipes. "These will make less surface noise than a cotton bud." He had beckoned Mark outside of the door to explain. The next arrival; a robot vacuum cleaner, of course, needed no instructions and it set to work at once. In the meantime, Mark and the Captain retired to a nearby office with the spectre which stood apparently doing nothing at all until it announced in a metallic voice "Sounds attributable to a working vacuum cleaner have been detected," and it reported the specific radio frequency and played back a been recording. "It is most certainly a vacuum cleaner," the Captain averred, "and that loud crackling sound it developed later must have been when it was sucking up the grains of sugar I put down."

Mark had returned to his office when a call came through from Anda confirming that the lab report said that there was no trace of pathogens in the swab. "So tell me what does my Cold War expert recommend in this case?"

"May I cordially suggest that we leave it with the conference room monitoring cameras switched on and focussed on that space underneath the table. That is where somebody would have to go if they wanted access to check on the bug. In that way we will, also, be able see if we have an undercover agent from Terrabot in our midst because from time to time Terrabot will wish to check it to reassure themselves that it has not been disturbed. I will tell the Intelligence Branch of the Defence Ministry. My bet is that they will want to leave it untouched so they will be able to feed its listeners with misleading information should the need arise."

"Please do that and let me know if there are any comments from the Ministry. You know I am beginning to enjoy the world of spy and counter spy. Could you recommend any novels on the subject?" Anda asked.

"Indeed, I can, I will send for some from Earth for you; I think you will find those by *John Le Carre* interesting."

After Mark had returned to his work place he made a trip to the AmOn code and cypher team to discuss this hidden microphone, first telling them that their conversation was under the caveat of 'High Temperature'. They listened and then gave a unanimous opinion that if it was transmitting information to Terrabot then a simple radio signal would be too slow. In their opinion the physical size of the bug confirmed that it would not contain a very powerful transmitter which would have required more space for larger components.

The evidence suggested that it was signalling to a DMT relay, probably located less than one hundred thousand kilometres distant. This prompted Mark to formulate a plan to locate the DMT relay using thirty of the ship's darts of a type that were usually used for space mapping. Buoyed, too, by the possession of the news that Anita may still be alive, the first thing he did when he returned to his quarters was to kneel and pray to God that she was safe and well and ask for guidance to find her.

Chapter 18

A BLACK FOREST ENCOUNTER

Four days later, word came through that they had found the Terrabot radio relay for the bug. It was in a fixed position in space and, as experience had taught them, its functional apparatus was contained in a garden shed, identical to the ones that they had found previously. Up until now the significance of the structure had not really been investigated but now Mark's thoughts turned to the subject of why; and he realised that the obvious had escaped him. A shed, of course, did not reflect a radar beam but neither, also, would plastic or a dozen other construction materials. The sloping roof was inconsistent to its purpose. It does not rain in space so why was it that shape? His mind drifted on from there to when he had replaced his own leaking garden shed back on Earth. It had arrived as a flat pack. 'Flat pack'! he kicked himself, mentally of course. If it were ready made and simple to reconstruct then why not. The shape of it had nothing to do with its intended use. Terrabot would only be concerned with its availability and if it could house their equipment. Most sheds came with a fixed internal bench shelf which made them ideal to seat radio equipment. But where were they buying them?

Returning mentally to the job in hand, Mark formulated a plan to ask Anda for one of his cloaked habitat probes that were normally used to investigate newly discovered small life forms without unduly alarming them. Cloaking, although impossible for an object the size of a spaceship, was quite possible for smaller objects such as a dart. Effectively, what was hidden behind the dart was projected in front of it. It was not perfect but near enough, against a complex backdrop to fool all but a close examination. The chosen probe was fitted with a huge crocodile jaw in its nose cone. When this was extended it could grab specimens and objects on the hoof, as it were, and bring them back to a launch site.

The cover for its activity against the Terrabot shed was to be a shower of small space pebbles fired toward it from a distant dart. This would undoubtedly be recorded as an asteroid shower and in the midst of it the probe would snatch away a portion of the structure's roof and convey it on to AMC for examination.

The operation was laudable and everything went exactly to plan. The AMC labs had signalled back that a substantial sample measuring about half of the wooden roof had been torn away. Finally, after a few days, they said the composition of the wood they had received matched no known trees among the planets comprising AmOn. Of now, they were spreading their search wider to include other planets that AmOn was aware of that were able to support trees large enough to be used as timber for construction purposes. Nothing more was heard for a week and then a priority DMT probe arrived from the Ministry. It contained a single short letter which explained that, as a result of their farming out the investigation, the wood had been identified on Earth as coming from the Norway Spruce. Chemical analysis suggested it had been grown in central Europe, especially relevant to the German Black Forest area. Bearing in mind, the letter said, 'That because the original tree had come from the planet Earth, it was felt that Mark Gelder was best placed to follow it up there in person.'

Apart from his constant anxiety over Anita, Mark was looking forward to his trip back to Earth. He would have to ask Vivienne in her ambassadorial capacity to clear his arrival with the United World Government, but the present treaty only allowed space ships to set down at the AmOn enclave at the site of L.F. Wade airport in the

Bahamas, and from there he would have to catch a normal service airliner to Germany. Vivienne replied without delay, stating that all was arranged with a personal 'welcome home' message. They met on arrival at L.F. Wade and he kissed her on the cheek. She knew about Anita and she expressed her sorrow to him and for her. Apparently, she had deposited a case of ten jars of coarse cut marmalade with the AmOn transport staff at L.F. Wade for him to pick up before he returned to the QvO. "Thanks," he smiled. "They can do remarkable things on AmOn but the art of good marmalade has escaped them."

"Sounds like a good export opportunity for the future then," she laughed. "I suggest that you take a few orange pips with you so when you go back you will be able to make your own!"

"There is something I have have to tell you," Mark changed the subject abruptly. "I have been asked to relay good wishes to you by none other than the Chairman of AmOn; and he wishes you to brief the President of the United World Government on the reasons for my visit. You will be aware of the recent demand that in return for a peace-treaty Terrabot wanted the Earth along with the whole solar system. AmOn were to depopulate the Earth and relocate them in its own territories. The answer from AmOn to that proposition is to be a resounding no."

"Gosh I wasn;t aware of that," Vivienne's hand flew to cover her mouth. "Why would they want that?"

"It is all to do with what they term 'Machine aw.' The solar system has everything they require and, so far, they have not been able to find like, for like, anywhere else. They believe their logic is irrefutable and people of Earth will recognise the force of their argument and agree with them and willingly vacate Earth in their favour."

"Gosh again," Vivienne was astounded "surely, they can't be serious?"

"I am afraid they are, without emotions; that luxury is just not catered for in their programming so they do not take sensitivity into account. That makes them virtually impossible to to make a treaty with."

"Clearly impossible," Vivienne picked up on the last remark. "The word 'virtually' seems to be unnecessary,"

"True," Mark replied, "I imagine it was added to give the impression that there may be a glimmer of hope but as I understand it, there is none. But there is more. The wisdom of AmOn takes the view that if the population of the Earth will not move out, then Terrabot will conclude that they have offered a reasonable alternative to the people of Earth which has been unreasonably refused, and they may attack the planet. Their objective would be to wipe out all human life forms upon it. To this end, the QvO and its escort of five-hundred war ships are to be deployed in close orbit around the planet Earth. They will be supported by a further three thousand torpedo gunships. The chairman has asked me to tell you so that you may pass it on. That is all the ships he can spare at the moment and a really determined attack upon such a small force could easily be devestating for Eartht. But the good news is that when Terrabot was decidedly defeated in the recent encounter with them, their losses amounted to many thousands of ships. If they were to mount a full frontal assault upon Earth now it would militarily leave their tail end thinly protected and vulnerably exposed a counter attack by AmOn"That is a small blessing, I suppose, but just the same I wouldn't feel safe living here permanently until this is settled," Vivienne replied.

"AmOn will do what is necessary. The Chairman has also told me to tell you that the number of ships allocated to the defence of Earth may vary according to risk assessments. Military thinking is that Terrabot may wish to preserve as much of Earth as possible. If they simply irradiated it, that would inhibit Earth's use to them if they then took possession. This has led to thinking that they may attempt biological warfare. Picture, a lone ship comes out of dark matter and sprays a deadly virus over the most populated areas. So please tell the President that AmOn will make available a large quantity of our new BugX preparation and they will make arrangements to talk to him about it."

"BugX, I have never heard of that either?" Vivienne voiced the question.

"It's absolutely hush hush," Mark held a finger to his lips. "Well, it was until just now," he laughed. "It is AmOn's new defence against bugs known and unbeknown. The Chairman has asked me to give you these." He produced a small pill box. "It is for your personal protection. Both he and his wife send their love and they hope to see you soon."

There followed a more personal conversation in which Vivienne told him about her formative years, many of which were spent on the QvO. "Is our cottage still there in English Village?" she asked.

"Indeed," he smiled, "the one with a thatched roof. It is near the duck pond with the artificial ducks resting on its surface. It is still there and it has a preservation order on it so nobody else can live there; and it is now owned by the Social History Museum of Ongle. When we are not fighting wars, it gets many visitors. I have visited it myself and I have seen your bedroom and your teddy bear is still sitting in there looking rather annoyed."

"Oh!" Vivienne squealed, "we always thought that he had such an aloof disapproving look as if he felt he was really too good to play with us. My sister, Sophia, now on Marina, named him Prince Snotty."

They parted on that note and Vivienne hurried off on her mission to report to the President of the United World Government. At the same time, a mini bus arrived to convey Mark to the passenger terminal of the international airport for his flight to Stuttgart where he was to meet emeritus dendrologist, Ehren Retca, who had identified the origin of the wood used in the construction of the sheds used by Terrabot for their clandestine activities in space. He was an upright man, with almost snowy hair, who approached Mark at the inbound gate and greeted him with a firm handshake. "You are Mark Gelder?" he asked.

"I am indeed that person," Marked affirmed.

"Good to see you," he said in perfect English,"I am Ehren Retca late of the German Forstverwaltungor, Forestry Commission, in your language. Your mission must be important because the Forestry Commission have never received a direct communication from the United World Government before. I understand it is in response to a small piece of timber that we analysed for them a week ago. What is it all about?"

"I can't really discuss it," Mark replied solemnly, "it is a police investigation and we are only at the evidence gathering stage. Whether or not we can bring a prosecution remains to be seen," he lied.

"That is fine then," Ehren smiled. "I can see your reasons, it is not suitable for discussion,"and he steered Mark though the terminal to his car. The journey started with an autobahn then a turn off into a two-way road. "Do you have an escort," Ehren was glancing at his rear-view mirror.

"I hope not," Mark turned around in his seat to look out the back of the car.

"It is just that the grey car has kept up with us all of the way since the airport. I have slowed down twice deliberately but it mirrored my movement and remained behind."

"It is probably innocent," Mark replied. "The crime we are working on is not connected with Germany so it is unlikely to be of criminal interest here." By now the road had become a lane and then an unmade-up track leading into the forest.

"No, it was my imagination, it was nothing sinister," Ehren confirmed. "Perhaps having a real live policeman with me triggered boyhood cops and robbers' fantasies because actually we lost him when we turned off. I saw him flash past in my mirror once we had entered this lane." But the track had led them into a forest glade and they had stopped at a single building in the middle of the forest clearing. "Welcome to my home." Ehren seemed pleased to inform him.

"You live here?" Mark questioned seemingly unnecessarily, but with a hidden agenda to create a conversation with Ehren.

"Indeed, I do, it is really an old Forestry Commission research station but they let me have it when they ceased their operations in this area. I have my private laboratories here. My wife used to live here with me until a year ago but she has died of cancer. On that note of both having lost their wives to cancer they had founded a compassionate friendship.

"In a way I have been fortunate because a local woman comes in daily to clean up, change the bed linen and keep everything else hygenic and civilised," Ehren swept his arms to encompass her theatre of work, "but not a lot of cooking takes place here. Anyway, I am banking on the fact as you are a widower so you will, no doubt, be handy with a microwave cooker, just pick any ready meals you want from the chest freezer," he pointed, causing Mark to laugh.

As they sat at the table over a functional meal Mark questioned Ehren about the timber and his analysis. "How could you be so certain that the fragment of wood came from the Black Forest?"

"It is a matter of cross referencing really," Ehren shrugged. "It is not entirely accurate in every circumstance because sometimes there can be a random localised effect that changes the content of the soil or there has been human intervention in some way. But by and large it is reasonably accurate because the call for the geographic identity of the specimen was worldwide but there were only two contenders. One of them was at the place where I am going to take you tomorrow, the other was over in the Russian Urals. But I have learned, the location in Russia is stocked with not yet fully mature trees and there are no plans there to fell them for timber just yet. I will take you to see the local site tomorrow, but it's been a long day, so I guess it is time for bed, your bedroom is over there," he pointed, "you will find everything ready for you and I wish you a good night," he rose. Mark found the archteture of his room relied heavily upon timber which seemed to reflect perfectly the forest setting outside and he fiddled with his mobile phone for a while texting Vivienne and asking her to relay an 'all is well' message to Clench, then he had a shower before he turned in for the night.

Mark was woken early to the sounds of the wailing of sirens and a yellow glow flickered through his windows and he could see water streaming down the windows of his bedroom. There was a noise like thunder on the roof, along with a strong smell of woodsmoke. At which point, Ehren barged straight into hisbedroom without knocking. "Best get up and get dressed quickly, the forest is on fire." Mark bounded to the window and as far as he could see there were trees burning.

"It is all round us, so we must stay inside until the rescue services reach us," Ehren cautioned.

"Do you have a cellar we can take refuge in?" Mark shot back.

"No, there is no cellar but we are safe in here, the forestry commission were aware of the risk of forest fires so they fitted external sensors. When smoke and flame are detected, the sensors automatically trigger a ring of water cannon which, for neatness, are normally stored below ground. They have now elevated above ground and they are dousing the building with water. There are oxygen storage tanks and masks if we need them but we will probably be alright without them."

"Pretty smart thinking, I detect a little of the fabled German efficiency at work," Mark raised a thumb in salute and when he looked through the windows of the house, he could see through the gaps in the inferno that there were distant flashing blue lights which were drawing closer. He could also hear the sound of sirens of fire engines, louder now, as they raced in to contain the fire. Thus, they stayed up, drinking cups of coffee and swapping yarns until six-o'clock in the morning when a change in the wind direction blew in rain clouds and the fire yielded reluctantly to a timely deluge with a mixture of choking smoke and steam.

For a while Mark and Ehren were kept busy by the arrival of firemen, ambulances and the police. The latter were very impressed with Mark's credentials because in a life time of policing they would, otherwise, never get to meet the head of the Global Police Force even though his current duties had taken him off world. It became noticeable that, as the morning progressed and the news radiated within their communications networks and the pattern of police presence was aggrandising to include ever senior police officers and Mark was kept busy sidestepping their invitations to lunch. Above all he was insisting on no television appearances or newspaper reports which included his name and status, by reason that this was an undercover investigation.

Ehren had garaged his car the previous evening and the garage was within the circle of water cannons so it was unharmed; yet it was after twelve, noon, before they were able to make a getaway. There was still the fire brigade, police officers and the Forestry Commission present on site when they left for the location where the wood used in the construction of the sheds was said to have come from It was a fairly steep hill to climb to reach the area pinpointed by Ehren as the most likely spot. The site was unremarkable when they reached it and it was now covered in a mixture of two-to-three-year growth of shrub, bramble and long grass. "They will leave it like that for two to three years," Ehren told him, "It helps the soil to recover. You notice that this is the highest point as far as you can see in any direction. That fact assisted me to make a preliminary assessment. Being higher than its surroundings invites increased lightning strikes and that produces more nitrates in the soil. It is a very rough end guide and there is was a lot more research needed to tie it down."

"I am particularly interested in who purchased the timber. Do they keep records?"

"Yes, they do," Ehren replied at once. "The Forestry Commission could tell us but there is one difficulty because an area this size is felled progressively so there maybe more than one buyer."

"If it does turn out to be a single buyer, I would be very interested to speak with the director of the company tomorrow if that is possible?" Mark asked.

"I am sure it could be arranged," Ehren smiled. Mark felt pleased with himself that night as they were making investigative progress. It was slow but when you are investigating something across the void of space, it was much more complex especially if the people you were investigating were ruthless. On the upside the Forestry Commission had furnished them with a buyer's address.

The managing director himself met them the following day and he was able to search the company records and provide Mark with the contact details for their main buyers of shiplap timber. Mark satisfied his curiosity by telling him that they might be buying sheds in quantity, subject to price and suitability, to be used as storage buildings for a planned base on Mars. "Easy to erect, they pack well for shipment, they do not weigh as much as metal and they are more durable than tents," he told him and cautioned himself inwardly for spinning as many lies in the past two days as he had in the decade before. As they left the factory Mark told Ehren that he would not be conducting that aspect of the investigation. "It could take weeks of surveillance operations and communications interceptions before we are ready to pounce."

The police were waiting for them when they returned and they had with them the preliminary report by the fire department. The fire department sniffer devices had revealed that an accelerant had been used to start the fire which had been started in six places, presumably with the objective that once it had caught hold there would be no avenue of escape. The firemen's search of the surrounding area had recovered twenty, randomly scattered, thirty litre cans which had previously contained paraffin. A wider search nearby had discovered a burned- o u t car which contained the charred remains of four garden, weed control, flame lances. Mark interceded at this point to tell them that this was a part of a much larger investigation and from this point the Global Police Force headquarters on Bermuda would assume control and any further information should be sent to them. They acknowledged this but obviously, from their expressions, they knew they were onto something big and they were not happy to have the investigation snatched from them but there was something more for them to add. A man whose farm ran right up to the edge of the forest had seen the fire and saw blue flashing lights in the vicinity; he knew that the rescue services were aware, so he went to get his night binoculars to enable him to watch the events. He then sat by a window which he opened to ensure optimum clarity.

He was surprised because the top edge of the fire was obscured from him by a dark shape and he knew there were no obstructons in that area of the farm so he went to find a tissue to clean the binocular lenses. When he next looked through them the dark blob was still there although underneath he could see through to the flames of the forest, feeling something must have come adrift inside one of the lens barrels he shook them and looked again. When he resumed his study, he was amazed to see a doorway flooded with inner light open outwards in the centre of the dark blob that he was observing. He was then startled to see three figures spring one by one into the doorway which closed and a moment later he felt a puff of wind through his window and the dark mass had gone. There was no sound so he knew it was not a helicopter. By his estimation the figures he saw boarding the vessel must have leapt at least four metres from the ground to access the open door. The policeman reporting all this folded his notebook and looked hard at Mark to see if he had taken it seriously. "I can tell you this," Mark said, "please do not dismiss it as delusional on the part of the farmer. I wouldn't want him to suffer ridicule because what he has told you may well tie in with the investigation that we are conducting. Please also make a note of that in your report. Perhaps you could take me to see your superintendent of police right now and I will explain more to him. And, by the way, I would like you to play this down if the news services become interested."

It was late by the time Mark returned and Ehren met him with a smile and a can of beer. "It has been a busy day" he remarked. "I have put a dinner in the microwave; you only have to press the button."

"Thanks for that," Mark sounded grateful too. "I am sorry for the trouble I seem to have caused you, it was by no means envisaged."

"I can guess that, but I can see that this is no ordinary police investigation. We were followed from the airport, then last night we had a mysterious fire. A blacked-out craft landed in a nearby farmer's field, its passangers leapt four metres to get into it. Thereafter, it took off and soundlessly disappeared. The fire, which I had thought was a very local matter, turns out to be deliberate and was an attempt to kill you or both of us. The German police force have been asked to tone it down and keep the press off the scent. A farmer who could, otherwise, have easily have been accused of hallucinating, is not to be disbelieved. In the meantime, the whole matter has been passed to the Global Police Force headquarters, far away on an island in the Atlantic Ocean, for investigation. Forgive me, but it all sounds a bit remote from dendrology."

"I take your point," Mark sighed. "You are correct this is to do with a little more than just timber. Because there were various buyers from the logging company we have just visited, I have passed that aspect over to the local police to follow up. I suppose I really owe you an explanation. There is a problem as well because you probably already know too much for your own safety."

"Explain why I would be in danger, surely knowing a lot about trees is pretty inconsequential to the criminal mind?" Eren inquired.

"Let's sit down and enjoy a beer and I will try to get this all-in context for you. It means that I must tell you some highly classified information, so from now you will be subject to the Official Secrets Act and you must not discuss it with anybody else who is not actively involved with this case and cleared to the highest levels of security." At this point Mark commenced to tell an incredulous Ehren the whole story of Terrabot and AmOn and Terrabot's recent claim to the planet Earth. "It is not what you know that puts you in danger, it is what they may think that you know which would decide how you are to be treated if they captured you. Because of that, it is no longer safe for you to live here and we must get you away to a place where you will receive full protection until this is all over. The safest place I know is on the QvO which is currently in this sector."

"That is by far the most extraordinary story that I have ever heard," Ehren was aghast, "but I understand where you are coming from. Silly of me, I never in a month of Sundays would have dreamed that your inquiry about a piece of wood had at its root, if you will pardon the expression, in space wars and inter planetary intrigue and robots. Of course, I have heard of the QvO, who hasn't on Earth, but what would I do on a spaceship?"

"I imagine that you would be very happy on the QvO," Mark assured. "That ship has some of the finest research facilities and laboratories in all AmOn. You could have your own department to study trees from two solar systems numbering twenty-one planets," and a rising interest was clearly visible in Ehren's eyes as he listened.

Chapter 19

BREAK THROUGH

Mark decided it was too dangerous to use the approved route of flying to Bermuda and from there pick up a shuttle to the QvO. Instead, he used his Clench authority to arrange an emergency DMT shuttle to drop in to convey both of them direct from the Black Forest to the QvO. When it arrived, the shuttle would approach the forest glade using its stealth mode and it would make a pass over the landing ground to make an infrared and a magnetic sweep to ascertain that there were no hidden persons or robots to observe them. Right on time, Mark's hucom pinged to announce that the shuttle had arrived and was ready for them to board.

It was amusing and amazing for Mark to see Ehren. Here was a person who had never been on a space craft and who had never seen one close up before. Yet it was not with dumbstruck awe that he boarded this one for his first trip but with an open scientific mind. He took nothing for granted and he wanted to know how, what and why even routine tasks were undertaken. What was happening, why was it happening, his questions were endless, leading Mark to joke to him that before the short trip was over Ehren would probably know more about shuttle craft than he did. The only time Ehren did show a sign of awe was when they materialised out of DM near the QvO and he caught sight of probably the largest artificial construction anywhere in space. " It's a world in its own right," he enthralled.

"That is probably as good a summary as I have yet heard to describe it," Mark agreed as he escorted Ehren to see the ship's Captain. For this errand Mark had already briefed Captain Anjar via his hucom and the Captain was already out of his chair to greet them by the bridge portal when they arrived. This allowed Mark to introduce Ehren hurriedly and to slip away to return to Clench and to be updated on their latest news. Petan stood up and welcomed him back as he came through the door and he made him feel welcome by vacating Mark's chair and he pushed it in to assist Mark to sit behind the desk. "Glad you are back; I gather that you have a story to tell me about your visit. The staff will undoubtedly be glad also because I think my morning briefings to them were not so interesting as yours."

Mark laughed out loud. "Oh, I can remember when I was a very junior policeman how boring the long winded the briefings given by the chief superintendent were. They probably view mine in much the same way. Put it down to an occupational hazard!"

"Well, if that is the case in this instance, I may have out-bored you." Petan chuckled.

"Whatever, we still have a problem with security because somehow Terrabot got to know where I was and who I was visiting Earth, so it seems that we are still infiltrated," Mark observed.

"Yes, I think we have pinpointed a weak spot in your absence. Naturally the various ministers of government employ robots to do everyday tasks, in their homes, but we have discovered that quite a few ministers have grown attached to their robots, regarding them as pets and are protective of them. In fact, they act rather like people who keep vicious species of dogs at home but firmly believe that their beloved pet can do no wrong. We have discovered that some of them have been shielding their robots from undertaking loyalty checks. I have spoken to the Chief Minister, Martin Fraser, and he is going to take it up with the Chairman of AmOn. All our other checks, both scheduled and random, by our outstations are returning negative results and have been for a whole week now."

"So, we are on top of it!" Marked nodded briefly.

During Mark's absence new information had come in; concerning the two Terrabot ships, which Mark had previously observed where the alien ships had mistakenly. tried to emerge in the same area of space and were now locked and welded cruciform. It had happened in the Ongle sector and now the two ships were being examined rivet by rivet.

They had already discovered that one the ships was a Terrabot headquarters vessel and it was commanding the Terrabot attack; it was already in place when the other arrived. They had discovered a gold plated antisplash helmet with the name Doyan 1, in high relief, emblazoned across the front of it. Thus, it probably belonged to the selfsame robot that had mooted the impossible peace treaty to AmOn. The ships were a mine of information including many computer codewords and digital acronyms. "We do not know how they were used and what their individual significance is," Petan commented "but it will be reasonable to assume that the fastest and the most sophisticated computers possessed by AmOn will be working hard to tease out their secrets."

"So, we have a name for him at last," Mark remarked to Anda Anjar at their scheduled meeting the next morning, to resume their abated daily two-way briefings.

"There has been no Terrabot incursions for three days now," Anda told him. "The really important news is this. If you recall when the robot, Doyan 1, arrived on this ship he had been ferried across from his ship on one of our levitated landing platforms. Military intelligence asked us, beforehand, to seek ways of turning this to our advantage. I think it was one of those interdepartmental rivalry things not to tell you as well. Anyway, I don't want to keep it from you so I have decided to brief you regardless. When the platform was sent back carrying the terrabots it had one of our own robots laced up underneath it. When the platform got to the silver Terrabot ship, the person operating it was told to hold it right up against the ship as the passengers got off. To cut a long story shorter, while the platform was in that position our concealed robot super-glued a transponder beacon to its hull below the lip of the landing stage, hence out of sight due to the ship's curvature. The transponder was in a silvered metal box to match the ship's hull. To a casual observer it blends with the ship so would appear to be an external sensor."

"Brilliant," Mark laughed, "is it working?"

"We have tested it twice and it is working fine. For the time being we have switched it off to conserve its batteries and lessen the chance of it being detected; that ship is probably out of range now anyway."

"I can feel it is all coming together now," Mark was upbeat.

"Yes, I feel that, too," Anda agreed. "It seemed very much a touch and go situation when AmOn first launched its attempt to contain Terrabot. We are only now getting the hang of it and your Cold War information has given us new ideas. The latest step I can tell you is that strategists on AmOn have substantiated through their own sources that Terrabot may attempt to depopulate the Earth by means of biological warfare. As you know, we are in talks with the United World Government with the intention of supplying them with BugX but now it is to be in a new format. It seems that because BugX is a live germ it can be spread naturally by the indigenous population and that will be highly beneficial to Earth. It has been engineered only to selectivey attack pathogens that can live in warm blooded creatures. It can be loaded into aerosol cans and sprayed into the atmosphere in crowded places and nature will do the rest. They say just five tons, for Earth, will be enough."

"Wow!" Mark exclaimed. "No more flu, it has got to be beneficial," but he was brought back from bonhomie chat with Anda by an urgent alert on his hucom from Ehren.

"Sorry to press the urgent button." It was Ehren. "Something has cropped up. I have been re-examining the wood sample using your more up to date and sensitive equipment and I think there has been an error on my part or at very least a failure in the equipment I was using on Earth. After I retested it on QvO equipment the origin of the sample now points towards Orda in Russia."

"I thought they claimed that none of their trees had been felled for timber," Mark asserted.

"That is true but the facts now revealed suggest that it can only come from the Russian site."

"Hang on, I'll be right there," and he glanced at Anda. "Sorry I have to go, it seems like something I thought was all but solved has now become a mystery again!" Ehren greeted him at the door of his laboratory when Mark arrived and led him inside.

"A truly wonderful ship," he breathed. "I am so glad that you brought me here, I could never have had these facilities anywhere on Earth, but I am sad to say that they have disproved my earlier theory of origins of the wood sample being the Black Forest. The finger now, most certainly, points to a spot near Orda in the Urals and I have managed, with a lot of help from the lab staff, to send one of your DMT probes to the AmOn Ambassador, Vivienne Holder. She has confirmed that the Russians still say that the forest described to them has not been harvested at all."

"What do you suggest we do?" Mark enquired.

"There seems only one thing we can do and that is to go down there and take a sample and look to make sure that there has been no thinning of the forest. Sometimes when thinning is carried out it is recorded as forest management and that is not regarded as a commercial undertaking. The Russians, of course, have so much woodland, they would probably not bother too much about trivial amounts. It is, therefore, necessary to obtain a visual confirmation."

"That seems to point to you as the person to go there.

Are you up for it?" Mark came to the point.

"Yes, it will not take long, I could go whenever you wish."

"A few things to work out yet," Mark smiled. "The first thing is to get hold of Vivienne and get clearance for a DMT shuttle to land at Orda. I am mindful also that last time we were on the Earth somebody tried to kill us, so you had better go armed and I will accompany you for added safety. Also, I am not sure how long you will need down there but we had best be prepared for a day or two so we will need all the paraphernalia of a camping trip. I will organise that. In the meantime, I will arrange for you to be taught to use a ponenillium pistol on the ship's ranges down by the lake."

To avoid public disquiet the direct DMT flight to the forest site was to land in an unfrequented valley near Orda and from there it was a short hike to their targeted grid reference. For reasons of discretion, they were to land at night and afterwards the craft would take off on its own and loiter in space to await their recall. "We certainly look the part," Mark chuckled because they were both dressed in disruptive pattern army clothing and they wore their energy weapons wild west style, at their hips.

"Remarkable weapon," Ehren glanced down at his side arm and remarked "it is quite extrordinary. Earth is so far behind in such matters."

"Earth 'ball shot' weapons are still quite effective," Mark replied, "but they have some disadvantages. Our ball ammunition in quantity is bulky and heavy; conversely, a ray weapon, as you know, can be used all day on a single crystal and you could carry a hundred crystals in a matchbox. Peraps the greatest asset the poenillium pistol, as you have said, is that you can acquire a target with it and it keeps it in its memory."

"Like many things I have seen on AmOn, it is just remarkable," Ehren replied.

At the prearranged rendezvous they were met by a Russian forest ranger who told them his name was Ludis. His job was, he said, to keep a weather eye on various tracts of commercial forest over a wide area. Most of his time was spent ensuring that fire breaks had not been bridged by combustable vegetation. He also kept his eye out for illegal logging and poaching, observing the health of the forest and providing samples and grid references when he had concerns. "It's a wonderful job,"he was genuinely enthusiastic. "I pity those people who have to work in offices and in the cities, like Moscow or London. What sort of life is that?" and Ehren and Mark agreed readily. with him on the benefits of an outdoor life. Thereafter he provided them with maps of the forest they were to visit, he further explained how to read the official Russian route marker signs.

Formal inspections were carried out every three years, he told them, and trees were assessed for readiness as timber and any fallen or dead trees were removed and the firebreaks were reploughed. Thereafter they exchanged contact details with him, and he lingered for a little while, then with an exchange of platitudes, Ludis left astride his quad bike and roared off, as an utter silence closed in around them.

The bulk of their equipment was still in the valley and hidden up where they had landed, along with an electrically powered garden cart, so they started back to it and from there they moved the camping equipment to a spot some half a kilometre into the forest. "At least Ludis told me that no dangerous animals have been reported in this area for several years, so at least we do not have that to worry about," Mark said cheerfully as they erected their camp of popup tents and sampled their self-heating military survival rations. At nightfall they retired, still dressed, to be ready for an early start the next morning. However, just after midnight, they were awakened by the rending crash of a large tree falling, and they came out of their respective tents to check it out. Both stood listening and watching a flicker of orange lights a few hundred metres away, followed by another loud crash of yet another tree falling. "No lights," Mark cautioned "let's use the night goggles" as they cautiously proceeded to rationalise these unexpected events. Yet another tree crashed down but much closer this time. They froze at the sound of branches snapping and the brushing noises made by an unwieldy object being forced through the forest somewhere to the front of them. Both of them instinctively sought positions, each with a bowl of a tree between themselves and the source of the approaching sounds. Through their goggles they witnessed a slow column of figures carrying three fallen trees between them. Then, waiting until the sounds were more distant, Mark and Ehren set out in pursuit, each not daring to speak for fear of being overheard. When they did get a chance to speak in whispers it was Ehren who asked. "What can they be up to, lumbering in the dead of night?"

"We are onto something big here" Mark replied, "I noticed there were only four of them to each tree and no party of four humans could have carried those tree trunks, let alone force them through the obstacles to be overcome by carrying them through a fairly tight forest, all without lights at night. I suspect they are robots and if that is correct then they can only belong to Terrabot. I intend to follow them to get a better picture of their activities. I cannot ask you to come along because this is a police matter and nothing to do with dendrology."

"Hmm, I would like to see what they are up to as well." Ehren was adamant.

"Ok, let's follow the sounds they are making." Mark started off by following distant noises which led them out of the forest to the edge of a derelict field in which they could both lay down, screened by low growing shrubs. In the middle of the field, their night goggles picked out the three felled trees lying together. There was no sign of the robots and they waited another hour but nothing further happened before they retired back to their tents.

In the late morning, Mark and Ehren went out into the forest to get an idea of the quantity of trees that had been stolen. "There are always gaps in a forest to sapling failure," Ehren advised. "It is probably best to look upwards because when a tree grows it creates and defends the space above for itself. If it were not there the canopy of the trees next door would have grown over the empty space below." He stopped and got down on his hands and knees and pushed away the detritus of the forest floor. "Ah, yes, take a look at this. They have cut down this tree below soil level and they have gathered up deposits elsewhere from the forest floor and covered the stump. By the time the next inspection is carried out the trees above will have spread their canopy outwards to cover the gap. The covering over stump, as it matures, will make it indistinguishable from the rest of the forest floor. So above ground level there would be no sign that there was ever a tree in this spot unless you looked as I have. They will probably put down gaps as the result of natural selection. It is really only quite recently that some forestry managers use digital tree counters, they then know the exact number and the individual health of every tree, which they keep can then keep on their computers. This plantation was planted about twenty to twenty-five years ago and, at a guess, not very detailed records were kept at the time. In those days it would have required wholesale theft of their trees before it became noticeable."

"I am learning a great deal about woodland and forestry management," Mark laughed, "but there is proof of criminal behaviour here; it is now a question of how we react to it." They next moved on to the fallow field, where the felled trees that had been deposited the previous night, were now gone. Mark studied the indentations left by a craft that had recently settled upon the surface. After pacing out the indentations, he found them to be roughly fifty metres in length. "It's not very large in spaceship terms but large enough to carry a tree or two," was his conclusion. "I think it is time to return to the QvO for consultations and a rethink, then gather intelligence,"he said as they made wended their way back to pack up their campsite.

Back in office, Mark asked for DMT traces, other than their own, in the vicinity of Earth coinciding with the time when they were there and he was referred to a ship specifically on station with the task to record them. When he got in touch with the ship, he was to learn that there were traces but they did not make sense because they seemed to be between two points, one of which was two kilometres from below the surface and after a short interval they went back down again. The observations had been routinely reported to their sector control. It was not immediately clear to Mark why he had not been told of these movements and he raised the query with the AmOn Defence Ministry who investigated the incident with their sector control. This resulted in the discovery of a combination of a computer glitch and human error. The reports received had been automatically filed which was a programming fault. However, the 'what in case of error' argument within the computer, which should have compelled it to seek attention to unread files in its memory, seemed to have failed. In the case of these particular files, they had been selectively tagged as 'archive only.' "A general cockup then," Mark added when he relayed the happenstance to Captain Anjar, who replied wryly "It happens, so what are your plan now?"

"I guess that there is a suspicion that the computer may have been deliberately tampered with but that it is all in the hands of the Defence Ministry. I do admit I would like to see this one through though!"

Chapter 20

INCURSION

As if they had read Mark's thoughts, the Defence Ministry had despatched a high priority message dart with an urgent notification to return to his office to read it. Once there he tapped his password into his computer to read the message which said that noting that he was familiar with the lay of the land at Orda, would be prepared to go back there with another person. They also wished to attach a surveillance officer (SO) to the party. Mark's job would be to guide the SO to the spot where they had made their observations. He was then to provide cover for the SO who was to attempt to attach a telemetry device to the hull of the vessel. On receipt of the request Mark contacted Ehren who spontaneously agreed. "I am starting to enjoy this new career; I thought I had been retired by the world, too," he chuckled.

They arrived back at the original landing spot the next day and once again returned their vehicle to space to wait for them to call it back. At night time they took up positions at the perimeter of the field where they had first encountered the Terrabot space craft and where they had previously laid silently watching through their night goggles, but a herd of deer and a colony of rabbbits grazing on the field was their only entertainment. Then, abruptly, orange flashes of light in the forest indicated another tree felling exercise was taking place, which they knew had been completed when the laser lights abated. Then suddenly, out of the shadows twelve robots carrying three trees between them appeared and dumped their load together in the middle of the field and stood motionlessly waiting for the load to be picked up. After a time, Mark's party was beginning to wonder if it ever would be. "One thing is certain," Mark whispered to the others, "they will not wish to spend the day here. The discovery of wood thieving robots would most certainly make the headlines and not only in Russia." The first indication of the event about to take place was by the group of placidly grazing rabbits had sat up ears pricked, then enmass raced from the field in a flurry of white tails on view, whilst the deer, their heads up, trotted regally away. Immediately afterwards, each of Mark's party jointly suffered a flicker of eyesight as their vision readjusted to compensate for the spacecraft that had soundlessly appeared. From it, a loading ramp was dropped down and twelve robots descended, and the twelve that were in the field boarded the craft. "Going to get their batteries recharged," Mark quipped. The SO nudged Mark's arm to indicate that he was about to set off and Mark and Ehren drew their pistols to give him protection if it were needed. Breathlesssy they watched him slip away, crouching, as he approached the landed ship on the blind side from its ramp. When he reached the craft, he stood up and pressed a hand against the hull and dropped down again and a minute later he rejoined them.

"Job done," he sounded relieved. "That particular nodule has multiple cameras, so we will get a good all-round view from wherever it goes."

Now back on the QvO, Mark was to receive a file of pictures from the Defence Ministry and it was a revelation The stills were of a massive underground cavern for which the telemetry gave a length of just over four kilometres and a high point of half a kilometre. A lot of work had gone into the structure and the roof and sides had been buttresses by massive cathedral like pillars and arches.

"Many robot hours will have gone into securing it," Mark remarked to Anda in their next two-way briefing. "They tell me that the cavern is naturally formed in a gypsum deposit and mirrors the world famous, water filled caves at Orda, nearby. In this case, however, there are no entrance and exits to the surface, so it has remained undetected for millions of years. The only conventional way to it would be to drive a shaft down to it, but speed is of essence, so that is not an option. From the pictures taken we can see sawmills in the near space area, but there are all sorts of other activities and workshops. Also, towards the far end, there appears to be a complex control console."

"So, what are the plans now?" Anda asked.

"I can tell you, but only you, "Mark replied. "At the moment we have got a seismic team above it to measure the exact size and depth of the cavern to the nearest tenth of a millimetre. Following that, we are going to approach the United World Government and brief them on our intentions. The AmOn government have already decided that they cannot invade the Terrabot site using its own military forces on a sovereign planet. Instead, they are going to ask the United World Government to earmark a contingent from the World Army to supply the military support for the job. However, they will be conveyed by AmOn warships and they will probably be come here to the military barracks in the empty quarter, where they will be taught to use poenillium weapons."

"That seems to tie up the loose ends," Anda summed up. "When is the master plan to be put into practice?"

"Sorry, I don't know that yet," Mark spread his arms, palms upraised to denote anytime!

As it was, the Earth United World Government was delighted to be invited to provide the strike forces to carry out the operation in the newly discovered Orda cavern and the AmOn Defence Ministry decreed that henceforth the operation would be given the secret code name 'Whiplash' that would conceal the nature of its concept and geographical identity. In the days to follow a selected Canadian special forces unit arrived on the QvO. At first, they were overawed both with their recent journey and with the sheer majesty of the QvO. Mark was, himself pleased because they seemed to be sensible men and women who took their training seriously indeed and, within a week, they had applied themselves diligently and had been declared combat ready, their next step was was to visit the ship's combat stores to be equipped with uniforms which could deflect an energy beam bolt in all but a direct hit.

Mark was to accompany them as an independent police investigator for the mission thus he was invited to attend the final briefing given by the Canadian general in charge of the special forces. Their interest in even the final detail of the plans convinced Mark that if the job could be done, they would do it! During the briefing photographs shown of the cavern. From these photographs the force was able to pinpoint the galleries that had been built into the columns of the buttress arches. With their commanding view of the cavern below it seemingly indicated that they were intended for defensive purposes. The general pointed them out with his cane, telling them that it was their first objective to render these galleries impotent. From the photographs they also discussed and planned the possible avenues of advance that were shielded by floor standing equipment and how to use them to make cautious advances. There would be five craft involved and they were to land, subject to standing obstacles, at an equidistance to each other, with one vessel at either end of the cavern and the other three between them. They were all to fight their way towards the centre and then turn and retrace their steps to mop up any remaining pockets of resistance which they may have deliberately by passed for reason of mission expediency.

Mark would not be required to take part in the operation because they were a trained fighting unit, he was told; a stranger in their midst might upset the balance. Immediately after the briefing the Canadian general in command of the operation sifted through all the documents and information available, as he sat silently with a large cup of coffee in front of him, going over the battle plan in his mind. Finally satisfied, he snapped into his executive mode, then issued his short military directive of 'Whiplash Go,' and the mission slipped into gear.

Mark stayed aboard the ship after it had landed up against an end wall of the cave and watched the military compliment move into action. First two men armed with poenillium rifles ran down the ramp and took up positions either side of it, lying on the ground against the ramp which would offer them some protection if there was a fierce exchange. Following them down the ramp was an armoured vehicle and immediately behind that the remaining soldiers ran down the ramp and spread out. The interior of the ship, otherwise in darkness, was illuminated by an almost constant flicker of red and orange lights accompanied by bursts of noise sounding like wood being machined which Mark knew was the sound generated by energy weapons. The battle was moving further away from the ship now so Mark ventured to stand at the top of the ramp. The two soldiers were still there and they had just resighted their rifles on to one of the galleries that were threatening the attacking force. The soldiers fired both rifles at the target at the same time and the gallery disintegrated. Its remains fell to the ground along with the two robots who had been manning it. The destruction of the gallery revealed that it had concealed the mouth of a tunnel leading into the rock face and other robots appeared out of it and fired down at their attackers. a Snapshot later half a dozen energy weapons zeroed in and poured fire into the opening of the tunnel for five seconds afterwards; flashes of ever decreasing light emitted from the tunnel as the bolts ricocheted into its depths and there was no further resistance from that quarter. Further over, Mark could see that the armoured vehicle had stopped and had elevated its poenillium cannon at another gallery, then he saw the discharge from it blow the gallery apart and before the debris had even reached the floor the vehicle had fired a second shot straight into the tunnel behind it. The battle was more at ground level now and soldiers could be seen crouching low and moving in the alley ways between machinery but ever moving forward. The Terrabot craft which had been used to convey the trees underground was still there but then disappeared into DM. The defending fire was growing more spasmodic and the Canadian special forces were mopping up, but there could be no negotiated end to the battle because the Terrabots were programmed to fight until they could fight no more; in consequence even though some of them had lost limbs or were on fire from internal electrical shorting they continued to level their pistols at the special forces. Selectively, one by one, the tailend Terrabot resistence was eliminated and the cavern was eerily silent.

Mark witnessed several stretcher parties, so obviously the Canadian force was not entirely unscathed but the element of surprise and good planning had enabled them to overcome a force larger than their own. In their favour, each of the craft which they had arrived in, carried a medical robot, so wounds were promptly attended to. But now the general approached Mark to make a request. Apparently, they had found a secure XPM compound which contained thirty civilians, and he asked Mark to make contact with the fleet and call for a craft to uplift the unexpected passengers. Meanwhile, his soldiers would cut the XPM fence to release them. Mark did as request by sending a DMT dart to the QvO.

Realisation came slowly to Mark. Could it be, he wondered? Could it be that Anita was there in that compound? His status prevented him from running but he was walking very quickly. Perhaps a kilometre away he could see a group of people and as he neared them, he could see that the compound's XPM fencing was peeled back so the group was probably the compound's former prisoners. A lone figure detached itself from the group as he approached and gingerly, at first, but with growing urgency they were soon running towards each other. When they met, Mark and Anita were blended together, in a single entwined hug, with laughter and tears of joy that lasted for a full ten minutes, until one of the Canadian soldiers, possibly slightly embarrassed to witness their depths of affection, brandished a flask and invited them to have a coffee.

"I never thought that I would see you ever again, but you lived on in my thoughts all the time," Mark's speech was hoarse.

"Me too, but it grew more impossible to believe as each day passed. Terrabot intends to go on a larger hostage gathering spree here on Earth and in AmOn. They have a plan to amass one hundred hostages then murder them, dissect their bodies, and leave them in public places on their original home worlds. Their reasoning was, this would force public opinion on AmOn to forcibly evacuate the Earth people. If that failed the massacres would continue for hundreds of years, if necessary, until a point where public demand gave AmOn no alternative but to concur. But you, my hero, have come to rescue me!"

She held his hand close to her. "Don't ever let go of me again, ever!" her voice quivered.

"No, I never will," he replied. "Does missus Gelder suit you?"

"Admirably," she replied.

Chapter 21

BATTLE STATIONS

When Mark and Anita returned together, Anita was, of course, very busy and despite her recent incarceration there were things that had to be done off ship immediately. For a start she had to attend almost endless meetings and the television cameras followed her everywhere. Socially and politically the whole planetary system was right behind her. Moreover, she could not decline the many well-meant invitations she received. It was not unusual for her to retire home exhausted from having attended functions on three or four planets in the course of the day. It was to be a full ten days before the demands for her presence had levelled down to what she described as 'manageable'. Her mail did not reduce however, and it arrived by the sackful and extra secretaries were hired just to acknowledge the many out pourings of support and loyalty she received. In between, there were also many formal engagements. In theory, she had automatically resumed her position as the Chief Minister of the Ongle System of Planets but she resigned from the government by reason that she needed time to recuperate from her recent ordeal. There was one duty, amongst many, that did give her great satisfaction and it involved the Candian special forces troops who had taken part in her release. These were taken to Ambrocognia Mundi to meet the Chairman of AmOn and all of the heads of the planets of AmOn. Then, before a vast horde of people gathered in a stadium, each soldier was awarded the solid gold AmOn star for bravery and outstanding service to the Government and the people of the Ambrocognia-Mundi Colligate and the Ongle System of Planets. Anita, naturally, had been chosen to pin the stars on their tunics as their names were read out by an announcer.

Privately, Anita told Mark more about the ordeal. She told him that Terrabot also intended to terrorise the people of Earth in addition to their planned murders. If that did not lead to possession, they were going to up the stakes dramatically and even more selected prisoners would be slaughtered and their remains would be deposited at various national congregation points on the relevant planets. The corpses would bear graphic evidence of having been tortured before they had been slain. Thereafter, Terrabot would routinely abduct people to replace their stocks as necessary. The objective being to destabilise society to the extent that nobody anywhere would ever feel entirely secure.

Terrabot intended to maintain the momentum until AmOn relented and depopulated the Earth. How Terrabot came to be on Earth at all, she told him, was due to a navigational accident many years ago, when one of their craft had ended up in the cavern at Orda, it was the first really secure place they had discovered in the universe. Of course, they had since discovered more caves now they knew where to look, for them but their Earth mishap was their first mission underground and they had started to develop the cavern as a redoubt. Later discoveries convinced them that the Solar System could supply all of their needs and Earth was suitably positioned in the solar system for defence in depth. In this, Terrabot had made a clear mistake in thinking that they were invulnerable, hence able to discuss such matters with their captives. Although Anita had not been mistreated in captivity, she did say that the attitude of her captors was best described as austere. Within the XPM compound each prisoner had a low walled, open-ended cubicle and outside it there were dining tables. Food preparation and cooking was done by the inmates. They had made good use of their individual skills available. For example, one of the ladies was a skilled hairdresser and that was put to good use. Immediately outside the XPM compound Terrabot had constructed major workshops and eventually the cavern was to be the launch point for their takeover of Earth. On a more gruesome note, because of her status as Chief Minister of the Ongle system of Planets, the Terrabots regarded Anita as a prize possession. In the tactless, dispassionate way of robots it was explained to her that if the negotiations did not go to plan, she would be killed; but because she was such a very high-status public figure her death would have a huge public impact. Thus, in her case, it would be a prolonged procedure and filmed in detail with copies of the video widely distributed among the AmOn planets and on the planet Earth. Afterwards, her body would be left on the steps of the AmOn parliament. At this point Mark felt decidedly sick. Alls well that ends well," she said when he returned, "but I fear it will still give me nightmares to the day I die. I am probably what one would term 'damaged goods' now."

Mark said nothing and simply held her to him, willing his strength to bolster her.

The security services of AmOn had already assessed the threat to Anita because they believed that Terrabot would try to avenge themselves by recapturing her, so for her defence they had provided two warrior robots who were day and night to never be further away from her than four metres. Albeit it was of necessity, the scrutiny of two robots watching her every move and reporting back, live, to an unknown, unseen security officer, did interfere with their natural desires and Mark slept in a bedroom next door to Anita. But things were to get even worse in the days to follow because reports were coming in that the Terrabot fleet, after their rout in the last battle, was reforming. With that in mind, the security services decided that the QvO could be a victim in the looming warfare or perhaps even captured, the upshot of their deliberations being that Anita was to be transported to AMC to take refuge in one of their high security underground bunkers; and once again she was saying goodbye to Mark.

The reports coming in from the forward listening posts indicated that the Terrabot fleet was massing in a manner which suggested it was to be a full-frontal attack with the objective of punching a hole right down the centre with a massive concentration of warships.

"I thought we nearly finished them off last time, so where are all these ships coming from?" Mark was asking Anda.

"I don't know," Anda replied, "but conjecture reports that Terrabot have overrun other species out in open space and they are using captured ships."

"Then their resources are virtually unlimited!" There was a tone of anguish in Mark's reply.

"That could be the case," Anda looked worried, "but let us hope that is not the reality, otherwise we will be fighting a lost cause." There were already some skirmishes with the Terrabot fleet but the AmOn fleet would not be drawn away from the three-star systems they were to defend; although Terrabot tried to encourage them to break ranks by making forays towards them, then retreating when the going got hot. It was true that Terrabot left behind more wrecked ships than were lost by AmOn but they just didn't seem to care about the mathematics. One of the most depressing battlefield statistics pouring out from AmOn to their fleet was that Terrabot could afford to lose up to three ships for every AmOn ship they managed to cripple, so, numerically, Terrabot would win.

If the AmOn Defence Ministry statisticians thought their neat statistics forecasted the end of AmOn then they had not reckoned on outside help. The advance part of this commenced when a needlelike, black space ship came alongside the QvO and she went into lockdown with a dozen cannons trained upon the black vessel. Their fears were allayed when a lighted hatch was opened in the black craft's hull and the QvO's ships public address system howled a warbling note before it settled down and, by induction, a rasping voice said "Hello Qee van Ongle, we are the Formacidae. It is a long time since we last met." A staff member standing next to Mark moved forward to tap the word 'Formacidae' into a desk computer. Of course, he knew their story of old but he was rusty on detail. The Formacidae were an ant-like society and they were capable of walking on their back legs and in that stance, they were two and a half metres tall, but by preference they walked on all six legs.

In the background the conversation with the Formacidae strangely continued via the ship's public address system, until the radio engineers installed a closed link over which they could communicate But Mark was reading the computer download concerning the Formacidae and the story of how they had first met them, as recorded in the book Dark Matter transit 2. The Ongle ship, the Passing Star, had stopped to make urgent repairs with all of her ports and hangers open, and in that vulnerable condition it had been invaded by Formacidae space pirates who had taken command of the ship and had begun to strip it of all moveable equipment and transportable items of value. Geoffrey Holder (Vivienne's father), the AmOn-wide known Earth man, had mysteriously, through an accident and technology, been beamed aboard the QvO.

He could not be returned to Earth because at that time the Earth people did not know of the existence of the QvO and it was not yet appropriate to reveal its presence to them. Geoffrey went on to join the Ongle System of Planets Space Force in which he had served with distinction. He was aboard the Passing Star when Formacidae pirates appropriated it for the purpose of petty theft. Geoffrey was in possession of an experimental transceiver, disguised as a wristwatch, and through it he had conspired, by radio, with a ship's robot (R351) to send an alarm to Ongle which then sent a powerful fleet to secure the ship from the pirates. However, they had been hampered because all of the Passing Star's access ports had been closed by the Formacidae. To blast a way into it would undoubtedly result in blue-on-blue casualties. Eventually Geoffrey, working through his secret wristwatch transceiver to robot 351, had also managed to override the ships computers to open the ship's ports, through which the Ongle forces had regained the ship. As this was unfolding, the Formacidae police, who had been hunting for the pirates, had arrived, and the captured pirates were turned over to them.

Captain Anjar called Mark to the bridge where, despite his briefing, Mark was still taken aback to see that there were two Formacids resting there against their folded back legs. Apparently, they, too, had trouble with Terrabot who had attacked them. In their hissing, grating voices the Formacids told them that when they got the pirates home after they had been captured on the Passing Star, they discovered the pirate horde. What they had found had enabled them to advance their space technology and weaponry. On reflection, after they had returned to their home world, their thoughts had crystallised and they realised that, of all the species and cultures they had previously met, a similar incident, if it had occurred, would surely have resulted in the slaughter of the pirates. But the Passing Star had given captured Formacid pirates to them to face the Formacidae judicial processes. That action was seen to be honest and trustful, which was also a founding principle of a Formacidae hive. Ongle was, of course, now a part of the AmOn Federation and the Federation was an enemy of Terrabot but they knew AmOn supported the same values as themselves. The reason for their visit today was to propose a lasting mutual defence treaty between Formacidae and AmOn. At this very moment they had a fleet of two million vessels earmarked to join the battle against Terrabot.

It was not within the scope of Captain Anjar to make decsions of that magnitude on behalf of AmOn but he wasted no time in getting the two Formacids to see the right people on AmOn and they were in conference with them less than twenty minutes later.

"This could swing it in our favour," the Captain remarked and Mark nodded his agreement. The details of the new alliance were issued to the fleet by the Defence Ministry. In effect the Formacidae were to be updated with the movements and intentions of the AmOn fleet. There would be no central coordination centre but the Formacids would augment the actions of the AmOn fleet with their own activities based upon how the battle was played out.

The Terrabot fleet was advancing steadfastly now, like a World War One attack they were massed in numbers with the objective of presenting more targets than the AmOn fleet could simultaneously engage; and they had also perfected a system that was preventing AmOn's self-homing mines from activating This meant it was ships fighting, gun to gun and missile by missile into the distance of space. With a naked eye, all one could see were the energy beams and the explosions made by dying ships Right now the AmOn front was beginning to look decidedly ragged and exploitable gaps were opening up between their ships as they continued to engage their enemy, shot for shot. It was at this critical moment, like a swarm of angry hornets, the black Formacid fleet attacked the Terrabot fleet from behind.

In an instant all space was seen to be filled with so many energy beams that the galactic background was entirely blotted out. The Terrabot fleet's tactics had been formulated on the basis of known fleet strengths which had been based upon intelligence reports. Hence, they were now suffering catastrophically from a major attack by a million more ships than they had expected. It was a turning point; Terrabot's computer brains were, in consequence, reassessing the outcome of the battle. Obviously, their conclusion had been a no win, no gain scenario and they disappeared from the field of battle.

The Formacidae ships remained in space around AmOn for a week or more but they kept themselves to themselves. The messages of gratitude and promises that AmOn would come to their defence if they were ever threatened were sent to them; but in a trice they were gone. In thinking of ways to disable Terrabot, of course computer viruses had been considered, but it was thought these would have only a temporary effect, they would still be insecure and unable relax their military state of alert. At some time Terrabot would be back. But this was about to change dramatically.

The Captain came through to Mark via a hucom secure link. "Do you remember the gilded robot 'Doyan 1,' that came to the negotiations and how we spiked his ship with a transponder to give us a fix on it?"

"Yes, the silver ship," Mark said to confirm.

"Well, that ship was in the centre of their battle fleet and the secret transponder was locked onto by one of our ships and the Terrabot ship was disabled in the ensuing firefight. When they boarded it Doyan 1, was there, but it had been decapitated by a metal shard propelled by an explosion. They are going to bring him aboard here for your department's laboratories to examine and they are going to bring the code breaking team back here to help decode him.

"Do you ever have a feeling that this could go on forever?" Mark asked.

"Gets to feel like that," the Captain's voice was flat.

The gold plated Doyan 1, was unceremoniously carried aboard and taken to the Clench laboratory where he was laid out on an inspection table. The code breaking team had been working on Terrabot wrecks extracting the activity code words from the robots of stricken Terrabot ships had arrived, too. "We now know for a fact that the gold-plated robot is the Master Robot and his title is confirmed as Doyan 1," they explained to Mark.

"Not a very original name. perhaps. but a spade is always a spade in their culture," Mark laughed. "Sorry I have not been told your name, but what have you got to tell me?"

'I'm Joe, and I am a computer engineer and I specialise in computer security. We have made some progress over the past week. We now know lots of their codes and how they are used.

Normally when a robot from Terrabot is threatened with extinction, or is captured, a protective protocol purges its memory of all useful information as well as destroying its processors. The centre for Terrabot protocols is in a robot's head and its memory is in its chest. This looks interesting because Doyan's head was unexpectedly severed from its body so it is likely that it has never initiated its self- destruct code. We aim to operate on its head and the body independently now to see what we can find out."

"Go to it and good luck because we can pretty much guess that Doyan 1, has some very important information contained within it; is there anything you need?" Mark replied.

"Indeed, there is" Joe nodded. "We need a few captured robots that have not self-destructed; there are probably some to be found in the remains of the battle."

"How will we know if they have self-destructed?" Mark asked.

"That is an easy one," Joe replied, "all Terrabot robots have a human looking eye and indeed it more or less functions the same as a human eye. It is controlled from the central processor. If the processor is not working their eyes will be black with no sign of a pupil in them."

"I guess I should have thought of that," Mark replied as he walked away from the group to contact Captain Anjar; filling him in on the present situation and asking if he could arrange to salvage a few Terrabot robots from the remnants of the battle.

Two days later Mark was presented with five Terrabots and the advice, with a laugh, that it was all they could find that 'still had pupils.' These five appeared to have been blown clear when their ship went up. They must have been held in reserve and switched off, it was suggested and Joe and his two colleagues were delighted to receive them, with Joe teling Mark that their investigation of Doyan 1, was progressing faster than they had anticipated."Joe explained, "it has a very sophisticated but in some ways easier to understand operating system and we were making sense of the coded instructions that he used, moreover, how they were delivered, but most of all their meaning when they were sent to other robots."

There was to be very little sleep for Mark that night because the engineers had been making extraordinary progress and they were simply too excited to stop work. At one o'clock in the morning they called him and asked him to come down in a dressing gown and bedroom slippers, if needs be, because they had some very, very important news to impart. Mark wasn't quite so laid back as suggested but he was casually dressed in just a shirt trousers and bedroom slippers with no socks when he arrived in the workshop where the engineers were standing impatiently waiting for him. He also saw that the five robots they had been supplied with were lined up and three of them were bent over with their heads and arms hanging down. "Watch this," Joe said as he tapped a sixteen-figure code into a computer, then he picked up two wires and held them together. There was a small flash inside one of the robots and it sagged down just like the other three and there was a strong smell of burnt electrical insulation in the air afterwards.

"Extraordinary," Mark was genuinely interested. "What have you done to create that effect?"

"It is all to do with the status of Doyan 1 - whom we call Goldie." Joe was like a boy showing his skill. "We have discovered that Goldie has a very special code secreted in a tiny auxiliary processor in his head and if he used the special codeword from it and a specific robot's individual designator together, then he could command that robot to self-destruct. But we have also found that he possesses a general code for all robots as well and that has nothing to do with instructions to terminate. It is a collective call sign for the whole hive, if you will imagine it to be. It's probably used for computer updates or general command instructions to all Terrabots. The two codes do not even share the same processor. It is vulnerability they have overlooked because athough the way Goldie is designed those two codes could never be strung together; we are working outside of those constraints. In short, we are able to link together the collective call sign for all Terrabot robots, plus the instruction code to 'terminate.' Any Terrabot receiving the two linked codes simultaneously will unquestioningly self-destruct."

"Could that code be transmitted by radio?" Mark was nearly as excited as the engineers.

"Indeed, it can. "He was told. "That is how Goldie sends his codes to them anyway and that is what I have just done; and you have seen the result. They just never have envisaged that Doyan 1, would be decapitated in an instant thus giving him no time to erase his memories or self-destruct."

'Well done team!" and Mark clapped them. "Sorry it's late but I want you to go to the Defence Ministry right away because time is of essence. We can't sit on this one! It will do the Defence ministry no harm to work a night shift anyway; I will wake them. On arrival you are to report to the Chief of Staff personally because only he has the power to motivate this quickly. Get your things together, a DMT craft will be waiting in the hanger bay in ten minutes." Then he broke off to speak with the duty QvO controller who authorised a shuttle without question. Mark was certainly not to get any further sleep that night and he woke Captain Anjar because he had anticipated that they were going to receive visits from some very high powered defence personnel during the night. In this, he was not mistaken.

"They seem to be coming by the coach load," Mark joked to Anda who nodded back.

"It's a good night to be a ship's Captain" he laughed. The guests were ushered into a conference room where Mark outlined the discovery that had been made by the engineers. "If we act with alacrity this could render Terrabot impotent forever," he told them. Even though it was the small hours of the morning, a plan had already been developed. Forthwith, all ships of the fleet were ordered to set aside fifty-percent of their stock of DMT darts and to modify them to constantly transmit the two codes they were given. They were then to send the darts out to materialise space at the vectors indicated in the instructions that they were about to reeeive. From there the darts were to be allowed to travel freely in the cosmos, endlessly transmitting the Doyan 1, combined instructions telling all Terrabots that received the message to self-destruct. If each ship only sent one DMT dart that night, they were assured, there would be more than a million of them in space by the next day and in time they could build that up to more than a one billion darts out there. There would be natural losses of darts from collisions and malfunctions. Also, some of them would be captured by gravitation fields so the aim must be to renew them as necessary. Additionally, there was to be a screen transmitting the Terrabot destrict code, circling Ongle, AMC and Earth. With poenillium batteries, it was said, each dart's broadcasts would be maintained for fifty years, whereafter they would automatically return to AmOn to be refurbished and returned to their mission, until the day it was decided that no more needed to be sent. Any Terrabot within fifty million kilometres of a dart would receive and act upon the signal. "The beauty is," Mark was briefing Petan " the self-destruct message is attached to a general call sign for all robots and once it is received by them they cease to exist, so there is nobody able to jam the signal or to warn other Terrabot ships to do so."

By now Anita had rejoined Mark, and Captain Anjar had made available to them the farm house down by the ship's lake and their own cabin cruiser to explore the lake and its islands. Captain Anjar was, also delighted, earlier, to declare, at a simple ceremony, that they were now husband and wife.

From time to time, in the years to come and often far out in deep space, far ranging AmOn ships would come across Terrabot ships, some drifting lifelessly and others erratically, still under power. When they boarded them, they found all was deadly quiet and their previous robot crews were slumped and lifeless and for the most part even their ship's computers had also destroyed themselves in response to the fatal Doyan 1, message. They left them as they had found them, to an eternity in space or, perhaps, they would, one day, fall foul of blazing stars or be dragged into a spiral orbit around a planet where perhaps other races, even millions of years hence. may find them and try to unpick their mystery.

AmOn formerly marked the victory as all governments do with pageant and ceremony where they bestowed gifts of thanks to the Formacidae High Command which had been asked to attend AmOn. It was there that they were presented with access to the prepared darts along with the know how to make more of them. Both species also exchanged illuminated scrolls confirming an everlasting pact of mutual defence.

"Job done," said Mark as he sat on a bench with Anita, overlooking the lake.

"It seems so odd to think of those Terrabot ships," she said. "Forever silent and forever on the move but going nowhere in particular. Those ships are the graves of an extinct race. I hope if other species find them, they do not feel badly about us for this," Anita observed.

"I don't think that they will do that; they will most probably see it as a malfunction. Should they ask us, though, we will tell them." Mark said.

Printed in Great Britain
by Amazon

80877530R00203